Leanne was gone.

Cassidy trembled with the sudden, chasm-opening realization.

Daryl's wet lashes lifted, and his eyes searched hers. "What happened?"

"I don't know. How am I in America?" She clutched her blanket. "In Carbondale?"

"I was hoping you could tell me."

The image of Leanne's number appearing on Cassidy's cell phone flashed in her mind's eye. "She—she called me."

A strangled noise escaped him. "When?"

"What's today?"

He named the date and she froze. Six days ago. She was missing almost a week of her life. The conversation she'd heard outside her door returned: whiplash, concussion, post-traumatic amnesia. Short-term memory loss brought on by an injury. In her case, an unexplained car accident with her estranged sister.

Her *dead* sister.

Oh, God.

"What did she want?"

"I don't remember. What happened to Leanne?" Cassidy had to know, had to understand her sister's last moments, their final time together. Why couldn't she remember?

Dear Reader,

Welcome back to stories about the Cade and Loveland clans you've gotten to know and love over the last five books in the Rocky Mountain Cowboys series. The ranching neighbors have finally solved the mystery surrounding their one-hundred-and-thirty-year-old feud's origin, resolved their water-access dispute and even became related when the heads of each household finally wed. They should be living in peace and harmony...right?

Not so fast! There's plenty of drama ahead in this Western family saga, and it continues with Daryl Loveland in an emotional book about loss, redemption and second chances. Daryl is a single father and a widower struggling to make sense of the disturbing end to his troubled marriage. When his first love, his estranged sister-in-law Cassidy, reenters his life, he discovers a path to forgiveness, healing and lasting happiness.

I hope you enjoy Daryl and Cassidy's one-of-a-kind love story and will return to the Rocky Mountain Cowboys series in summer 2019 to find out if champion bull rider Maverick Loveland can find his happily-ever-after with Ella Parks. She's a fiercely independent sheep rancher who's got too much on her plate for love, including being pregnant with twins!

I love to hear from my readers. Feel free to visit me on my website at karenrock.com or write me at karenrock@live.com.

Happy reading!

Karen Rock

HEARTWARMING

A Rancher to Remember

———

Karen Rock

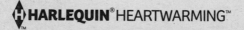

Recycling programs
for this product may
not exist in your area.

ISBN-13: 978-1-335-51061-7

A Rancher to Remember

Copyright © 2019 by Karen Rock

Printed in U.S.A.

Award-winning author **Karen Rock** is both sweet and spicy—at least when it comes to her writing! The author of both YA and adult contemporary books writes sexy suspense novels and small-town romances for Harlequin and Kensington Publishing. A strong believer in happily-ever-after, Karen loves creating unforgettable stories that leave her readers with a smile. When she's not writing, Karen is an avid reader who also loves cooking her grandmother's Italian recipes, baking and having the Adirondack Park wilderness as her backyard, where she lives with her husband, daughter, dog and cat, who keep her life interesting and complete. Learn more about her at karenrock.com or follow her on Twitter, @karenrock5.

Books by Karen Rock

Harlequin Heartwarming

His Kind of Cowgirl
A Heartwarming Thanksgiving
"Thankful for You"
Winter Wedding Bells
"The Kiss"
Raising the Stakes
A League of Her Own
Someone Like You
His Hometown Girl
Wish Me Tomorrow
Bad Boy Rancher
A Cowboy's Pride
Winning the Cowboy's Heart

Visit the Author Profile page
at Harlequin.com for more titles.

To Anne, my grandmother, who lost the love of her life at a young age. Thanks for sharing your romance novels with me, along with your faith in true love and happily-ever-after.

CHAPTER ONE

"This way! Quickly!"

Cassidy Fulton scrambled after her gesturing guide through the Philippines' tropical forest on unsteady legs. In the distance, another round of rapid-fire blasts from semiautomatic weapons peppered the sticky-hot night. Screams followed it. Her breath rasped in her throat and her blood raged. Something wet and scaly slithered over the top of her boots. Cicadas buzzed in her ears. From a strap slung around her neck, her trusty Canon Rebel T5i banged against her jumping belly. It traveled with her on every journalism assignment, from the frigid heights of Siberia to the sandy shores of the Dead Sea.

Her guide held up a hand and they halted to crouch on the edge of Quezon City, their position hidden by thick vines and ferns. She lifted her camera, aimed it through a gap in the foliage and pressed the shutter-release button in quick, muffled bursts.

Do not think.

Do not feel.

Document.

Through her lens, she recorded officers tossing limp-bodied men onto a truck. Some of the policemen joked. Others smoked. None seemed in any rush to transport the injured to the hospital in accordance with their "official" protocol for battling suspected drug dealers. As part of her investigative piece about the rumored executions of suspects— a secret policy to rid the island of its drug trade—she'd traveled the Philippines for the past month, interviewing government officials, locals and hospital personnel to uncover the truth.

And here it was…in black-and-white. The knowledge was like getting hit by a speeding train, and then getting stuck under the wheels and dragged down a bumpy track. Her camera captured the stained ground and the wide-eyed children clinging to their wailing mothers' skirts. Behind them stood crumbling industrial complexes serving as makeshift living quarters for this drug-riddled community. Stray dogs scurried into dark alleys.

"What's she saying?" Cassidy whispered in

her guide's ear, her camera trained on a gesticulating young woman. Her bare feet peeked from beneath the ragged hem of a sundress and tears rolled down her sunken cheeks.

"He is innocent. My husband is innocent," the guide murmured.

"And that woman?" Cassidy captured image after image, her heart breaking despite her resolve to remain detached. Regardless of her ten years as a conflict journalist and despite having exposed some of the most heinous crimes against humanity, she'd failed to acquire the hard shell other professionals adopted. Her heart had not yet turned to stone…though she wished it would in times like this.

"Why? Why? Why?" the guide relayed. "Another is calling the officers murderers."

"Those are close-range shots." As she zoomed her lens, the evening's meal rose back up to the base of her throat. *Think of the greater good…not what you see…but what you will expose. Change.* "They had no time to defend themselves."

"I see no weapons other than the police's."

Sweat broke out across her hairline. At the guide's astute observation, Cassidy swapped her lens for a wide angle to capture the crucial shot. Such pictures brought worldwide condemnation against brutal regimes like this. Consequences. Sanctions. She leaned forward, and a twig snapped beneath her foot. Cassidy's heart tumbled as officers froze at the loud crack. Heads snapped in their direction, and narrowed eyes scanned their hiding place. At a shouted order, a trio of rifle-carrying officers raced their way.

No!

A tremor coursed through her as the guide grabbed Cassidy's hand and yanked her back through the thick bramble.

"Pagagil! Pagagil!" the officers shouted behind them.

Halt! Halt!

Her body sparked like a live wire, humming and crackling with the adrenaline zipping through her. If caught, she'd either meet the same fate as the victims she documented or worse, languish in a Filipino prison for the rest of her life. Death or imprisonment. Neither was uncommon in her dangerous career, yet she'd never quit. She'd worked too hard to let fear drive her away. This tale of corruption, violence and cover-up had to be shared with the world. Too many lives depended on it. Too many lives had been lost already.

Shoving aside prickly branches, stumbling over slippery, moss-covered ground, she charged through the forest. Her heartbeat raged in her ears. *Faster. Faster. Faster.*

The sound of large bodies crashing through the foliage behind them grew louder. Closer. More shouts then—

—something whistled past Cassidy's ear and struck the trunk of a palm tree just ahead. Scorched black encircled the embedded bullet. Another blast of gunfire shredded the overlapping fronds and leaves around her. Her heart thundered in her chest and each rapid breath grew shallower and more painful as she hurtled after her guide. A brief glimpse of his T-shirt appeared to her left and she swerved to follow. Without him, she'd be lost. Even if she managed to evade the shooters, she'd never make it out of this lethal wilderness on her own.

Her eyes stung, and her muscles screamed as she labored up a hill, gunshots raining through the air. A piercing scream rang out and her guide crashed to the ground. In three steps she was upon the writhing man. He clamped a hand to his ragged ear. He'd been shot, but not seriously. Her own war injuries included a knife scar in the stomach, shoulders marked by shrapnel spray and a bullet embedded in her left hip.

"Get up!" she urged. With every ounce of reserve strength, she dug her heels in the spongy earth and pulled the guide to his feet. "Hurry!"

The man swayed slightly before recovering. "This way!" He lurched forward, and they resumed their headlong flight.

The officers' shouts grew louder still, the barrage of bullets unrelenting. Something sliced her upper arm, sharp as a wasp's sting. Pain bloomed and spread. Sticky warmth gushed from the wound. She'd been shot, she thought, with a strange sense of detachment, her adrenaline keeping her from feeling too much. When they crested the hill, the guide yanked her down, then scuttled backward into a shallow hollow in the embankment. A downed tree shrouded the entrance.

A moment later, footsteps pounded overhead. Cassidy held her breath as the men conferred with each other. The world's spin seemed to slow. Time stopped. So did her heart. Then, after what seemed like an eternity, they moved on. Their agitated babble growing fainter and fainter until it quieted altogether.

Still, she and her guide remained motionless until her muscles cramped, and her body grew prickly, then numb. The guide mumbled a prayer beneath his breath. The rosary. She'd heard it in enough languages to recognize it. The rank smell of their sweat and blood permeated the cramped space.

After peeling back her sleeve to examine the wound, she tied a bandanna around it, one-handed. Her teeth clamped on one end as she pulled it tight. She'd been grazed, not struck. A relieved breath flew from her. She would tend to it later in her hotel room, since seeking medical treatment wasn't an option. Not if she hoped to live anyway, because they would be scouring the hospital within the hour.

After what seemed like an eternity, her guide poked out his head, then led them down the hill. All around, the forest pulsed, alive and deadly in the dark. They moved cautiously, but swiftly, following the glimpses of the moon through the thick canopy overhead. At last, they reached the Jeep hidden in the brush, flung themselves inside, then raced down the back road, holding their breaths. After several glances in the empty rearview mirror, Cassidy sank back in her seat.

"We did it." She traced her camera with trembling fingertips. Its critical memory card had survived...as had she...this time.

How many more assignments before her luck ran out?

She tipped her forehead out the window to let the rushing air cool her flesh. No time to think about that now.

Or ever.

Growing up near Carbondale, Colorado, she'd worked on enough cattle ranches to know the only thing stopping a beast from killing you was convincing it to fear *you* instead.

It was mind over matter.

Courage over danger.

An hour later she hunched before her laptop inside her hotel room. Her fingers flew as she transcribed the day's notes.

"It's not possible they were alive," said Mahalia Cruz, 39, whose husband, Danilo, was among the dead. "We saw them thrown in the back of a truck."

Cassidy stopped typing, brought up the images she'd downloaded from her camera and studied the last one. A picture was worth a thousand words, especially when it corroborated witness statements. She dropped the picture into a digital folder, attached the folder to a brief email and sent it to her editor. She'd be arriving at her Manhattan office soon. Cassidy minimized the screen and resumed writing.

"In police operations, we don't know where the bullets may hit," Police Chief Torres said. "Some suspects retaliate, fight us. We are only defending ourselves."

"Didn't look like that to me," she muttered. When she reached for her coffee, pain lanced in her arm. Little more than a scrape, the wound should heal on its own. Her guide hadn't been so lucky. He'd lost his ear tip.

"The police do the shooting, they do the killing—and they investigate themselves," Rosaria Del Mortel, a forensic scientist and chair of the University of the Philippines Manila Pathology Department, said. "Impunity, that's what's happening. Such practices can leave the system open to abuse."

Cassidy pressed the tip of her tongue to the roof of her mouth and nodded, every nerve ending afire. The familiar sensation accompanied every important story she'd ever broken. Every journalist lived for this…if nothing else…

Bereaved relatives and other witnesses said

the bodies were taken to a hospital an hour or more after the shooting, and that none of the victims showed signs of life. "They weren't moving. They weren't breathing," said Fernando Reyes, the local district medical director. "They were cold to the touch."

She stared at the screen, picturing the doctor's anguished face, the widow's grief. Her vision blurred, and her head dipped. So much injustice in the world and not enough time to expose it all in one lifetime.

Her cell phone buzzed, and her editor's number flashed on-screen. "Hey, Brenda."

"Quite the scoop!" Brenda crowed. "If you don't win the Pulitzer this year, I'll eat my Birkin."

"Would that count as a protein?" Despite her fatigue, Cassidy's lips curved up in a smile.

A Pulitzer. She'd been striving to win the highest recognition of her profession since she'd declared herself a journalism major her freshman year in college. Growing up in poverty, her father's difficulty holding on to jobs amid layoffs meant they'd sometimes had to choose between rent, food or heating. Lying in bed, her empty stomach growling in the dark, she'd vowed to fulfill her pa's unshakable faith. She'd break the cycle and achieve greatness someday. He'd spent every extra dime he'd scraped together on her, from her first camera, a battered, secondhand Nikon, to the uniforms required of the private school she'd attended on scholarship.

"You were robbed last year," Brenda said, then swore a blue streak about suing Starbucks over third-degree burns after what sounded like a scorching sip of coffee. "Your work on Erdogan's strong-arm tactics should have beat that *New York Times* Ebola series. I'm so sick of sickness stories."

"Maybe this year." Cassidy's fingers dented her jeans. When a work injury caused her father's permanent disability, she'd vowed to prove his sacrifices weren't in vain, that his belief in her was warranted and she was worthy of all he'd given her, especially his love.

Her eyes flitted to the framed family photo she carried with her on every assignment. Only an arm showed of the person she'd carefully snipped out...her younger sister, Leanne, who'd betrayed her in the worst way imaginable.

"How much longer before you send the final piece?"

Cassidy ignored the pressure banding

around her chest and scrolled through the text-filled screen. "By noon. Your time."

"That's my gal. I owe you a bottle of Pinot when you get back."

Cassidy's eyes closed as she imagined the crisp white wine. "I'll hold you to that. So what's my next assignment?"

"You mean after we hate-watch Season Sixteen of *I Didn't Know I Was Pregnant*?"

Cassidy groaned. "I thought we kicked that habit."

"I just can't quit it, Cass."

"Fine…but seriously, have you got anything in mind for my next storyline?"

Now it was Brenda's turn to groan. "Do you ever stop and just enjoy your accomplishments? It's always about what's next with you, isn't it?"

"I—I love my work."

"Hmm." Brenda slurped more coffee. "I wonder."

"You wonder if I love my job?" Cassidy's voice rose. A buzzing window fan dragged in muggy air scented with something fruity and cloying.

"Sometimes, Cassidy, I wonder if your drive is fueled by something else."

"A paycheck works nicely."

Brenda laughed. "There is that. Okay. Gotta go. We'll chat about your next piece when you get back. You can stay with me."

"I appreciate it." Since Cassidy lived a no-mad's life, all her possessions in her suit-case, it didn't make sense to pay a Manhattan apartment's astronomical rent. The rare times she returned to America, she rented an effi-ciency room.

"I'll introduce you to my brother. He's been dying to meet you. And his divorce is final…"

"I'm sure he's lovely, but I—"

"Am too busy, traveling too much and a type A, perfectionist workaholic," Brenda finished for her with another laugh.

"Pretty much. Bye, Brenda." Cassidy punched off her phone and sighed. She longed for a lasting relationship and a real family, yet her career came first.

Sure, she was lonely, but her demanding schedule, her dangerous life and the stan-dards she drove herself to meet didn't allow for long-term connections. She picked up the framed picture and the memory of that day—an annual family picnic in the Colorado Rockies, which she'd mostly avoided over the years—rushed through her like laurel-scented sunshine.

Her fingers tightened around the frame. She stared into the smiling eyes of her younger self, recalling the photographer who'd made her that happy. Daryl. Her college boyfriend had snapped the photo when they'd returned home between semesters. He was the only man who'd tempted her to abandon her career aspirations for love...

The only man to break her heart.

No amount of time or distance had healed it. Hurt remained like slivers of broken glass, impossible to see and liable to draw blood even after she thought she'd swept them all away.

How different her life would have been if she'd said yes to Daryl's proposal instead of making him wait.

Her oppressive, jumpy thoughts drove her downstairs and out into the stifling night, her cell phone's flashlight feature illuminating the dark. She peered up at the crescent moon.

When it'd gotten too hot, she and Leanne used to crawl onto their roof and stare up at the sky. They'd called themselves moon sisters. No matter how they grew and changed, they'd sworn to always be a constant in each other's lives. Crescent had been Leanne's favorite whereas Cassidy had preferred the full.

It saw everything, just like she'd wanted to someday.

Funny how blind she'd been after all. They hadn't spoken in over a decade, not since Leanne's crushing treachery, not since their worlds collided and they'd spun into different orbits, infinite space between them.

Cassidy's cell phone buzzed and then, as if conjured from her very thoughts, a familiar name appeared on the screen. Her mother had made Cassidy enter the contact because of her father's fragile health.

Why would *she* call? It was the most shocking, dangerous sight Cassidy had witnessed today. She'd rather face Duterte's firing squad than answer. Something had to be very, *very* wrong...

It took her three tries before she managed to push the answer button. Her phone shook as she lifted it to her ear and opened her trembling mouth.

"Leanne?"

DARYL LOVELAND CRANKED the heat beneath a pot of water, snatched up his landline's wireless handset and stopped by the kitchen counter where his children, Emma and Noah, labored over school assignments. "Be right back. No stabbing each other with pencils."

To his relief, they nodded without looking up from their homework. No signs of stress. No deviating from the routine he'd established to provide his teetering family stability. He ducked into the bathroom, shut the door and flipped on the shower. The phone slid in his damp palms as he dialed the next number on his list.

"Hey, Kevin. Daryl Loveland calling. Was wondering if my wife was at your bar today." He paced the narrow, tiled floor.

"What?" Kevin asked. "Can't hear you. Sounds like you're in the car wash or something."

Daryl raised his voice slightly, one eye on the door. "I'm in the shower."

"Dude. Call me when you're dressed."

"No… I've got clothes on… Just… Have you seen Leanne?" Daryl wiped the fogging mirror and met his dark eyes. Dilated pupils turned them black, and a deep, vertical line cut between his brows.

"What about your clothes?" Kevin asked.

"It's about Leanne!" Daryl shout-whispered. "Have you seen her?" He whirled from the mirror and leaned against the vanity, his chest so tight he struggled to breathe. Puffs of white steam billowed over the shower curtain and slicked his skin.

"Leanne? What about her?"

"She didn't come home last night." Daryl raked a hand through his hair.

"Hey. You don't have to shout," Kevin protested. "Haven't seen her since the other evening."

"And the night before that, and the one before that," Daryl said wearily. He thanked Kevin and punched off the phone. Leanne spent more time at Silver Spurs than she did with her family.

He reached behind him to grip the vanity's granite edge and hung his head, thinking fast. Where was she *this* time? For the past year and a half, she'd checked out of their ten-year marriage, demanding he sleep up at the ranch's main house when she was home. Otherwise, she was barhopping with friends and staying out until all hours, sometimes not returning until the next day.

She'd never taken a suitcase before, though. When he'd returned to their cabin after his ranch work, he'd found his stepmother, Joy, with the children. Some of Leanne's clothes, shoes and jewelry were gone, save for the wedding band he'd given her before their shotgun wedding. Had she left him?

He rubbed his temples. His head ached as though he'd spent the night banging it against the wall, which would've been more enjoyable than staring at the ceiling, replaying all the quiet arguments, the bitter silences, the scathing asides he and Leanne had shared these past eighteen months.

"Pa!" The knob turned, and his nine-year-old daughter, Emma, peeked her head around the door. "The water's boiling over."

Shoot.

With his thoughts swerving in every direction, he'd be lucky if he didn't burn down the cabin. "Thanks, darlin'."

"Is Mama coming home soon?" Emma tore the top off the pasta box and handed it to him once he lowered the cooktop's flame.

Daryl nodded firmly. "Of course." He dumped in the spaghetti, grabbed a wooden spoon and pushed down the brittle noodles until he submerged them beneath the bubbling water.

"Where is she?" Noah hopped off a stool and passed over the salt shaker.

"It's a surprise," Daryl temporized, adding a pinch of the white crystals.

"Are we getting a puppy?" Noah clapped his hands together.

Daryl ruffled his six-year-old's dark, silky hair. "We already have Beuford."

Hearing his name, their geriatric beagle, Labrador mix opened his eyes, raised his head and thumped his tail against the wooden floor. Then, as if the effort had worn him out, he dropped his head again with a long, suffering sigh.

"But all he does is sleep and fart," Noah complained. "He never wants to play with me. Nobody does."

Daryl's heart clenched at Noah's hurt expression, knowing he wasn't talking about just Beuford.

Leanne hadn't spent much time with the kids lately either. She'd begun organizing a country store on his family's ranch, Loveland Hills, and planned on selling the heirloom apples they grew along with produce and homemade baked and canned goods. When she'd first begun talking about it, he'd been encouraged, believing she'd recommit to their family, their marriage, but she'd only become busier. More distant.

And now she was gone.

Why? He'd failed to make her happy, clearly,

but the kids and the store she'd invested so much time into?

Something must be wrong.

Very, *very* wrong.

He'd swallowed his pride alongside the deep-rooted Loveland need for privacy and called his brother Travis, Carbondale's county sheriff, earlier to report Leanne missing. Had they found her yet? Located her white Jeep?

"Can you help me with math, Pa?"

At Emma's question, he grabbed a can of peas and an opener and carried them to the counter. Books, paper and crumpled candy wrappers littered the stone surface. "Sure."

"A bat and a ball cost one dollar and ten cents in total," she read from a worksheet. "The bat costs a dollar more than the ball. How much does the ball cost?"

Daryl fitted the opener over the can's metal line and cranked the turner. Approaching headlights glared through the window above the sink. His heart resumed beating when they swept by to the main house. "Ten cents," he said lightly, careful to keep his tone neutral.

Where was Leanne?

"Nope! It's five cents," Emma announced, checking the answer in the back of the book.

Five cents? What did he know about anything anymore?

"Pa?" Noah mumbled around the pencil clamped between his teeth. "What's a pie-mary source?"

"A pie what?" Behind him, water hit the metal grate and hissed. In his hurry to whisk the kettle off the heat, he dropped the now open can of peas, splattering the floor with sticky fluid and preserved vegetables.

His cheeks bulged, holding back a string of oaths. Heat burned from his chest to his ear tips.

Emma flicked back her wispy blond bangs and stared. "Are you having a stroke?"

"No." He pulled the overflowing pot off the burner and the boiling water splashed his fingers. "Ow!" When his boot slipped on the bean mess, he crashed to one knee, biting his tongue.

He forced himself to his feet and gave his gaping children an exaggerated bow. "Greetings from Clumsy the Clown," he pronounced, donning the persona he'd created to make Emma laugh when she'd been teased for the orthopedic gear she'd worn to straighten her pigeon-toed gait.

"Please, no." Emma's mouth quirked.

Noah giggled. "Clumsy's funny."

"He's also not getting any younger." Daryl rubbed his aching knee, then peered at Beuford. "Any chance you want to help me clean up this mess?"

Beuford cracked open an eye, studied the mushy peas, then lowered his lid again, adding a loud snore for effect.

"Man's best friend my butt—er..." Daryl yanked open the broom closet and pulled out a mop.

"Butt! Pa was going to say *butt*!" Noah grabbed the plastic jar on the end of the counter. "Now you have to put in a quarter."

"Two quarters," Emma corrected. "And *you* owe them since you said *butt*. Twice."

"Well, so did you!" Noah fired back.

"I did not!" Emma jabbed her pencil at Noah. "I repeated what you said, *butt*."

Noah spun on his swivel stool. "Now you owe two quarters, potty mouth!"

"Take that back!" Emma screeched, lunging.

Daryl grabbed Emma's pencil inches from Noah's eye. "Enough!" he thundered, then sucked in a shaky breath and started again. Slower. Gentler. "What's the number one homework rule?"

"Don't get caught cheating?" Noah grabbed the counter edge and stopped the rotating stool.

"The other one."

"Don't feed it to Beuford?" Emma subsided back in her seat.

"Nope. Pencils aren't..." he prompted, waiting.

Emma and Noah exchanged confused looks.

"Weapons." Daryl heaved out a sigh. "Pencils aren't weapons. For the millionth, gazillionth time."

"Gazillion," giggled Noah. "Who wants to be a gazillionaire?"

"Aunt Jewel said she stabbed Uncle Justin's hand clean through with a protractor once," Emma supplied.

"I believe it," he muttered, picturing his petite, roughrider stepsister. Her mother, Joy, had married his father, Boyd, a year ago, blending the neighboring Cade and Loveland ranching families and ending their 130-year feud. Now Jewel was engaged to his brother Heath, their wedding set for Christmas Eve. Would Leanne attend it with him?

If she came home...

Noah pulled the tip of his eraser from his nose and sniffed. "Is the house on fire?"

The smoke detector shrilled.

"And what's a pie-mary source?" Noah shouted.

"It's primary," Emma answered as Daryl dashed to the stove.

Black smoke billowed when he yanked it open, coughing. Inside lay the charred ruins of his famous cheesy garlic bread.

"I'll call 911!" Noah snatched up the phone.

"I'll get the extinguisher." Emma hopped off her stool and raced to the broom closet.

When it came to disasters, he and his kids were becoming a well-oiled machine. "Put down the phone and don't spray the—" An explosion of white foam drowned out his next word.

"Did I put it out, Pa?" Emma lowered the red canister.

"Sure did."

"Then how come you still look upset?"

He mashed his lids shut, counted backward from ten and wished like hell for Leanne…for an extra pair of hands even, since that was all they'd been to each other for a very long time, he realized, looking further back than just the past year and a half. He was lonely, and somehow, crazy as it sounded, it was harder to be lonely when you were with someone. He wasn't making Leanne happy, and his family was falling apart. "Who's upset? You saved the day, sweetheart."

"But what about dinner?" Noah pointed at the white goop dripping from every surface, including the pasta pot. "I'm hungry."

"How about grilled cheese sandwiches and tomato soup once I clean this up?" He filled a bucket, dipped a mop in the fluid and raked it over the sticky floor in quick, jerky half circles. Beuford's tongue flicked out to sample the foam. "So now you're helping?" Daryl growled.

"You don't make them as good as Mama." Noah's lower lip trembled. "How come she's not home?"

"Does she still love us?" Emma warbled.

The mop clattered to the floor and, in three quick strides, Daryl caught them in a tight hug. "She loves you very much."

"Because she's our mama?" Noah buried his head in Daryl's shoulder.

"Yes," he affirmed, though that hadn't been his experience growing up. He fought to provide his children the happy, loving and stable home he'd longed for as a kid before the

Lovelands adopted him…the reason Leanne's erratic behavior tore him up. The children hung on each of her rare smiles and called out a good-night to her, even when she wasn't home to hear it.

Long ago, he'd messed up and sealed his and Leanne's fate…though he'd never regret the impulsive action that'd created Emma. He'd lost the future he'd wanted with another, a woman he'd never been able to forget, but he'd committed to this marriage, this family. Leanne made him content, if not truly happy, and deep down, he wondered if she sensed this, if his inability to give her his heart fully drove her away.

She'd rebuffed all his attempts to reconnect. When he'd signed them up for ballroom lessons, she'd gone line dancing with friends instead. The new saddle he'd tooled with their initials and wedding date gathered dust in the stable. She was miserable, and the children suffered because of it.

Where are you?

Come home to your family…

A loud knock broke up their family hug.

"Mama!" Noah flung himself at the door, sliding on his stocking feet in his haste. When he wrenched it open, his brother Travis stood outside wearing his gray sheriff's uniform. Noah's face fell. "I thought you were Mama."

Daryl's heart beat faster at Travis's somber expression. "Come inside."

Travis doffed his hat and mashed it between his hands. His jaw was set as if to control some powerful emotion. "Would appreciate a word with you outside if you have a minute."

Daryl struggled to lift his heavy feet from the floor, to move, to breathe even. Haziness made his head lurch and spin.

"Daryl?" Travis prompted, his voice grave.

"Yes. Uh—kids, get back to your homework and then I'll take you out for pizza."

Travis's stone-faced expression suggested Daryl had just made a promise he might not keep.

"Yay!" Emma and Noah whooped.

Once the door clicked shut behind them, Travis's blue eyes blazed into his. Their sister, Sierra, huddled on the bottom step with her arms wrapped around her shivering body. Travis must have picked her up at the main house, then brought her here to…to… Daryl's thought hit a dead end, unable, unwilling to complete itself.

"Did you find…" His throat closed around

his wife's name, as if by not naming her, he'd shield her, protect her from whatever turned his siblings' faces pale.

"Leanne." It was a whisper, and Sierra's face contorted tearfully around it.

Goose bumps raced across his skin like a squall through a hayfield. He swallowed and just that small physical reflex felt like an effort. He felt as if the blood had drained from him, and with it the strength that he had left, the fight.

Travis gripped Daryl's shoulder. "There's been an accident."

CHAPTER TWO

CASSIDY WOKE TO the sound of her heartbeat. Strangely, it seemed to pulse outside her body, a synthesized, electronic pulse. She struggled to pry her eyelids open, but they weighed a thousand pounds. Even that small movement made her moan, but at least the sharp pain along her right side revived her. Through heavy lids, she made out the small room she lay in, and her mouth was so dry she felt as though it were stuffed with cotton. She had to sit up to find water, but the heavy blankets, tucked around the edges of a narrow hospital bed, imprisoned her.

Hospital?

Her thoughts and vision sharpened, along with the rest of her senses. She'd been hurled into a brick wall if the agonizing hurt racking her body was any indication. Each breath felt like fire, and she was pretty sure a few of her ribs were broken. She could barely see out of her right eye, her left eye was swollen shut and a collar encased her neck. What happened? Had the Filipino police found her? Beaten her? A chill spread through her chest. She had to get out of here.

She nudged down her coverings and leveraged herself upright. The pain had her dry heaving into a pan beside her bed, seeing stars, fighting to remain conscious. She clutched the metal bed rail for several minutes until her cramping stomach eased. Three fingers on her right hand swam into view. They were missing nails. The smallest finger on her left was broken. When she drew in a shallow breath, the subtle scents of antiseptic, bleach and hand sanitizer crept into her nose. She was somewhere clean and modern. A wall-mounted TV looked new as did the IV pump dripping fluid into her arm and the monitor recording her heartbeat.

This was no backcountry Filipino hospital. Not the kind they'd hide *her* in…a journalist preparing to expose government corruption. So where was she? She cocked her head, wincing, and strained to distinguish the language spoken by the health professionals conferring outside her doorway. She heard her name then—

Concussion.

Whiplash.

Post-traumatic amnesia.

Unrelated, recent gunshot wound.

English. They spoke English with an American accent, which meant... She was stateside and had amnesia. A head injury.

How?

Last she remembered, she'd been typing up her notes halfway across the globe in Quezon City. Her editor had called. They'd talked about a stupid TV show and then...

Brisk steps snared her attention and halted her thoughts. She stared in shock as a large, well-built man loomed in the doorway. A familiar cowboy. One she'd avoided these past ten years. He strode to her bed and his contorted features mirrored her anguished confusion.

"Daryl?" she croaked.

Was this another of her dreams featuring her first and only love? She'd had countless nights of them...except he'd never worn the beard now accentuating his square jaw. And he hadn't had the crinkles flaring from the outer corners of his coffee-colored eyes. Thick, clipped hair still ended above dark, arched brows and framed his lean, handsome face. His cheekbones were as broad and high as she remembered, his nose straight and fine-boned. Those lips, with their fuller bottom, were parted. The C-shaped scar on his temple also looked the same, the one he'd never explained to her.

"Cassidy." His low, bass voice rumbled from his throat. A black T-shirt stretched across a chest that she knew was well-defined and a toned stomach—the kind of stomach that put six-packs to shame. Wranglers hugged slim hips and mile-long legs.

"What are you doing here? Am I—?" *Dead*, she finished silently. Surely someone as otherworldly gorgeous as Daryl would appear to her at the pearly gates…not in this lifetime… not after she'd promised herself she'd never speak to him again. Right after she'd vowed to hate him for the rest of her life.

Thinking about him, though, was another story. Her thoughts flew to him each lonely night, no matter the time or distance. He'd left her battered heart a crime scene, yellow "do not enter" tape blocking it off, his fingerprints everywhere.

The bed dipped slightly as he sat on its edge and his large hands swallowed hers, gentle around her bandages. "Are you…are you okay?" His soulful eyes skated away from her face, then back, as if she were a magnet, attracting him against his will.

She could only imagine how she looked—hair matted and tangled by the feel of it, her face bruised and swollen, the shapeless hospital gown smelling faintly of sweat and sickness. She wanted the floor to open and swallow her whole.

Or maybe she just needed to *wake up*.

This was a bad dream. A very bad dream.

At her recoil, Daryl released her. This close, she made out the dark circles beneath his bloodshot eyes and the paleness of his lips. The urge to smooth the line cleaving his brow seized her but she swatted it away, welcoming the heated rush of anger toppling her concern. This was no dream. She might not know where she was or how she got here, but she knew she didn't want to see *him*. *Ever*.

"Get out."

An overhead PA system called out a Code Blue. Footsteps pounded in the hall outside her room.

"Cassidy, I—"

She gritted her teeth and turned her aching head in search of the call button. It took her a painful eternity to locate it. *Code Blue. Code Blue.*

"Please," he urged, and the plea in his voice made her finger hesitate on the remote's switch. "I need to ask you about…about…" He stopped, and his mouth worked.

She searched her memory as a word—no, a name—teased its borders. A white Jeep flashed in her mind's eye. Whose? The familiar chorus of a Garth Brooks song echoed in her ears followed by raised voices, squealing tires… The call button dropped from her nerveless fingers. "Leanne," she gasped.

His anguished eyes flew to hers. They were red-rimmed and raw. "What happened?"

"What do you mean?" The remembered sound of squealing brakes filled her ears followed by a thunderous boom. She knew something, a memory she couldn't quite get to materialize. Something horrible. A dark fear crept up her spine. "Where's Leanne?"

"You were in a car accident."

She stared at him unable to speak. His tortured expression robbed her of words, drawing the air from her mouth so that she could barely breathe.

"Together," he elaborated when she remained silent.

"Leanne and I were in a car accident?"

He nodded slowly, as if his head might roll off his bowed shoulders if he moved too fast.

"Where is she?" Her heart thrashed behind her ribs. She searched her mind for some recollection of what happened, but only the aroma of burning exhaust returned to her.

His nostrils flared. He strove for control and his face was a mask of pain.

"Where. Is. Leanne?" Cassidy reached for his wrist. She fought not to cry out as her shredded fingertips grazed his sleeve.

"She's—she's gone."

"Gone?" Cassidy felt the cold-hot shock that came from being struck without warning. The wheels of a machine, pushed by a health professional, rattled past the door. It barely registered. In fact, everything receded save the harsh rasp of her breath and the thrum of her accelerating heartbeat on the monitor.

"You were wearing a seat belt. She wasn't. When you hit the guardrail…"

"No," Cassidy murmured. Numbness stole over her, anesthetizing her. Even her voice sounded distant, as though she were listening to a recording of it. Was she really speaking? Was Leanne truly gone? This was happening to someone else and she merely observed the unfolding tragedy as usual, ever the documenter of others' disasters. Not her own.

"You're lying."

"I never lie."

She'd heard that vow before. Had believed it, too, before he'd chosen her sister over her… "You did once."

He swallowed hard and his voice, when it emerged, was a hoarse croak. "She's dead, Cassidy. I identified her remains myself."

"Her remains?"

He didn't elaborate and in the silence the reality of it all hit her. A tsunami of grief rushed through her, destroying everything, even the hopes she hadn't known she'd harbored for reconciliation with her only sister, her one-time best friend. They'd survived their desperate childhood because they'd always had each other when they'd had little else.

And now Leanne was gone.

Dead.

Cassidy trembled with the sudden, chasm-opening realization.

Daryl's wet lashes lifted, and his eyes searched hers. "What happened?"

"I don't know. How am I in America?" She clutched her blanket. "In Carbondale?"

"I was hoping you could tell me."

The image of Leanne's number appearing on Cassidy's cell phone flashed in her mind's eye. "She—she called me."

A strangled noise escaped him. "When?"

"What's today?"

He named the date and she froze. Six days ago. She was missing almost a week of her life. The conversation she'd heard outside her door returned: whiplash, concussion, post-traumatic amnesia. Short-term memory loss brought on by an injury. In her case, an unexplained car accident with her estranged sister.

Her *dead* sister.

Oh. God.

"What did she want?"

"I don't remember. What happened to Leanne?" Cassidy had to know, had to understand her sister's last moments, their final time together. Why couldn't she remember?

"The EMTs pronounced her dead on the scene. They said she didn't suffer."

Cassidy swallowed painfully. She'd uttered this phrase to others during her hazardous career, but never saw its inadequacy before. Its emptiness. Dead was still dead. Suffering continued for the living, regardless, and she'd carry this grief, along with her unresolved anger, for the rest of her life. A dead, empty space opened inside her.

Leanne.

"Did she ask you to come home?"

"She'd never… We haven't spoken since…" Cassidy's voice cracked. Her tongue swelled as if to block her from saying aloud the words she'd silenced long ago.

"Since you returned home and discovered we'd married," Daryl finished for her, his eyes hot with remorse.

"I don't want to talk about it." She couldn't breathe fast enough, not as the door inside her mind opened and closed, and the images of Daryl that Cassidy had made herself forget flashed before her eyes. She closed them, wishing for darkness.

"We never talked about it," he said, his voice as broken as her heart. "That was the problem."

"It doesn't matter." Cassidy's frail, damaged hand trailed an IV tube when she flicked it backward, as if she swatted the memory, their falling-out and Daryl, away. "Not *that* anyway. Not now."

"You're right. It doesn't matter." Only it did, Daryl realized, marveling at the powerful emotions the sight of an injured Cassidy stirred in him. Her bruises and bandages clenched his churning stomach. They set fire to his chest. Even though he hadn't seen her in ten years, the strength of his reaction was overwhelming and disproportionate given he was married—had been married, he amended—to her sister. Loss swamped him with fresh grief.

He bowed his head, trying to hide his tears from Cassidy, willing back the rush of guilt and pain when his eyes landed on her hand. The one that he thought would be bearing his wedding band—had she said yes so long ago.

One of her fingers was broken, wrapped in a thick splint, while several fingernails were missing on the other. The outline of bulky bandages around her torso showed beneath her thin hospital gown, and a neck collar framed the beautiful face he'd never forgotten, swollen and discolored as it was. Seeing her hurt sent him right back to the day *he'd* hurt *her*...

He fought the impulse to hold her hands again, to reassure himself that she was alive, whole and going to heal. If he could, he'd trade places with her in a heartbeat to take away her pain. Her suffering. Seeing her like this affected him more than it should. He was a widower, a man grieving the mother of his children and the wife he'd committed to for life, even if she'd emotionally left him long ago. She had stopped being a true partner in their marriage, but when a Loveland pledged himself to another, he meant forever. He'd imagined the rest of his life with Leanne.

Yet the sight of Cassidy brought everything back, the love, the guilt, the loss, the regret… It was as if she'd never left and nothing had changed between them. The idea of her living her life in the abstract, following her dreams—he could handle that. But the idea that she could have died and not been here at all was unbearable… As devastated as he was over losing Leanne, he was equally relieved that Cassidy was still here, one of the most disturbing emotions of these past few days.

He was wrecked. Not thinking straight. It had to explain his distorted view.

Like Cassidy said, their history together didn't matter. She was nothing more than his children's aunt to him, his deceased wife's sister. And as a responsible man, he'd do his duty to check in on her and ensure her care.

That was the end of it.

Daryl tore his eyes from Cassidy's ashen

face. "Leanne didn't mention you were visiting." In fact, they never spoke of Cassidy at all except when dropping their children off at their grandparents' when she visited.

"I was on assignment in the Philippines." Her hand rose to feel the bandage covering what he'd overheard the doctors describe as a recent gunshot wound.

"You were shot."

She shrugged. "Barely."

Barely? What kind of a life did she live where a gunshot didn't register?

Not your problem...

"I need water."

"Be right back." Relieved that he finally had an excuse to put space between them, space to think, he grabbed the pitcher beside her bed, strode down the hall. A nurse pointed him toward a utility room.

Inside it, the machine ground and sputtered before spewing ice into the container. His distorted face reflected in the steel surface. He resembled the figure in the painting *The Scream*. Felt like it, too. Looking at Cassidy was difficult, comforting her near impossible. She was as beautiful as he remembered. Her electric-green eyes, despite being swollen, one nearly shut, still sparked with a restless energy. Her mouth, split and puffy, was just as expressive and her bruised chin square enough to take the many knocks life had given her…including the one he'd landed ten years ago…the worst of all.

He slid the pitcher to the water dispenser and tapped the button. Her cheeks had lost their curve, though, and dark circles rimmed her eyes. Some of the changes might be from the accident, but he suspected hard living also played a role. It aroused his protective streak, the instinct to shield her from her worst impulses to fling herself into dangerous, unstable situations—the biggest points of contention in their former relationship.

Clear liquid gushed over the ice, lifting it. When it reached the top, he replaced the lid, grabbed a stack of paper cups and strode back to Cassidy's room. He paused at the sight of her, her head turned toward the windows, her shoulders shaking with silent tears, hiding her pain. It was the stronger, tougher side of her that Daryl remembered, loved and, at times like this, hated…his being protective and all.

"Cassidy." He set down the pitcher, grabbed a tissue and blotted the tears streaming down her face.

"Stop." She jerked away, and his hand dropped. "Did you have the funeral?"

"Yesterday." The fresh shock, the grief, the regret on her features echoed the emotions racking him. He'd had a few days to process, though. For Cassidy, this was all just sinking in.

"How are the kids?"

Her concern for them tugged at his heart. Despite the way they'd parted ways, she'd been a devoted aunt. Presents and postcards and pictures arrived for them from every country she traveled through over the years. Whenever she'd visited her folks, the kids had begged to see her, and she excitedly brought home stories Leanne refused to hear. Leanne let them see Cassidy at her parents' behest, not hers.

"Emma and Noah are broken up. They've been sleeping with me." They'd huddled under the covers every night, holding on to each other lest they lose another family member. But it wasn't enough to ease their suffering. As hard as he tried, he couldn't make this better for them, protect them from this pain, and it killed him inside.

"Poor sweethearts. Tell them I love them."

"I will. Oh. Here." He grabbed the homemade cards they'd begged him to deliver from the back pockets of his jeans and passed them over.

Cassidy examined the construction paper missives carefully, her good eye brimming. "They're beautiful kids, Daryl. You and Leanne did a good job."

Yes, they had.

And what would he do now?

Though he'd been struggling without Leanne for a while, he'd had faith it was a temporary separation... Now his single-fatherhood was official and terrifyingly real. "Thank you. They wanted to visit you today, but I thought it was best if I came alone first."

"First? Why come at all?" she demanded, her anger returning along with a rush of red into her cheeks.

"I had to see you, had to know you're all right."

Wanted to see you open your eyes...

"I've survived this long without you," she snapped.

"I still needed to know you were being taken care of," he insisted. Cassidy had never needed him. Not like Leanne... "I also wanted to ask you about Leanne...see what you remembered about the accident. I didn't want the kids to overhear that."

Some of Cassidy's anger seemed to dissipate. She closed her good eye briefly and her brow furrowed. When her thick lashes lifted, her eye had darkened to a forest green. "I—I can't remember anything else."

He blew out a breath. "Who's taking you home when you're discharged?"

"No one."

No one? How could she have no one? The isolation of her life hit him hard. He couldn't stand the thought of Cassidy alone against a chaotic world, but that was how she'd preferred to live, in flux and in danger.

"Come home with me." The impulse came to him so swiftly that the unexpected offer flew from his mouth before he had a chance to think it through.

"What? No!"

"Your parents are living with your aunt's family in Phoenix now. They barely had room for them… If you have nowhere else to go, you can recuperate at my cabin," he pressed, despite every instinct ordering him to shut up and leave.

Why was he intent on taking care of her? Was it out of family loyalty or something deeper? He felt guilty about her injuries and how he did her wrong. Plus, he wanted to be close when she recovered her memories. He needed to know why she was in the car with his wife and where they were going with suitcases for both stowed in the trunk.

"I don't want your charity."

"It's not charity." Daryl didn't shrink from his responsibilities, the reason he lingered by Cassidy's bedside, surely, and why he'd stuck by Leanne, no matter how hard she'd pushed him away. He'd always tried to be one of the good guys, careful not to end up like his incarcerated biological parents. After the Lovelands adopted him, he'd devoted his life to proving his worth, to ensuring they never regretted their decision to take him into their home. He sacrificed all for the family he owed everything to, even his heart once... He'd never told Cassidy this about himself.

"I don't want anything from you."

His conscience stabbed him when Cassidy looked into his eyes. He'd been anything but a "good guy" when it came to her. No wonder she wanted nothing to do with him. Understandable, but not acceptable. She needed to be cared for, the doctors said, for at least a couple of weeks. As his children's aunt, he was honor bound to help her. "Where will you go?"

Cassidy glared up at him. "I have friends."

"No husband? Boyfriend?" The idea of Cassidy with someone else unsettled him when he had no right to feel that way or any way about her.

"No," she said. Terse.

A strange sense of relief washed over him. "Who are your friends, then?"

"My editor."

"And where does she live?"

"Right now..." Cassidy's brows knitted. "...she might be in the Hamptons with her family...or they own a yacht...or..."

"Or?"

Cassidy groaned. "I don't know, Daryl. I'll figure it out. I've somehow gotten through the last decade without you. I'll manage on my own, though I'd like to see the kids."

He blew out a breath. "Fine." Maybe it'd be for the best if he let her go. Cassidy was like an earthquake, shaking up lives, upending them, and he didn't want that when his family needed to regain its stability. "Tell me one thing. Why were you driving?"

Cassidy's eyes widened in shock. "I was behind the wheel?"

He nodded. "It was Leanne's Jeep. Where were you taking her?"

"Was it a white Jeep?" she gasped.

He stiffened. They'd leased the vehicle last year. Cassidy wouldn't have seen it before. "You remember!"

Cassidy's brow furrowed. "Just the Jeep. That's all. And a Garth Brooks song."

"Garth was Leanne's—"

"Favorite singer," Cassidy finished, visibly shaken. "But why were we together? It makes no sense!"

He gripped the bed rail and leaned forward. "Think, Cassidy... You must remember!"

"I don't. I don't," Cassidy sobbed, and her tears ripped another hole in his heart.

"Mr. Loveland," said a nurse behind him. She eased Cassidy back down to her pillow and poured her a glass of water. "I think it's best if you leave now."

He opened his mouth, then closed it. What more was there to say? "Get well," he choked out, then marched himself through the hospital room door, feeling as though he'd experienced another loss, crazy as the emotion was...and wrong. He'd given up on him and Cassidy long ago. They'd both gotten what they'd wanted, him a stable family and she an adventurous career. Was she happy?

Had he been happy?

And why did he care?

As she'd said, it didn't matter.

"Mr. Loveland!" The nurse caught up to him as he passed the utility room door. "Cassidy has retrograde amnesia. The trauma of the accident caused her to lose her memory of events immediately before and after it."

"Will she get them back?"

The nurse shrugged. "Head injuries are unpredictable. Only time will tell."

He nodded his thanks and strode out into a day so cheery he wanted to punch the sun in its bright yellow face.

Time would tell…

So far, it'd only revealed that his past feelings for Cassidy remained, despite every effort to erase her from his memory and heart.

If only there was amnesia for that.

CHAPTER THREE

A WEEK LATER, Daryl passed his sister, Sierra, a pan filled with frozen mice through a raptor enclosure's slot. The morning was bright, the late September air crisp with a hint of hickory smoke wafting from her wildlife veterinary practice's woodstove flue. It was the kind of day that made you breathe deep, smile for no reason and feel glad to be alive. Or it should.

Since losing his wife, Daryl had been sleep-walking through a twilight of grief, regret and confusion. He needed closure, answers, stability and peace, none of which seemed possible—at least in the short term. Careful not to agitate the sick bald eagle inside the structure, he inched back. "How long have you had this one?"

"Eleven days." Sierra lightly pressed the top of its beak with one hand to distract the large bird while feeling beneath its breast feathers. "You're such a pretty thing," she cooed softly. "And you're gaining weight."

"What's wrong with him?" Daryl recalled the forceps she'd asked him to bring when he'd phoned to say he'd be stopping by this morning. He crept to the chicken wire door and dropped them through. Funny how he didn't blink an eye when squaring off against a bucking mustang or a raging bull, yet birds strong enough to sever a finger in one bite put the fear of God in him. Not his sister, though. She'd been rescuing animals all her life, from a fallen nest beside their bedroom window when they were kids, to big game like raptors, elk and bears in her sought-after practice.

"Lead poisoning." In an experienced move, Sierra scooped up the eagle and, cradling it against her side, grasped its bone-crushing talons with one hand. "Shh…" she breathed when the predator wriggled in her arms, then settled.

She grabbed a large syringe filled with a thick brown mixture and gently tapped its beak until it opened. "There you go." She pushed the plunger to release the fluid into its mouth. "You're taking your medicine so well."

"Where was he found?"

"It's a she." Sierra set the majestic, white-headed bird back on a low perch and, with slow, deliberate movements, picked up the forceps and pail. "Jed Swanton spotted it beneath some cottonwoods on his ranch. When he checked the next day, it was still there, so he called me. I didn't think she'd make it, she was so weak, but I'm feeling a little optimistic since she tried to bite me earlier. I hate when they don't try to bite."

Daryl shook his head at the crazy logic of his animal-loving sister. The only female in a family of five brothers, she kept him, Maverick, Cole, Heath and Travis in line as easily and effortlessly as she managed this dangerous bird of prey.

Using the tongs, Sierra picked up one mouse after the other and fed each to the bird, sometimes wiggling it when the eagle didn't clamp down.

"How do you know it's lead poisoning?" Daryl asked once she'd fed it the last mouse and felt beneath its neck.

"You've got a good crop in there," she murmured to the bird before turning to Daryl. "Absence of any injuries. No nearby power lines or roads."

"What are the symptoms of lead poisoning?"

Once she secured the enclosure entrance

behind her, she set down the empty pail, planted her hands on her hips and raised an eyebrow at him. "Cut the crud, Daryl. You didn't drive all the way out here just to talk about lead poisoning."

He lifted his hat, resettled it on his head and cupped the brim. "Can't a brother help his sister once in a while? Plus, I wanted to tell you Pa got a letter from Neil's lawyer," he added, referring to a stranger claiming to be their half uncle and eligible to inherit half of Loveland Ranch.

"Yeah. Two weeks ago."

"Just wanted to keep you up to date."

She slid him a side-eye, silently communicating she wasn't buying whatever he was selling, and led the way to her office. It was a rustic building with natural pine siding, green shutters and window boxes that, in the summer, overflowed with pink, white and red geraniums. The second story housed Sierra's new apartment.

"I brought you some hay bales and corn stalks." Autumn was Sierra's favorite season, and she decorated every inch of her practice with Indian corn, overstuffed scarecrows, carved pumpkins and potted mums.

"Thanks." The screen door creaked as she

pulled it open and stepped inside the dim interior of a spacious kitchen.

An oversize stainless-steel sink broke up a tiled countertop littered with cooking and veterinary instruments, baking ingredients and medical tinctures, ceramic cats and a real calico curled in a pool of sunshine. Magnets held dosage charts, wildlife population maps and cheesy animal-sayings posters to a refrigerator as likely to hold baby raccoon formula as it was to contain milk. The room was cluttered and homey and welcoming like his sister. It even smelled like Sierra—of fresh flowers, the outdoors and a faint trace of cinnamon and vanilla, ingredients she favored when indulging her second passion: baking.

Daryl flicked on the lights, crossed to the round antique table she'd refinished and dropped into a spindle-backed chair.

"How about some coffee?" Sierra thrust a glass pot under the faucet and twisted it on.

"I can't stay long."

"Sure." She elongated the word, calling him out as only a sister could. "How strong do you want it? Chuck Norris or Thor?"

"How about Chuck Norris as Thor?"

"That bad, huh?" She popped the top off a canister and added an extra, heaping scoop to the coffee machine the way he liked. No one knew him better than Sierra…no one but…

…Cassidy. Despite his determination not to think of her, his mind had turned her way all week. Between bouts of grief that wrung him inside out and left him sleepless and struggling to smile for his children, he worried about her recovery. Had she finalized plans for her discharge? According to her visiting parents, whom he'd called earlier, she'd leave the hospital this afternoon. He needed to make sure she was cared for.

Sierra turned on the machine, grabbed a container of homemade chocolate chip cookies and sat beside him. She nudged the treats his way. "How are you doing?"

He shrugged, bit into a cookie and chewed the crispy thin sweet in lieu of an answer.

Sierra twisted her fine blond hair into a long rope. "How are the kids?" she asked around the elastic band clamped between her teeth.

A ball formed in his throat. "Emma's afraid to go to sleep by herself and I caught Noah looking up pictures of dead bodies on my phone."

"You don't have it password protected?" Her hands stilled midway through twisting the band around her hair.

"He remembered I'd set it to 'Beuford,' but I've changed it." Daryl swallowed down the lump, recalling the horror, the profound sadness, the confusion he'd felt in discovering his little boy looking at graphic images. "They're trying to make sense of everything."

"What have you told them?" The coffee maker spat out a few drops before sending a stream of pungent brew into the carafe.

"Their mother's gone to heaven."

"That's it?" The elastic band snapped in half.

He spread his hands. "What else can I say?"

"They must want to know what happened."

Emotions weighed down his tongue. He flipped over a couple of cookies and assessed the number of chips until his blurred vision cleared enough to pick one.

"Have you spoken to Cassidy?" Sierra's voice dipped at the name his family had assiduously avoided using.

He nodded, chewing so hard his teeth banged together.

"And…" When he didn't answer, Sierra shoved back her chair, stomped to the now quiet coffee maker and grabbed two mugs hanging above her sink. "Lord," she said to the ceiling. "Give me the patience to deal with another tight-lipped Loveland man."

"I'm not tight-lipped, I'm confused!" he blurted, and the pressure in his chest eased the tiniest bit at the confession. He didn't have the situation under control yet, hadn't stabilized his family again. And it scared the hell out of him.

"Glory hallelujah." Sierra filled the mugs, then placed one before him. "He speaks. What did Cassidy say?"

"Not much." He held up a hand to stop whatever words puffed out Sierra's cheeks. "She's got temporary memory loss from the accident. Last she recalls, she was in the Philippines."

Sierra blinked at him over the rim of her raised mug. "She doesn't remember coming to the States? The accident?"

"Her last memory is Leanne's number appearing on her cell phone screen."

"Why would Leanne call her...of all people?"

He shook his head, withholding the detail of the suitcases in the Jeep. "Maybe she wanted to reconcile with her sister?"

And leave me...and the kids.

"Wouldn't she have told you?"

"We haven't—hadn't—been talking much," he confessed, his voice thick.

Sierra gripped his hand. "Were you planning on a divorce?"

He snatched it away. "No!"

"She'd been acting so distant. I worried she was planning to start a new life."

"Well, she wasn't," he said, brusquely, then downed a long gulp of bitter coffee.

Sierra held up a hand. "Okay. Okay. I get it. I'm sorry."

"Don't be sorry." Daryl hung his head and his fingers tightened around the mug handle. Deep breath in. Suck-it-up and face-the-music breath out. He'd come to Sierra to talk, not deny. "You're right. Leanne wasn't happy, although she hadn't said anything about leaving me."

"Leanne loved you."

"I thought she did."

"I'd never seen a happier bride the day you married." Sierra paused. "Or a more miserable groom."

His head snapped up. "What do you mean?"

"I know you, Daryl. I know your real smile versus the one you wear when your church lady fan club corners you at a social. You didn't want to marry Leanne in the first place."

"Yes, I did. She was pregnant with Emma. And I like the church ladies."

"You were doing your duty."

"And that was wrong?"

"No. But you weren't happy."

"I was doing the right thing, which is more important."

Sierra groaned. "Your halo's showing again."

"Cowboys wear Stetsons, not halos, darlin'."

"You've got yours tucked under it, then. Seriously, Daryl. You make the rest of us look bad."

"'Let sinners be consumed from the earth. And let the wicked be no more,'" he quoted, mimicking their minister's sanctimonious voice.

"Amen." Sierra shot him a lopsided smile. "Good thing you came to us, Daryl, to save us from our wicked ways."

"I do my best, though it's no easy feat," he drawled. "Speaking of honorable deeds, I'm thinking of bringing Cassidy home to recuperate."

Sierra's eyes bulged. "You can't do that."

"She has nowhere else to go."

"A world traveler like her? She must have friends everywhere."

"Not according to her folks."

"You've got enough to focus on with the kids. The last thing you need is Cassidy complicating your life."

"I owe it to her." After his betrayal, the least he could do was give her space to heal, physically and emotionally, before seeking answers about the crash.

"There's the real reason." Sierra drummed her fingers on her leg. "You feel guilty."

"Shouldn't I?" Since visiting Cassidy, remorse and guilt consumed him, nearly as powerful as his mourning. "We'd dated through college and I'd proposed to her. Next thing she knows, I took up with her sister."

Sierra shook her head. "That's a little over-simplified, don't you think? You talked about marriage and moving home together after graduation. You even had the engagement ring I helped you pick out—the one she'd admired in a magazine. She shot you down, so you moved on."

"She asked for time to think," he countered, reliving the moment when his dreams of starting a life with Cassidy went up in flames. "A national magazine had hired her to cover the conflict in Bosnia, her dream assignment, and she wanted to try it before committing to me."

"Why am I only hearing this now? And couldn't she have had both? Career and marriage?"

Daryl brushed cookie crumbs into a napkin, crumpled it into a ball and crossed to the waste basket. "She wanted to photograph wars." He stepped on the lever to lift the lid and tossed out the paper. "That meant travel, danger, chaos."

"But you majored in photography and journalism, too. Couldn't you have gone with her? Traveled together?"

He slumped back in his seat and dropped his elbows to the table. "She begged me to."

"Why didn't you?"

"The ranch had lost another hand. I had no choice but to come home and help out."

"Yes, you did! Maverick's chasing his dream as a bull rider, Travis is the county sheriff, Heath's a songwriter and I've got my practice."

"But I'm not like the rest of you!"

She gaped at him. "Because you're adopted?" When he didn't answer, she blasted on. "You're a Loveland, Daryl, in heart and soul, where it counts."

"Which is why I owe Pa," Daryl insisted. "He gave me a home, even when he already had enough to handle with Ma's issues, five kids and a struggling ranch."

"That was your past. You didn't owe him your future. Your happiness."

"That's not as important as—"

"—doing what's right." Sierra rolled her eyes. "Take off the halo, Daryl. Stop playing the martyr."

"I'm no saint." Not by a long shot. He downed the rest of his now tepid coffee. In the silence, another of Sierra's cats stretched her paws forward on the rag rug beneath the table and yawned with a curl of pink tongue. A wall-mounted Audubon clock chirped eleven o'clock. Whatever Sierra believed, he knew the truth. His birth parents didn't think him worth keeping, and the first woman to whom he'd given his heart had cast it, and him, away.

If he was a poker hand, he'd be the discard.

"What made you turn to Leanne?" Sierra dangled a length of yarn from her knitting basket to the swatting kitty below. "I never asked before because of the Loveland need-to-know information policy…but I have to understand how to help you."

"Cassidy needs help, not me."

"I disagree. You were crushed when you came home without her." Sierra tugged at the yarn ball the kitty managed to drag from her grip. "All this time, I thought you'd broken up at college. Why didn't you wait for her?"

Daryl's breath caught, and he swallowed back the black nausea, the bleakness of their parting. It was so fresh he could still taste it. "We'd never been apart a day let alone two months, and I got lonely. I kept running into Leanne at church functions, line dancing, fund-raisers, and she'd tell me stories about the two of them growing up. It helped."

Sierra arched a brow. "Meeting up with Leanne was just a coincidence?"

"At first, but then we started hanging out. She was a shoulder to lean on and an ear to listen to my doubts."

"You could have talked to me."

"You were doing that internship in Yosemite."

"Right. Forgot." Sierra waggled the string back and forth and the kitty's head swayed with it, jaw clamped. "So how did you and Leanne—" she stopped and cleared her throat, her cheeks pinking "—uh—get together."

"I don't remember."

"Come again?" Sierra quit pulling and, with a sigh, released the rest of the wool to the determined cat.

He broke a cookie in half, dunked it in his coffee, then lifted it, dripping, to his mouth. While he chewed, he struggled to recall his limited memory of the night that'd changed the course of three lives... Four, counting Emma. "I was trying a new moonshine recipe and Leanne stopped by. Cassidy hadn't answered my letters in over two weeks. The latest one came back return to sender. It felt like a rejection."

"And Leanne was there to listen."

"I rambled for hours, drowning my sorrows. Next thing I knew, I woke with Leanne in my arms. It was a big mistake that only worsened when Leanne became pregnant."

"Interesting choice of words."

"Which one?"

"Worse." Sierra scooped up the cat, yarn and all, and settled it on her lap.

"I don't regret anything leading to Emma being born," he said fiercely. He'd never put himself ahead of his offspring like his biological parents.

"Of course." A purr erupted from the cat as Sierra stroked its arching back. "But I bet you wished it was with Cassidy."

The statement was matter-of-fact and without any hint of censure, but Daryl felt his stomach churn with shame for being so foolish and careless. "Cassidy and I weren't meant to be."

Sierra scoffed and shook her head. "How can you be sure?"

"When Cassidy came home and found out we'd married, she wasn't bothered." The hollow feeling he associated with that moment returned. "In fact, she already had another assignment and was flying out the next day. I wasn't her choice anyway."

Sierra pursed her lips. "Hmm…" The cat lifted a paw to bat at her long hair.

"What?"

"Why come home if she had to leave the next day?" Sierra gently tugged blond strands from the cat's mouth, shoved them behind her ears and peered at him.

"To break up with me?" Daryl shifted in his seat, pinned under Sierra's direct gaze. "At least I spared her the task since I'd moved on."

"Did you?" Sierra probed.

His eyes slid from hers. "When Lovelands commit—"

"It's forever. I know. Pa was a case in point."

"He's honorable." Their gazes collided, the memories of their erratic mother, who'd suffered from mental health and addiction before taking her life, an unholy bond. "If I'm even half the man Pa is, that's an achievement. All my focus has been on Leanne and our family since we married, and I've worked every day to make her happy...and I still failed."

"Did you love her?" The cat's collar bell jingled as it jumped back to the floor.

"Yes." His voice broke, and he looked down at his clenched hands. "A different kind of love." It wasn't the intense, electric, edge-of-his-seat, can't-get-enough feeling he'd had with Cassidy, who'd always left him unsettled and wanting more. He, Leanne and their children had carved out a respectable, stable life that'd satisfied him most of the time.

"And what about Cassidy? Did she find someone else?"

"She's on her own." He ignored the relief accompanying her unattached status. It was none of his business.

"If she was fine with you and Leanne, how

come she never visited you when she came home?"

"I destroyed her relationship with her sister. It's unforgivable." He'd hurt her. No matter how stoic she'd behaved when she'd learned of the shotgun wedding, he'd sensed her same despair, the loss behind her shuttered expression.

Sierra leaned back in her chair and tilted her head as she contemplated that for a few beats. "What about Leanne? Did she feel bad about taking her sister's beau?"

"She said Cassidy wouldn't have been content tied down in Carbondale, to me or the ranch and it worked out for the best."

Sierra wrinkled her nose. "If that's what helped you cope."

"You don't agree?"

"Do you?"

"Carbondale couldn't give her the excitement she wanted."

And neither could I.

His need to do what was right, to follow the rules, had been a point of contention between them. His adoptive siblings knew their place in the world. Him? He'd had to forge his own path and found the straight-and-narrow one easiest to follow, even when it meant giving up what he really wanted to make correct choices…like Cassidy.

"What about you?" Sierra challenged. "Did you get what you needed?"

He rubbed his aching temples. "I wanted my kids to have a stable life. That made me happy. I thought that made Leanne happy, too. Then something changed a year and a half ago. Leanne started acting distant. Resentful. Nothing pleased her, and I worried the kids might lose her."

"Not you?"

"And me," he hastily amended, though it'd been the children he'd been concerned about. He knew what it was like to be abandoned, rejected by the people who were supposed to love you.

Sierra tipped her head to the side, her gaze reflective. "How does Cassidy figure into what happened to Leanne?"

"I don't know. The nurse said she may regain her memory over time, and I want her to be in Carbondale when she does, not thousands of miles away in some war zone."

"And you're sure you want to take care of her?" Sierra leaned forward and touched his tense forearm.

"Yes." He owed Cassidy that.

"Do you want my opinion?"

Her question was so predictably rhetorical, he couldn't help but smile. "Do I have a choice?"

Sierra's brief laugh trailed off, and her expression sobered. "If you bring Cassidy home, you won't be able to let her go again."

"Not true," came the automatic denial. "We've changed, grown up and want different things. I—I don't love her anymore."

"Not sure if I believe you."

"Believe it." He'd made his decision years ago and given his heart to the woman who'd wanted it: Leanne.

"The goal when rehabilitating wild animals is to release them. You can't get attached or interact too much or your heart will break when you let them go."

"Then why do you always cry when you release one?"

Sierra sighed. "Because I'm a softie who doesn't practice what she preaches. You, however, need to take my advice. Keep your distance, emotionally, at least."

He looked at his watch and stood. "I'd better hurry. Her discharge is at noon."

Sierra walked him to the door, then threw her arms around him. "You're just as good a man as Pa, Daryl, halo and all. Please don't add to your hurt."

"Not a chance." He ignored the alarm bells shrieking in his ears, hugged Sierra, then jogged to his pickup. On the road, his mind raced along with his truck.

Did Sierra have a point? If Cassidy could no longer affect him, then why had he never forgotten—or stopped missing—the relationship they used to have? Not a day passed without his thinking about the woman he'd walked away from.

He'd tried pushing the painful memories aside because there was no way to go back and do things differently. But sometimes, deep in dreams, he'd imagined himself making a different choice. A smarter choice. And in those dreams, he held the woman he'd loved first and lost…

And every time he dreamed of her, he'd awakened with such a heavy weight on his chest, he'd wondered how his broken heart still beat. Then he'd look at Leanne, asleep beside him, one or both kids nestled between them, and know he'd done the best he could. He'd grab some toast, head out to the range and throw himself into physical labor, as if driving cattle would somehow drive away his regret and guilt.

His foot eased on the accelerator as he approached the hospital minutes later, doubts battering him from all directions. Why was he really doing this?

Was he putting his already grieving heart in more jeopardy?

His fingers remained on the wheel long after he'd turned off the engine. He was older now. Wiser. A father and now a widower. A long breath whistled from him. Regardless of his reasons for helping Cassidy, he was doing the right thing.

Now how to convince her to come home with him… The pine-scented air freshener dangling from his rearview mirror caught his eye. It'd been a Father's Day gift from the only two people Cassidy could not refuse. He checked the dashboard clock, started up the engine and sped from the parking lot. If he hurried, he'd return in time to stop Cassidy from leaving him.

His sweaty palm slipped on the gearshift.

Whoa. Where did that thought come from?

He wanted to help Cassidy was all. When she left, he'd feel satisfied that he'd done right by her this time. Period. End of story.

Sierra was wrong about his getting hurt.

If he'd let Cassidy go once before, he could do it again…

"THE SWELLING'S GONE down quite a bit."

Cassidy winced when her mother gingerly touched her bruised eye, still healing from surgery five days ago.

"But will she get her full eyesight back?" Her father, a stocky man with ruddy skin, thumped his cane on the floor as he paced beside her hospital bed. "It'll break my heart if you can't take more photos, bug. You're the best in the world. You deserve one of them Pulitzers."

Cassidy hid another wince. Her father's opinion meant everything. "The doctor said it'll take some time."

"Wish we could bring you back to Aunt May's with us." Her mother poured Cassidy water and passed over the cup. A sad smile graced her pretty face, touched by years and love as she liked to say. "Your father and I only have one room and Aunt May's kids, and their kids, are living with her, too."

"I'll figure it out." Cassidy's mouth creaked into a smile reassuring enough to smooth her father's furrowed brow.

"Of course you will. No one's as bright as you." Her father limped to a nearby chair and lowered himself with his wife's help. "Knew it when you began drawing those birds. No stick figures like the other kindergartners."

Cassidy met her mother's slight eye roll as her father launched into one of his favorite stories. "You had all the colors right, the sizes and shapes, too. When you beat out fifth graders to win the school art show, I said to myself, 'Earl, whatever you do, give this girl every chance to reach her potential.' The sky was the limit, and I'd do anything to help you reach those stars."

"Thank you, Pa."

Her vision blurred as she took in her father's earnest face. He'd scrimped, saved and sacrificed to pay for college expenses not covered by her scholarship, helping her become the first to attend in her family. He'd rarely slept between back-to-back shifts and incurred a disabling spine injury for his efforts. All he'd ever wanted was to see her achieve her dreams.

Her glory was his glory.

What if she didn't regain her full sight and resume the career she'd given up *everything* to follow...even love?

Daryl's concerned brown eyes returned to her, along with the feelings she'd thought she'd buried. She couldn't think of him without hurting, or picture her sister, Leanne, gone, buried, beyond her reach, without crying.

Would she ever regain her memory of their accident?

"How are you two doing?" She set down her water and swung her legs over the side of her bed. Thanks to her mother, she wore a pair of new jeans and a soft pink T-shirt. The Jeep's engine fire destroyed her luggage and, more troubling, her ID and passport. She was grounded in more ways than one.

Her father gripped her mother's hand. "We're holding it together, bug. A parent should never have to bury a child." Their youngest child at that.

Her mother released a shuddering breath. "It was a lovely service. There wasn't an empty pew in the church. I couldn't get over how hard the Lovelands and Cades worked to make it special. Such good people. Leanne sure was loved, and my she had a beautiful family."

As her mother described the service, Cassidy wondered who'd come to her funeral since her demanding schedule meant she lived out of a suitcase and didn't have time for close relationships. She recorded others' lives but didn't have one of her own.

Cassidy tuned back in and heard her mother say, "Everyone asked about you. Daryl mentioned he was planning to visit."

"He did," she replied, terse.

"Honey, I think you should stay with him while you recover." Her mother smoothed back a strand of Cassidy's hair.

She jerked away, then nearly cried out at the stabbing pain in her skull. "That's a horrible idea. Back me up, Pa."

Her father sighed heavily. "Not this time, bug. Doctor says you have to be discharged into someone's care, and we're not in a position to take you, as much as we wish otherwise."

"I'd rather sleep on the street. I'm used to it."

Her mother sucked in her cheeks. "We may not have had much, but we've never let you girls go homeless."

"I meant, when on assignments."

"You don't have a place of your own," her father said.

"I'll rent an efficiency."

"You'll need ID for that."

Cassidy frowned as her father's pronouncement sank in.

"Which is why you should stay with Daryl," her mother pleaded. "At least until you have your license and have healed a bit more."

"I don't need him." Cassidy slammed to her feet, felt the ground tilt beneath her and toppled backward into the bed.

"That answers that," her father stated.

"Think of it this way, honey." Her mother placed the back of her hand on Cassidy's damp brow. "Emma and Noah need a mother figure, especially this time of year when Daryl will be working long hours bringing in the harvest."

Cassidy's resistance melted a touch when she thought of her niece and nephew. Until her parents' recent move away from their home outside Carbondale, she'd visited with them at least twice a year and they'd grown close. She loved those kids and would do anything for them... Did that include moving in, temporarily, with Daryl?

Unthinkable.

She didn't want to recover in the home of the man whose memory she'd never outrun, no matter how far she'd traveled or how risky her environments. He'd destroyed her relationships with two of the people she'd loved most: him and Leanne.

But her choices grew more limited by the minute. Her editor had offered Cassidy a room in her Hamptons home, but how to travel there without an ID? Other than her parents and aunt, she had no blood relatives in Colorado, except Emma and Noah.

Her father glanced at his watch and frowned. "Bug, we're supposed to catch a bus back to Phoenix soon. I have a bit of savings for us to get a hotel tonight, though, if you need us to stay while you make up your mind."

Cassidy's mother's teeth worried her bottom lip. It'd be the height of selfishness to make them spend their meager nest egg while she waffled.

"No. Go. I'll call my editor again. I'm sure we'll work something out," she assured them. Tears burned the back of her throat as she stared into their concerned faces. They couldn't help her; no one could. She'd never felt so utterly alone, not since the day she'd learned Daryl and Leanne had married.

Her father heaved himself up and limped to her bed. "Promise me, bug." His wiry eyebrows lowered as his blue eyes bored into hers.

"I promise."

"I don't want to leave without knowing you'll be taken care of." Her mother wrung her hands.

"You don't have to," someone pronounced from the open doorway. A tall, handsome, deep-voiced cowboy.

Daryl.

"W-what are you doing here?" she demanded, hating the catch in her voice almost as much as the flicker of relief at the sight of his confident stride, the no-nonsense set of his firm chin. Deep down, did she want someone to rescue her for a change, that someone being the last person she'd ever trust?

"I'm taking you home, Cassidy."

She opened her mouth to refuse, then stopped at the sight of her niece and nephew as they ducked under their father's arms and flew to her side. Her heart melted when Noah buried his head in the crook of her arm while Emma grabbed her good hand.

"I miss you, Aunt Cassidy!" Noah's voice was muffled, lost in the folds of her shirt. "Mama's gone to heaven and she can't come back."

Cassidy laid her cheek atop his head. "I know, sweetheart. I'm so sorry."

"You're hurting her." Emma grabbed the back of Noah's shirt and pulled.

"Let go!" Noah's out-flung arm smacked Cassidy square across her bruised chin as they grappled.

"Kids! Off!" At their father's roar, they scrambled away.

"Now she'll never come home with us," Emma half yelled, half sobbed.

Tears rolled down Noah's red cheeks. "I'm sorry. Please don't go away, Aunt Cassidy. We need you. Pa makes bad grilled cheese sandwiches. And his mac-n-cheese is the worst."

Emma nodded sagely. "Too much butter, not enough cheese."

"And Beuford ate my Flamin' Cheetos and made a big mess."

Daryl squatted to face his son. "What's the rule about feeding Beuford?"

"Always stay downwind?" Noah's little face scrunched.

"The second one." The faint glimmer of humor in Daryl's eyes as they rose to meet hers had her biting back a tremulous smile. *Keep your guard up*, she reminded herself.

Emma planted her fists on her waist. "No Flamin' Cheetos, stupid!"

"I'm not stupid," Noah cried. "You're stupid."

"Take it back!"

"Behave yourselves." At Daryl's firm, authoritative tone, the kids quit squabbling. Eight pairs of expectant eyes, including her parents', turned her way.

"I'm sure this is mighty tempting…a dog with a hair-trigger colon, bickering children and a quest for the perfect mac-n-cheese," Daryl said gravely, fatigue weighing down his handsome features. "But it's the best we can offer. Will you accept?"

"Please," the kids pleaded.

She opened her arms to the children who needed her, suspecting she needed them just as much or more. They flung themselves at her, probably refracturing her aching ribs. Still, she'd have time to heal, physically and emotionally, on Loveland Hills if she took care not to let Daryl too close.

"Sounds irresistible." She ruffled Noah's hair, pressed a kiss to Emma's damp cheek and met Daryl's grave brown eyes, wondering if she was about to regret her next words. "I accept."

CHAPTER FOUR

"REAL PIRATES?"

Daryl followed his son's excited voice, paused outside Noah's room and glimpsed Cassidy perched on the edge of his bed, Emma beside her. Surprise rooted his boots to the floor. Noah's sound soother gushed pattering rain and the soft scent of body wash lingered in the air. Noah's damp head peeked above his Spider-Man cover, suggesting a shower, as did Emma's. Both wore pajamas, ready and on time to go to sleep, Noah in his bed, a first since Leanne's passing. The heaviness in his heart eased at this return to normalcy.

Stability.

It spoke to the level of comfort the children felt, and safety, from having Cassidy around.

Concern quickly replaced his relief. Why was Cassidy putting them to bed? She should be resting, recuperating. Bandages bulged beneath her yellow T-shirt, a splint covered her broken pinkie and a white gauze pad concealed her upper arm's gunshot wound. When he'd left this morning to drive cattle, Joy had been in the kitchen cooking breakfast. She'd promised to watch the kids until he returned. Granted, a pinkeye outbreak requiring medical attention to the herd made him late, but Joy was dependable, and Cassidy shouldn't be up and around.

The ranch demanded extra work during harvest season. It was on more stable financial ground recently since the Cades—their former rivals and now extended family—reinstated the land easement allowing them to drive their Brahmans to the Crystal River. Yet Loveland Hills still had a way to go before it operated at maximum capacity, the threat of foreclosure not fully behind them. Commanding top prices at this fall's cattle auction, as well as bringing in a large grain harvest for winter feed, was all-important. Worse, some stranger claiming to be his father's older half brother insisted the ranch partially belonged to him and demanded half the land and his share in the crucial profits.

"I'll take it from here."

Cassidy twisted around and winced at the move. Her green eyes were enormous in her heart-shaped face, her honey-brown hair framing it in a tumble of waves. She looked vulnerable, young without makeup, and pale. It reminded him of the day she'd learned of his and Leanne's marriage. His betrayal.

Emma flung herself at him and he staggered backward when he caught her. She wrapped her arms and legs around him like a spider monkey.

"Pa! Cassidy made us arrows con…!" Emma paused, and her brow furrowed.

"Arroz con pollo," Cassidy supplied with an indulgent smile that faded when her eyes rose to meet his.

"Sounds fancy."

"It is!" Emma answered him. "The rice was yellow, and the chicken was better than KFC."

"High praise indeed." Cassidy's gaze clicked with his again and the glimmer of humor lightening her eyes tugged up the corners of his lips. "Where's Grandma Joy?" He placed Emma back on her feet.

"She got tired and Grandpa took her home. Aunt Sierra was going to leave work, but Aunt Cassidy said we'd take care of each other and we did!" Emma pointed to the bandages on

Cassidy's hand. "I put those back on after dinner."

"And I took a bath and cleaned behind my ears," Noah said.

"You were a big help." Daryl crossed the room and ruffled Noah's damp hair, marveling at this unknown, maternal side of Cassidy. She'd never wanted a traditional life or family, yet she seemed a natural with the kids, their faces more relaxed and less pale than they'd been in the past couple of weeks. The ice encasing his heart since Leanne's passing melted slightly around the edges. "What about Beuford?" At his name, their geriatric beagle mix dragged his muzzle from the floor and peered blearily in Daryl's direction.

"He didn't throw up on anything." Noah shrugged his shoulders beneath the covers.

"Yes, he did!" Emma flipped her damp, blond hair over one shoulder. "Pa's slippers."

Daryl bit back a groan.

"I meant nothing of mine." Noah sat up and the covers dropped to his waist. "Plus, he ate the rice I dropped on the floor, so we didn't have to sweep."

"How about homework?" Daryl leaned in to hug Noah.

"I finished mine and I didn't cheat." Emma

gnawed her cuticle. "Mostly. But it's not for a grade so that's okay, right?"

"You checked your answers and changed the ones you got wrong… What's your father say?" Cassidy's eyes slid from his. Since she'd come home with him yesterday she'd mostly avoided talking or looking directly at him and he'd done the same, the two of them circling each other like boxers in the final round, sure the other one might deliver the knockout with one blow.

"Sounds fair to me." Daryl released Noah. "Now let's say good-night to Aunt Cassidy. She needs her rest."

"She was telling us a pirate's story!" Noah dropped back to the pillow and for the first time since losing his mother, his face broke into a smile. "A real one!"

Daryl glanced at Cassidy's ashen complexion, then back to his pleading children. Bedtime had been a struggle since Leanne began going out and keeping odd hours, throwing the kids off their routine. After her death, Emma refused to sleep alone, and Noah resisted sleeping at all, both afraid of the dark, suddenly.

"It's a short one," Cassidy assured him, her eyes on Noah.

"Okay. Mind if I stay?" He was dead tired but the hot shower he'd been looking forward to no longer appealed as much as the warmth filling this cozy room. A projector displayed twinkling stars on the ceiling and through the dim he gleaned Legos, trains and Lincoln Logs littering the small room's floor. Noah hadn't taken them out in weeks.

"As long as you don't scare easily… This isn't some kiddie tale," Cassidy cautioned. Her left eyebrow lifted.

"I think I can handle it."

Cassidy launched into her tale and his children lost themselves in the story, Emma slipping in beside Noah, their wide eyes riveted to Cassidy's animated face.

"I was asleep on the *Albedo*, a cargo ship on the Indian Ocean," she began, "when an announcement came over the loudspeaker— pirates are approaching."

"Where's the Indian Ocean?" Noah scratched his nose.

Emma rolled her eyes "In India, stupid."

"Don't call me stupid." Noah shoved Emma's shoulder. "Mama said…"

Horrified silence descended, so painful breathing felt like a stab to the lungs.

"Your mother said you were the brightest children and she loved you both." Daryl clamped his back teeth together to keep his mouth from wobbling. An image of a beaming Leanne holding a newborn Emma flashed in his mind's eye followed by one of her cooing over Noah when they'd brought him home from the hospital.

How had everything changed?

Why, Leanne?

What did I do?

"I miss Mama," Noah sniffled. Emma buried her face into the pillow. When Daryl rubbed her shoulder, she flung off his hand.

"I don't miss her," Emma cried, her face red when she turned. "And she didn't love us. She didn't!"

"Yes, she did," Daryl said tightly.

"You're just saying that!" Emma stormed. She threw off the covers and swung her legs over the side of the bed.

"What about the pirate story?"

Emma froze at Cassidy's question and her shoulders lowered. "Did anyone die?"

"Nope."

"Okay." Emma eased back down to the bed. "Sorry, Pa."

"It's okay."

"Did anyone get their arm chopped off?" Noah wiped his red eyes on the comforter.

"No. Though some teeth got knocked out."

"Well…all right," Noah grumped. "If that's the best you can do."

Cassidy's twitching mouth snared Daryl's attention, and he released a breath when the children snuggled together again.

"We were a thousand miles from the eastern coast of Africa…west of the Maldives, closer to India." Cassidy resumed her story. "I rushed up to the bridge, where most of the ship's crew had already gathered. The captain pointed to port."

"What's port?" Noah twisted around, planted his elbow into the mattress and dropped the side of his face into his palm.

"Left side," Daryl answered.

"I could just make out a distant silhouette on top of the waves, an open-bow skiff." When Noah opened his mouth, Cassidy added, "A skiff is like a speedboat. The captain sent out distress messages, then he directed the steersman to maneuver the ship in a zigzag pattern. He called the engine room and ordered full steam, but the *Albedo* was old and sluggish."

"Liked Beuford!"

Cassidy nodded. "Though not as smelly."

Beuford's lips vibrated as he snored, the dog oblivious to the censure raining down on him. He rolled onto his back and his rounded belly rose and fell.

"The crew had ringed the deck with barbed wire and affixed an electric wire to the gunwale, hoping to prevent anyone from boarding the ship uninvited," Cassidy continued.

Noah pulled up the covers so only his rounded eyes showed.

"The crew plugged in the electric wire. By then, the skiff was just a few hundred yards away. On board were four men wearing T-shirts and sarongs and carrying rifles. We watched, helpless, as the skiff pulled alongside the ship."

Daryl frowned, imagining the danger Cassidy described with such relish. Why put herself into risky situations?

Because she cared only about her career, the story, came the answer…not anything or anyone else, not even herself.

Or him, once.

Not that it mattered anymore.

"The pirates retrieved a long ladder with hooks on one end, hung it over the deck wall and climbed it without getting shocked from the wire."

Emma pressed her fingers to her mouth. "Did they have eye patches?"

"Were they zombies?" Noah's eyes bulged. "If you're dead you don't feel anything."

"No—to both."

Noah heaved another disgruntled sigh.

"Did the electric fence malfunction?" Daryl asked, caught up in the tale and invested in knowing how Cassidy had survived. She crossed the globe in the most treacherous circumstances, yet a visit home had nearly killed her.

Leanne hadn't been so fortunate.

With that question out, three pairs of eyes fell on him. He jerked his mouth into an approximation of a smile. "I was just imagining those rifles."

"They were scary, and yes." Cassidy's concerned gaze lingered on his face. "The electric fences failed."

"But you still had the barbed wire," Emma interjected.

"It didn't stop them. The first pirate charged through it, the metal cutting into his flesh." An artificial thunder roll rumbled from the sound soother, punctuating Cassidy's statement.

"He *was* a zombie!" Noah pounded his fist on the cover.

"No." Cassidy's honey-brown hair swished over her shoulders as she shook her head. "Just desperate."

"He wanted your booty." Emma giggled through her raised fingers.

Cassidy grinned. "They wanted to capture and ransom us."

Emma dropped her hand and stared, open-mouthed. "Kidnap you?"

"Like a princess?" asked an aggrieved-sounding Noah.

"Not that glamorous," Cassidy answered, wryly, her offhandedness at this life-and-death anecdote hard to comprehend. What drew her to danger? Chaos? Not the part he'd loved once…or had it been exactly that part, so unlike him, which had drawn him when he'd been young…foolish…full of dreams instead of responsibilities? "Cargo ships don't have much in the way of cash, but people can command a price."

"When does someone get their teeth knocked out?" Noah demanded.

"Soon, my bloodthirsty pirate." Cassidy tweaked Noah's nose. "The captain ordered everyone off the bridge, and down to the engine room. We heard gunfire and shattering glass above. After a few minutes, a heavily accented voice came over the loudspeaker. 'Come on bridge, Captain,' it said, in English. 'Come on bridge with crew, otherwise we kill.'"

"But no one dies, right?" Emma interjected.

Cassidy stroked her face. "No, sweetie. We went upstairs. One pirate yelled and jabbed at us with the butt of his rifle, and we all fell to our knees. Our captain had a hand to his mouth and when he dropped it, his front teeth were gone."

"Ewwwwwwww..." Emma shuddered.

"Awesome," Noah breathed.

"Then another pirate took over," Cassidy said. "He introduced himself as Ali Jabin. 'We want only company money,' he said. 'If company pay money, no problem.' He ordered us to collect everything valuable from our cabins—cell phones, cash, jewelry—and pile it on the bridge. 'Crew problem, Somalia problem,' he said. 'Crew no problem, Somalia no problem.'"

"What's that mean?" Noah's nose scrunched.

"We had to cooperate or there'd be trouble," Cassidy explained.

"Like getting your arm chopped off?" Noah snuggled closer to Emma.

"Something like that… The pirates ordered the captain to head to Somalia and they held us there for almost two weeks."

"Did they chain you to a wall?" Emma pushed Noah's drooping head from her shoulder.

"No. But I was in a room without windows, so I couldn't see anything." A distant expression crossed Cassidy's face and Daryl wondered at her thoughts, her memories, her experiences of traveling the world as they'd once planned to do together.

Emma shuddered. "I don't like the dark."

Since Leanne's death, Emma had demanded Daryl keep the lights on after she and Noah piled into bed beside him. With Cassidy in his bedroom and him on the couch, she'd started bunking in with Noah. "How did you get through it?" Daryl asked, hoping Cassidy's answer might help the children.

"I memorized poems from a special book someone gave me once," she said softly, and Daryl's chest tightened, recalling the poetry collection he'd given her as a Christmas present one year…their last holiday together. "I recited them over and over until I was freed. It helped me get through."

"What was the best one?" Noah asked through a yawn.

"My favorite is 'I Carry Your Heart with Me' by E. E. Cummings."

Her gaze locked with Daryl's for a heart-pounding moment. It carried him back to that distant Christmas, her warm body snuggled into his before a fire as he'd recited the poem, the words a perfect match, then, for his feelings.

A long, *long* time ago.

Day by day, year by year, Leanne had replaced Cassidy in his heart, love built on shared experiences, trials and joys. What he'd felt for Cassidy had been an untested love, fragile as a bubble drifting on a breeze…not meant to last.

Not like he'd imagined with Leanne.

When he'd followed voices down the hall a few minutes ago, he'd momentarily forgotten the accident and had expected to see Leanne with the children. The sight of Cassidy in her place was jarring. Unsettling. Would his heart ever comprehend Leanne was truly gone? How to accept losing a wife who'd already seemed lost to him before the accident?

"Bleh!" Noah made a face. "I hate hearty-farty stuff."

"Can I hear the heart poem?" Emma pleaded.

"I'm not sure..." Cassidy began. Uncertainty shook her voice.

"I carry your heart with me," Daryl began, his eyes stinging as he recited the rest of the poem by heart.

"That's beautiful," Emma sighed when he finished, her eyes growing heavy, her lashes drifting to her cheeks. "I hope someone gives me that book someday."

"I wish I could have given it to you," Cassidy sighed. "But it—uh—got burned."

He stared at her in surprise. Had it been destroyed in the car accident? "You still had it?"

"I carried it with me. Always."

Noah made retching sounds, which earned him an elbow from his sister that, in turn, morphed into a shoving match.

"Kids!" Daryl roared and they instantly subsided. "What's the rule about bedtime?"

"Toothbrushes aren't weapons?" Emma supplied.

Cassidy seemed to be fighting a smile suddenly and he wasn't doing much better.

"The other rule."

"No eating Flamin' Cheetos in bed?"

Daryl closed his eyes and counted to ten before saying, "No fighting."

"What about crying?" Emma asked, her voice tight.

"If you need to, and you always have me," Daryl vowed. He patted his shoulders. "These can take on anything—especially tears."

"I bet Aunt Cassidy never—" Noah cut himself off with an enormous yawn "—cries. She's tough." He twisted around until he faced the wall, his back to his sister.

"When I grow up I want to be just like Aunt Cassidy," murmured Emma before her eyes shut for the last time and her mouth slackened.

A chill swept down his spine as he eyed his little girl. He didn't want Cassidy's risky, chaotic life for Emma. Misgivings over his decision to invite Cassidy home swamped him. Clearly, Emma hero-worshipped Cassidy. She might grow too attached and want to follow in Cassidy's footsteps only to be devastated when Cassidy left.

"Good night." Cassidy slipped by him, leaving her familiar scent in her wake. It always reminded him of night-blooming flowers in faraway places. Beautiful and just out of reach.

Daryl leaned in the doorway and watched his now sleeping children, his heart in overdrive. Cassidy's positive effect on them was undeniable. She'd gotten them to sleep, even if it was with each other, on time and with the lights off. But the mixed-up feelings he was having for Cassidy, and the way her story turned Emma's head, had him wondering if it was a good idea to bring Cassidy home after all...

SHARP PAIN LANCED Cassidy's side as she stretched up to stack another dried dinner plate inside the cabinet a few nights later. She gripped the counter's edge and waited for the hurt to abate and the room to stop spinning. Nearly a week had passed since her discharge, her healing steady but aggravatingly slow. Her left-eye vision didn't seem to be improving much and her broken pinkie left her clumsy and unable to grip properly, especially something she'd have to keep steady, like her trusty Canon. Not that it mattered.

It'd disappeared in the accident with her cell phone, right along with her memory of what'd brought her to Carbondale.

To Leanne.

In the background, a grandfather clock rang nine times. Beuford woofed quietly as he dozed by the front door. Down the hall, she pictured Emma and Noah, each asleep in their own beds at last after she'd told them another nightly adventure story. They'd asked her to wish their father, who hadn't returned from the range yet, good-night.

She tensed at a noise outside the door.

Daryl?

When quiet returned, she drew in a ragged breath, grabbed the dishrag and dried another plate. Living with Daryl had her on edge. Everywhere she looked, especially while staying in Daryl and Leanne's bedroom, held signs of a shared life together. Everything from their framed wedding photos to the monogrammed hand towels drove home their happiness and their betrayal. Her emotions careened between old anger and fresh grief, to ongoing concern for a mourning Noah and Emma and a strange sense of peace when she cared for the children or lost herself in some domestic chore like drying the dishes.

She gingerly stowed the plate, closed the cabinet and peered around the snug cabin. It had a rustic, homey feel with dark oak floors and log walls. A leather recliner, matching a three-cushion sofa, sat off to the corner beside deep bookshelves that spanned most of the far wall. The kitchen was separated by an arched entryway, open to the rest of the living room. Every inch of space screamed *family*, from the photos lining the walls, to the children's drawings covering the refrigerator door. This was a home, not a house, a life, not a showroom.

The efficiency rooms she'd stayed in these past ten years blurred together in a sterile composite, the exotic locations she'd traveled to a sharp contrast. Her old life was exhilarating, but lonely in comparison. Staying in one place for a change, on this sleepy, bucolic Rocky Mountain ranch of all places, provided another kind of satisfaction. She was needed in a more personal way than on the world level she normally experienced.

Beuford barely left her side all week, sticking his nose in her hand, seeking attention and reassurance. As for her nephew and niece, their quiet grief and need for physical contact brought her to tears. The rush of love and desire to comfort them filled her with a maternal protectiveness she'd never encountered before. Her feelings for Daryl, however, were far from straightforward.

Every time she met his large brown eyes, regret and hurt filled her, as well as sympathy. He grieved his wife, her sister, just like she did. The more time she spent with him, the harder it became to keep from finding common ground.

Cassidy peeked in on a snoozing Emma and Noah, then let Beuford out the front door. A velvety darkness folded around her, the chill air making her shoulders hunch. She stood at the porch railing, rubbed her hands over her arms to keep warm and stared up at the stars, wondering which one was Leanne.

Will I ever know why you summoned me? Why you needed your big sister again?

Growing up, struggling through an impoverished childhood, she and Leanne had clung to one another, survivors, each other's only lifeline. They'd often talked past their bedtime, Leanne counting off the number of children she'd have while Cassidy had listed the places she wanted to see. Leanne dreamed of home and hearth and Cassidy had longed for adventure and accolades. They'd never imagined their paths would intersect as they did, hadn't imagined they'd lose each other along the way…and maybe…just maybe, Cassidy had been too harsh on Leanne.

Yes, Leanne had stolen the man she loved and the life Cassidy might have had, but ultimately, hadn't Leanne made a tough choice easier? Cassidy loved her career and the chance to fulfill the potential her father envisioned. Should she have made amends years ago, before it was all too late?

Or was her grief talking? You couldn't be mad at someone you lost. Only now she had no sister to forgive and no place for her bubbling emotions to go.

Beuford's welcoming bark, followed by footsteps, broke her from her thoughts. Her heart picked up speed at the sight of tall, broad-shouldered Daryl. Shadows shrouded his face beneath his Stetson, but she sensed his fatigue, his sorrow, from the clenched hands filling out his pockets and the bow of his head, as if he walked through a hurricane.

"Hey," she called in warning before he started up the steps.

He lifted his face and his soulful eyes landed briefly on her before swerving away. "Howdy." His boots stomped heavily on the treads as he climbed. "Did I miss the kids?"

"They fell asleep about twenty minutes

ago. They wanted me to wish you good-night."

Daryl stopped on the top step and his scent of horses, leather and the earthy musk of a day's work made her breathe deep. "Thank you. Getting them to bed's been difficult since…" He cleared his throat and lifted his gaze to the stars. "I'm supposed to be helping you, but it seems as though you're the one doing the helping."

"I don't mind."

He flicked a sideways glance at her. "Not feeling too hemmed in yet?"

She ignored the layers of meaning and history in the question and waved her broken pinkie. "My wings are clipped. I couldn't fly away yet, even if I wanted to."

"How's the pain?"

"It only hurts when I breathe," she joked, despite being dead serious.

"Well, if that's all," Daryl teased back, then seemed to catch himself, his half smile disappearing into his beard.

"I should go in and get some rest."

Daryl held up a hand, stopping her. "Travis gave me this. They recovered it from the scene." From a bag, he pulled out her Canon Rebel T5i.

Relief turned her knees to jelly. "I thought it was destroyed."

Daryl turned it over in his large hands, a look of longing on his face. "It was thrown clear."

A shudder tore through her body. Leanne had also been ejected from the car...but not cleanly. Or so she'd been told. Some memories Cassidy hoped never to regain. "Is the investigation report completed?"

Daryl raised the camera to his eye and sighted her through the lens. "Yes. The swerve marks suggest fast acceleration prior to hitting the rail."

"I was speeding?" Her heart burned, sending flames into her throat to scorch her tongue.

Daryl lowered the camera. "Yes."

"So I was negligent. At fault."

"We don't have all the facts yet. Don't..." He stepped closer and briefly touched the side of her face. "Don't blame yourself."

She squeezed her eyes shut. "I just want to know what happened. But sometimes, I'm afraid of what I might find out," she confessed.

"Me, too." Daryl shoved the camera at her as if it burned his fingers. "Some things are better forgotten."

"Do you still have your camera?"

"That's part of my past."

She turned his answer over in her mind, hearing what he didn't say as loudly as his actual words. "Who took the pictures in your living room? The ones of the kids, Leanne, the mountains…?"

Daryl shifted his weight. "Me."

"The composition's beautiful. You haven't lost your eye."

"I've forgotten nearly everything from college," he said curtly, then strode inside, shutting the door firmly behind him.

Including me?

She bit her bottom lip to hold back the ridiculous question. Of course he'd forgotten her. How else could he have turned so easily to Leanne?

And why was she still returning to their past? Clearly Daryl had moved on and she thought she had, too, until now, when the chance to resolve things with Leanne was lost forever.

Cassidy raised her camera, adjusted her shutter speed and flash for nighttime and fired off a couple of shots of the orange moon cresting in a purple sky over Mount Sopris.

Had she made a big mistake coming home

with Daryl? It seemed to be opening up old wounds.

Then again, maybe they'd never healed in the first place.

She'd avoided Daryl and Leanne all these years because she'd thought she moved on, when clearly she hadn't.

Instead of simply enduring or marking the time she was marooned in Carbondale, she should work to find the closure she hadn't known she needed.

CHAPTER FIVE

CASSIDY FOLDED ONE of the old maternity tops retrieved from the back of her sister's closet with shaking hands. Across the large master bedroom, Joy opened an oversize plastic bag with a snap and dropped another pile of Leanne's belongings into it. They'd been organizing things for Goodwill since Noah and Emma left for school this morning. Now the sun stood nearly overhead, the cheery azure sky at odds with their somber task. When the familiar apple blossom scent her sister favored wafted from the garment, Cassidy buried her nose in the soft material.

Leanne's voice drifted in Cassidy's ears, carrying her back to their childhood.

"What's your favorite fruit?" Leanne asked as they swung together on an old tire swing munching heirloom apples. They faced each other, sneakers overlapping inside the empty ring, free hands gripping the rope dangling from an overhead branch, a piece of fruit in the others. They still wore their school clothes, and a limp pink ribbon dangled from one of Leanne's glossy brown braids.

"Not apples." Cassidy winged the half-eaten fruit into the fields, then instantly regretted it. Besides her free lunch at school, food wasn't always a given and her mother didn't appear to be readying anything for supper. "I'm sick of them. Someday I'm going to eat mangoes. Passion fruit. Papayas."

Leanne eyed her golden-hued apple. "How do you know you'll like them?"

Cassidy tipped her head back and the wind, generated by the pendulum motion of the rocking tire, lifted her hair from her damp neck. "I don't know. That's what makes them exciting."

"I'd rather stick to what I know." Leanne gnawed her apple with small precise bites. "Then I won't be disappointed."

"But think of what you'll miss…"

Leanne peered skeptically at Cassidy with a pair of light eyes more silver than blue. "I'd miss apples."

"Honey." Joy's light pat on Cassidy's shoulder yanked her from her reverie. "Why don't you lie down and let me finish up."

Cassidy brushed the wetness from her

cheeks. "I'm fine," she croaked, refolding the top and placing it on the appropriate pile.

"You look pale as a ghost." Joy passed over a glass of sweet tea. "Drink this."

Cassidy obliged and closed her eyes at the first sip of the cool drink. It tasted of sunshine, of cozy chats on long summer nights, of family, friendship...home. She'd missed the taste. Revived, she lifted her lids and met Joy's concerned gaze. "Better, thanks." After another sip, she passed the glass back.

"How are your holding up?" Joy pulled open another dresser drawer and began transferring pajamas into another bag.

Cassidy drew in an aching breath. Her brain prepared a pat answer that dissolved on her tongue the moment she met Joy's sincere, hazel eyes. "Sometimes, not so good."

"You've been very strong for the children. Leanne would be grateful."

Cassidy refastened the buttons of another top. "I'm not so sure she'd agree with you."

"Because of your history with Daryl," Joy stated, matter-of-factly, as if it hadn't been the scandal of the year when he'd dumped one sister to impregnate and marry another.

"I never forgave her."

"Do you now?"

Cassidy searched her heart, but it slammed the door and turned the latch before she could see inside. "I—I…"

Joy patted her leg. "It's okay to still be mad."

Cassidy swallowed hard. "Is it? You're not supposed to speak ill of the dead, let alone hate them."

"Is that how you feel? You hate Leanne?"

Cassidy's chest grew impossibly tight. "I'm a monster for saying yes, but I loved—love her, too."

"Absolutely not," Joy said crisply. "Dying doesn't give us a pass on our mistakes or the wrongs we've done, and Leanne wronged you…as did Daryl. I love my stepson, but you love someone despite of the wrongs, not because of…"

"I've never heard that phrase before."

"My grandmother always said we like people because of the qualities that please us, but we love people despite the qualities that drive us crazy."

Cassidy turned that over in her mind. "Makes sense. I'll never get to make up with Leanne now." Her chest grew tight again. They'd never settle their differences, never replace their hateful last words, never hug, kiss or laugh together. Not ever again.

"She's still there." Joy pointed at Cassidy's heart. "Whenever you're ready."

"You think people are still with us after we pass?"

Joy's eyes shone, overbright, and her mouth trembled slightly. "I hope so."

Cassidy hurried to Joy's side. "Daryl told me about your mammogram results." Concern for the blended Cade-Loveland families' matriarch clenched Cassidy's heart.

Joy dipped her head. In the silence, Beuford whined to go outside and the oven timer on a pan of baking brownies dinged. After a moment, she brushed at her eyes and lifted a smiling face. "I'm sure everything will be fine. It's just a biopsy."

"Joy—" Cassidy began but Joy waved her off.

"I'd better go get those brownies."

Joy hurried from the room and Cassidy fought not to follow her. In a rare, private exchange with Daryl this week, he'd confided that Joy's mammogram showed possible tumors, a significant concern as her mother had died of breast cancer, and her mother before that. They were not, he'd emphasized, to tell the children.

Cassidy returned to her pile and picked up a T-shirt with the words *I'm with Dummy* and an arrow pointing to the right. A lump formed in her throat. She'd had the matching shirt, the arrow pointing left, stowed in the luggage burned in the accident. Why had Leanne kept it all these years?

And given Cassidy's limited packing space, why had she?

No matter how many times she'd crammed the single suitcase she carried through life, she'd always made space for it, along with the poetry book Daryl had given her.

Yet she hadn't made room in her heart to understand her sister...the first steps to forgiveness. Could she reconcile with a sibling no longer here? If she wanted closure, it might be the only path forward...

"I put Beuford outside, though I think he was more interested in the squirrels than doing his business." Joy breezed back in the room, the chocolaty-sweet smell of baked goods following in her wake. Her lashes were still wet, as was her hairline, her face rosy from having splashed water on it, Cassidy guessed.

"If there's anything I can do…" Cassidy twisted the top of a laden bag and wrapped a tie around it.

Joy paused in her task of matching pajama tops and bottoms. "You're doing so much already. I'm sure you're itching to go back to you job."

Even with the return of her camera, Cassidy hadn't given work a thought this past week, with Daryl and the kids. "I'm not much use documenting conflicts until my vision's back and this is healed." She waved her splinted pinkie. "I'm glad to be here, helping out. I just wish there was more I could do."

"There is one thing…but I'm not sure if you'd be interested. It's a big undertaking." Joy shook out a red-and-green flannel nightgown with a small white ruffle at the neckline.

Cassidy visualized it around her sister's throat, imagined her cuddling Noah and Emma on her lap while wearing it. All these pieces of Leanne disappearing into boxes and bags, bit by bit, was another form of death. A heaviness settled in Cassidy's chest. "What is it?"

"Leanne was planning to open a country store to sell the heirloom apples grown on

Loveland Hills, as well as local produce, canning products and baked goods. For the past year, she'd worked to convert one of the old barns for the store and it was supposed to open next month—only my energy isn't up to see her vision through." Joy dabbed at her nose. "It meant so much to her. She wanted to have something for herself, she said, something to be proud of."

"She wasn't proud of being a mother?" It'd been all Leanne talked about growing up. Cassidy had never considered her sister wanted anything else…a shortsighted view for an investigative journalist.

Then again, maybe the people you saw the least clearly were the ones you'd been around the most.

Joy nodded as she returned to sorting nightclothes. "Of course. But it didn't seem like enough anymore." She sighed. "Now I'll have to call off the grand opening, and I don't know what I'll do with the animals arriving for the petting zoo."

"A petting zoo?" Cassidy marveled at the scope of Leanne's ambitious plan.

"Not to mention the local vendors who'd been preparing the canned goods and other crafts," Joy added. "But with my—uh—procedure coming up, I won't be able to pull it off by myself. Oh—and I'll need to contact the church. Leanne was insistent we have a coat, hat and boots drive. She said it was the most important part of the operation, though I don't know why."

"I do," Cassidy said quietly, deeply moved. Growing up, they'd shivered through many a winter in ill-fitting or inappropriate-for-the-weather outer gear. Leanne always had to take Cassidy's hand-me-downs, and sometimes wear shoes and clothes that didn't fit. Her sister would have wanted to give others the kind of access to clothing she didn't have.

It meant a lot to Cassidy, too...

"Don't call the church," Cassidy blurted before she thought better of it. "I'll open Leanne's store. I can't promise anything beyond that, though."

"It's only meant to be open from fall until Christmas and I can step in once I've got my health sorted out." Joy rose and caught Cassidy in a hug. "Are you absolutely sure?"

"Yes." Cassidy dropped her chin to Joy's soft shoulder and eyed Mount Sopris through the window. She'd always seen it as a block between her and the horizons she'd longed to explore. Now it'd be her anchor, keeping her home to see her sister's legacy through.

Maybe this was her way of making amends with her sister.

Joy's words about reconciliation returned to her. Maybe, by making Leanne's dream come true, Cassidy would understand her estranged sister better, one step toward forgiveness if she decided to follow its path after all.

"I'M MAKING THIS one a witch!" Noah dipped his brush in one of the paint jars lined up along the kitchen island and lifted it, dripping, to his green mini pumpkin. Dozens of painted pumpkins filled the kitchen table to decorate Leanne's country store. Daryl still couldn't wrap his head around Cassidy's offer to open it, especially given all the hard work he and his brothers had been putting into remodeling—work that'd come to a complete halt after Leanne's accident.

"Keep the paint on the newspapers." Daryl dropped a few more pages on the kitchen floor for good measure and looked up in time to spy his son turn in a quick circle, spraying the wall with black.

Awesome.

Just awesome.

In a corner, Beuford chewed on the spilled pumpkin guts he'd snatched as they'd fallen, carried to a corner, then spit back up to enjoy at his leisure.

Daryl sniffed the burnt grease of their aborted doughnut making and eyed the Jackson Pollock version of his trashed kitchen. Martha Stewart he was not, but at least the kids were occupied, doing something healthy as opposed to watching death videos or turning everyday objects into lethal weapons.

"I *am* being careful." Noah brandished his wet brush for emphasis.

Cassidy chuckled softly, swiping a splotch of paint from his cheek. "You're doing a great job."

"I can't get this right!" Emma tossed down her brush and frowned at her pumpkin.

"It doesn't have to be perfect." Daryl smoothed a hand over his daughter's fine blond hair.

"It's for Ma's store." Emma added a silent "Duh" of an eye roll. "No one's going to buy my stupid pumpkins and then the store won't make enough money and it will have to close and Ma will be—"

"Hey..." Daryl cupped her shoulders, halting Emma's tirade. "You'll make your ma happy either way."

Emma jerked away and hopped off the stool. "Ma was never happy!"

"Yes, she was!" Noah cried. "She laughed when she fell down that time at the store."

"Because she was drunk," Emma blurted. She whirled, raced down the hall and slammed her bedroom door shut.

Daryl's heart wrung itself inside out. He started down the hall, but Cassidy put her hand on his arm and nodded at a silently crying Noah. "Let me."

He shot her a grateful look and gathered Noah in his arms. Noah buried his face in Daryl's sweater, hiding his tears.

"It's okay to cry."

"Boys don't cry," Noah sniffled. "Only babies and losers."

"Who told you that?"

"Jax Miller."

Daryl searched his memory but didn't recall hearing Noah mention Jax before. "Is that a friend from school?"

"No. He hates me. Everybody hates me."

Daryl's arms tightened around his son. "Who could hate you?"

"They call me dog boy because Beuford's hair's always on my clothes." Noah's voice dropped so low Daryl had to strain to hear. "And they make me fetch things at recess."

Acid burned Noah's gut. "And what do you do?"

Noah only dug farther into Daryl's sweater.

"Noah?" Daryl prompted, his voice thick as he fought to contain his rising anger at kids picking on his son...his six-year-old, motherless son.

"Sometimes I do it," Noah squeaked. "I want them to like me."

"And do they like you after you do what they say?"

Noah shook his head and raised his blotchy, tearstained face. "They just laugh."

Daryl strove to keep his expression neutral and made a mental note to talk to Noah's teacher. "Want to know what else dogs can do?"

Noah stopped sniffling and glanced at Beuford. "Fart?"

"Besides that, though he is a champ."

"Sleep?"

"That, too. But they also herd cattle, help people with physical challenges and even sniff out bombs. They're hardworking, smart and helpful."

A noxious cloud rose from Beuford's corner as if on cue and Noah pinched his nose.

"Okay," Daryl added wryly. "That wasn't so helpful, but look how Beuford always takes care of the floors for us."

"Dogs are dirty and get fleas." Noah squeezed his eyes shut. "Is that why Ma never wanted to spend time with me?"

And just like that, Daryl's heart cracked open like an egg, oozing into his chest. Daryl placed a finger beneath Noah's chin and tipped it up, waiting until his son's lids lifted. "Your Ma always loved you. She was just unhappy with certain things."

"What kinds of thing?"

Me.

"Grown-up things."

Noah scooched backward out of Daryl's arms and onto his stool. Down the hall, all was silent, and Daryl wondered how Cassidy's talk with Emma was going. If she hadn't stepped in, he would have missed what was really going on with Noah. Gratitude filled him. It'd been a long time since he'd had a child-rearing partner, and it felt good. He could get used to this…if he wasn't careful.

"Grown-up things like money?" Noah swished his paintbrush across the green pumpkin. "Uncle Cole and Grandpa are always worried about paying bills. What's bills?"

"Money we owe for things. Some big. Some small. It's not easy being a grown-up but it's even harder being a kid. I'll speak to your teacher about Jax tomorrow."

Noah's eyes rounded. "No! It'll get worse. Please, Pa. Don't. I can take care of it."

"How?"

"I'll growl. Dogs do that." Beuford stopped munching and woofed in response to Noah's attempt. "Maybe I'll snap, too."

"Just don't bite," Daryl cautioned. "But it's good to stand up to bullies."

"So you won't tell my teacher?" Noah painted a blobby black tooth in his pumpkin's wide mouth.

"I promise Jax will never know." Daryl still planned on talking to Noah's teacher. No more playing fetch. His son had gone through enough without kids piling on.

"Am I a dog?" Noah's voice quavered.

"Of course not. You don't even have a tail," Daryl joked, trying to make his little guy smile.

"I mean low, like a dog. Like not good enough."

Daryl slung an arm around Noah and pulled him tight into his side, alternately angry at Leanne for the uncertainty she'd given their kids about their worth and wishing she were here to reassure their son how much he was wanted. Loved. "You're more than good enough."

"Just not to Ma."

"Especially to Ma. She spent time away from home because she didn't want to make you and Emma sad."

"We would have cheered her up!"

"Yes. You would have."

Or should have...

When had Leanne stopped caring about everything she'd told him she'd ever wanted? And why? Cassidy hadn't regained any of her memory. Would he ever have answers? Closure?

Footsteps announced a returning Emma and Cassidy. His daughter's pale face appeared calm as she plunked down on a stool and grabbed a brush.

He shot Cassidy a questioning look to which she responded with a shrug and a nod, as if to say her talk with Emma went pretty well. When she inclined her head at Noah, he repeated the gesture and their shared concern flashed between them. It nudged some of the weight he carried from his shoulders.

"Kids, Aunt Cassidy and I are going to get more acorns. Behave," he cautioned, then headed for the door and grabbed their coats. After helping Cassidy on with hers, he shoved his arms through his fleece and they tromped outside into the gray autumn afternoon. The sky was as flat and heavy as granite, the birches' bright yellow leaves a sharp contrast. Overhead, geese honked noisily as they winged southward.

"I think there might be more over here." Cassidy strode to a copse of oaks. Her head was bent and turned away from him.

"Cass," he called. When she turned, the grief in her green eyes made his throat swell. "I didn't ask you out here for acorns."

She shoved her hands in the pockets of the white down coat Sierra had loaned her, along with the rest of her secondhand wardrobe. The color highlighted the honey strands in her brown hair and the rosy hue in her bow-shaped mouth. "What, then?"

"We haven't talked."

"There's nothing to—"

"About the kids," he broke in, knowing she'd never consent to talk about their past…

and maybe it was irrelevant now, but somehow he sensed it was tangled up in the mystery of what'd happened on Avalanche Road.

Cassidy scooped up a couple of acorns and turned them over in her palm. "Emma feels like she let Leanne down. Wasn't good enough. That's why she's trying to make every pumpkin so perfect."

"What about her eating?"

"You mean her *not* eating?" Cassidy countered.

He nodded. "She's losing weight. I'm worried about her."

"She could be trying to find a way to control some of her life since she's gone through a lot of upheaval." A breeze lifted a strand of Cassidy's hair and fluttered it across her face. She shoved it back and continued. "Why was Noah crying?"

"He's being bullied in school."

Cassidy's cheeks flushed, her eyes flashing with the same outrage he felt. "Who? When? We need to talk to his teacher." She clapped a hand over her mouth. "I mean you. *You* need to call the school. He had a failing grade on his class work today."

Despite her correction, the *we* lingered in the air and he suddenly wished for a real partner. He felt like the boy holding his thumb in the hole to prevent the dam from bursting. Every time he'd stopped one problem, another appeared. Would their lives ever regain the stability they needed? When Cassidy left, it'd be another loss for the children. She'd be gone, and he'd be forced to pick up the pieces, alone, once more.

"Thank you."

"For what?" She ambled away to stand at the split rail fence surrounding his cabin. A few lingering vine geraniums bloomed red along the posts.

"Helping me with the children."

"They're my family, too."

"I didn't expect you to feel..."

"Responsible for them?" She leveled accusing eyes on him. "I do."

"Is that why you're opening Leanne's store?"

She wrenched her gaze from him and tracked a low-flying hawk as it swooped off the mountain and glided over the tree line. "She had a dream and I want to make it come true."

"You hate Leanne...and me."

"I loved Leanne. That never changed."

And me?

He swallowed back the wholly inappropriate question and asked, instead, "Would you visit her grave with us tomorrow?"

Her head snapped around and her eyes bored into his. "Are you sure?"

"Yes. She'd want you there." He cleared his throat. "The kids need you there."

I need you there.

"But why did she want me *here*?" Cassidy's hands clenched. "I keep trying to remember... It's so frustrating."

Unable to help himself, he wrapped his palms around her fists until they relaxed. "Don't tax yourself. You're still healing. How are the headaches?"

"Less frequent."

He laced his fingers in hers, careful not to jostle her broken pinkie. "And your ribs?"

"Down to more of an ache now." She retreated a step and he released her.

"You'll be glad to get back to your own life."

She was quiet so long he turned to study her beautiful profile. Her long slender throat rose to a delicate jaw and shell-like ears behind which she'd tucked her thick hair. "I don't want to leave until I know why I came here."

All the air in his body whooshed out of him in surprise. And relief. He didn't want her to go…and was uncomfortable with how much he wanted her to stay. "Leanne's computer and phone were destroyed in the car accident. We won't get any help there."

"Until I remember, we're just living in the dark."

He watched her as she strode back to the cabin, silently agreeing. The longer Cassidy stayed, the murkier his emotions became. If he didn't keep his distance, it'd be even harder to let her walk away than the first time.

CHAPTER SIX

Leanne Marie Loveland, Beloved Wife and Mother.

Cassidy tucked her chilled hands into her sweater sleeves and read her sister's grave inscription for the third time, bracing for the words to sink in fully. Leanne was gone, yet it'd seemed almost abstract until now. Cassidy had avoided her sister for years, but it wasn't a choice any longer.

It was forever.

No takebacks... Leanne's voice echoed in Cassidy's mind and memories returned of them trading toys, candy, clothes, makeup, certain whatever the other possessed had to be better.

Only this wasn't a game.

No takebacks.

Her moon sister, best friend and rival lay beneath Cassidy's feet while she stood above, one hand clasped in Noah's, the other with Emma. Daryl brushed some fallen leaves from the top of the white marble plaque, straightened and stepped back. "Your ma always loved fall," he said, gruff. He shoved his hands in his pockets and blinked hard at the blue sky. Overhead, a single white cloud scuttled by.

His grief struck Cassidy hard enough to bruise her heart.

He loved Leanne.

Really loved her. In the isolated setting of a college campus, where life was more theoretical than experienced, the love she and Daryl shared had been a hothouse flower, not meant to withstand life's realities. Choices. His feelings for Leanne, however, were sturdy, tested and real. Cassidy ached to see him grieve. How could she wish to ease his suffering all while resenting it?

"Apple season was her favorite." Cassidy shivered and wished for the borrowed jacket she'd forgotten this morning.

"Are we still going to make pies after we pick apples?" Noah angled his head to look up at her and his brown hair slid back from his forehead.

"Is that all you care about? Pie?" Emma yanked her hand free and stomped off. In the distance, a trio of crows cawed as if passing dark judgment.

Noah's shoulders shook, and he moved into Cassidy's arms, crying. "I care about Mama."

She smoothed a hand over his hair. "Of course you do."

"Emma, apologize." Daryl's voice was deep and grave and brooked no argument.

"Sorry," she muttered, dragging her feet as she rejoined the group. "How long do we have to be here?"

Daryl's features tensed. When he opened his mouth, Cassidy stopped him with a hand on his arm. "How long do you want to stay?"

Emma pulled the pumpkin she'd painted yesterday from her backpack. A red heart wove around its stem. "Can I be alone?"

Daryl squeezed her shoulder. "Take as much time as you need."

"I didn't give Mama her candy!" Noah plunged his hands in his pockets and pulled out a fistful of Tootsie Rolls. "These were her favorite."

After he lined them up along the perimeter of the plaque, he followed Daryl and Cassidy to a bench beneath an ancient maple. Brittle green leaves mixed with orange rustled crisply in the autumn breeze blowing off

Mount Sopris. It carried the heady scent of fresh roses arranged beside a nearby headstone.

"Can I get some more acorns?"

At his father's nod, Noah scampered off to the nut-laden ground beneath an oak.

"She's doing worse," Daryl murmured, his eyes on Emma. The young girl sat with her legs folded beneath her, her head bowed.

"Give her time. This is a shock."

"Thanks for stopping me from reprimanding her. I didn't know she'd brought the pumpkin. How did you…?"

"I didn't. She must have painted the heart this morning and put it in her bag when she ran back in the house."

"You're good with them, Cass." The warm appreciation in his eyes made her slightly light-headed. "A natural with kids."

"I haven't spent much time around children," she deflected. Was she a natural? Mom material?

"No evil child dictators to expose?" His left eyebrow quirked, and his full mouth curled slightly in the corners.

Despite herself, she smiled. "Not yet anyway, though at this point, nothing would shock me."

A stocky man with cropped silver hair and dark-framed glasses strode their way. "Forgive me for interrupting, but are you one of the Loveland boys?"

Daryl nodded and stood. "Daryl Loveland."

Even white teeth, revealed in an easy smile, contrasted with the man's weather-beaten skin. "Thought I recognized you from a family photo my mother had of you."

Daryl's eyes creased in confusion. "Your mother had a picture of us?"

The man stuck out a hand. "Sorry to make this awkward. Suppose I'm nervous. I've been hoping to meet more of the family but your pa's been opposed. I'm Neil Wharton, Clarence Loveland's eldest son. Boyd's half brother."

Daryl sucked in a harsh breath and bristled. "Emma! Noah! Time to go."

"But you said—"

"Now!" Daryl cut off the children.

"I didn't mean to intrude." Neil's face fell. "I'm here to pay my respects to family, same as you."

"You don't have family here."

The lethal edge in Daryl's voice took Cassidy aback. He'd always been easygoing and courteous; this dark side made him seem like a stranger.

"My father's buried there." A gold wrist-watch gleamed when Neil pointed to a grave-stone.

"Don't come near my family again," Daryl growled. He hustled her and the children down the path and into his truck.

"Who's that, Pa?" Emma asked, craning her neck to watch the waving man through the rear window.

"No one." Daryl jabbed on the radio and the children donned their respective head-phones.

"Your dad didn't have a brother." Cassidy twisted forward in her seat when they passed through the cemetery's gates.

"Correct," Daryl bit out, his knuckles blanching against the steering wheel.

"I don't understand."

"Neil claims my grandpa fathered him while stationed in Germany and that he's owed a stake in Loveland Hills."

"Poor Boyd!" Cassidy leaned the side of her head against the truck window's warm glass. "What's he going to do?"

"We've hired a lawyer. Right now, there's no direct paternity link other than he has my family's watch, which we thought Grandpa lost in the war, and letters Neil's mother exchanged with Clarence referencing a child. They don't specifically say the baby is or isn't Grandpa's."

"So it's his word against Boyd's."

"Unless he gets the judge to grant his request to have my grandfather's body exhumed for a paternity test."

She gasped. "That's horrible."

"Neil challenged Pa to do a DNA test, but Pa says he won't cooperate with that grifter. He's already got a lot on his plate as it is."

First Joy's health scare and now a new threat to Loveland Hills? She touched Daryl's leg briefly. "This must be so difficult. I know how much the ranch means to you."

More than me.

"Pa's the one who's deserving. He's worked it all his life whereas Neil… What's he done before crawling out from under a rock to stake a claim?" Daryl shook his head in disgust. "The will states ownership is to be split evenly between offspring. Since Pa's sister and brother passed early, the entire ranch went to him. If Neil wins his case, he'll gain fifty percent, which he plans to sell, and we don't have the cash to buy it back."

"Is that why Leanne was opening a country store? To bring in more revenue to the ranch?"

"I don't know. She never mentioned her reasons, but I'd like to think so."

Cassidy did, too. Had Leanne asked Cassidy to come home and help with the store? It seemed unlikely, but no other reason made sense other than, perhaps, a wish to reconcile... Cassidy's resolve intensified. She wouldn't stay on Loveland Hills indefinitely, but she'd see her sister's plan to fruition and leave the ranch, and Leanne's family, in a better place. Stronger. "Has Joy gone in for her biopsy yet?"

"Tomorrow. I'll wait with Pa for her if you don't mind watching the kids. I've been putting a lot on you lately."

"It's no problem." Daryl lapsed into silence and the tires hummed in the quiet as they drove. When they passed a spot where a guardrail bent inward, her heart stopped.

"Please! Let me go!" Leanne's voice reverberated in Cassidy's head. She squeezed her eyes shut and gasped, "Is that where..."

"Yes," he said quietly, then blasted the radio's volume, his profile stone.

Her lungs seemed to fill with water and she forgot how to breathe as she searched the dark, blank spots in her memory for more of what sounded like an argument with Leanne. Burning exhaust, a wave of heat, screaming… then nothing, as if her mind had hit a wall she couldn't get past.

When would she get the answers, the closure she sought?

Hours later, Cassidy rocked on the back porch, listening to the bullfrogs sing from the edges of a burbling stream. Tendrils of warmth emanated from the dying fire inside a chiminea. They'd toasted marshmallows after dinner, speaking little after their emotional day. To her surprise, Emma announced she wanted to go to bed—on her own—and Noah asked his father to read him a story, leaving her with her thoughts.

Which wasn't a good thing.

Leanne Marie Loveland, Beloved Wife and Mother.

Cassidy's fingers tightened around the glider bench's armrest as she pictured her sister's grave marker.

What would Cassidy's headstone read?

Pulitzer Prize Winner?

Maybe…and maybe not.

If she didn't earn her profession's highest

accolade, had she really been successful? Did her life have meaning? Worth?

And what was an award compared with a child? A marriage?

The former recorded your name in a file whereas the latter kept you in his or her heart forever.

Would she ever be a wife? A mother?

She hadn't seriously considered those roles until now. The work, sacrifice and rewards of helping Noah and Emma revealed motherhood to be one of life's greatest achievements.

Were her goals just as worthy?

A door opened behind her, breaking her from her thoughts.

"Fire's nearly out." Daryl paused by the glider. "Head in. I'll throw some more dirt on it."

"I'm fine." She tipped her head back. "It's peaceful out here." It'd been a long time since she'd stopped her life long enough to simply soak it in.

"Thought you preferred conflict." The glider squeaked when Daryl lowered himself in it beside her.

This close, the subtle spice of his aftershave teased her nose and the brush of his shoulder against hers pitched her heart into a funny rhythm. "Only when I'm working."

"What were you working on before—before you came back to Carbondale?"

"An exposé on government corruption in the Philippines." She stared up at the stars, marveling at how frantic she'd been to uncover a truth that seemed far removed from the tragedies unfolding here in the Rocky Mountains.

Her editor dubbed it her strongest piece yet and advised Cassidy to take the time she needed to heal and grieve. Was she losing out on the next big scoop spinning her wheels in Carbondale?

Granted, her ribs and pinkie hadn't fully healed, and her left eye vision was still poor, but she could hire a photographer. What if she lost her peers' respect and her father's pride in her...? Who would she be then?

"Your piece on child trafficking in Malaysia was eye-opening."

"You read my stuff?" She stared at him in surprise.

"Don't miss an article." His eyes slid from hers, back to the house. The lights in Emma's room flicked off. "I need to do something about Emma, but she's not talking to me."

Her throat ached at the quiet despair in Daryl's voice. "Why do you think she's withdrawing?"

Something rustled in the dark, shaking a berry bush just beyond the deck. "Maybe she blames me."

"You?" She glanced at him in surprise. "That's crazy. Emma misses her mother. She's mad at the world."

"Noah's not doing much better. He just asked me when I'm going to die."

Her heart squeezed for the little boy trying to make sense of such a big concept as loss. "What'd you tell him?"

"God only calls the angels home early. He doesn't want a tough piece of boot leather like me around, mucking up the place. At least, not for a long, long time."

That drew a reluctant smile from her. "What'd Noah say?"

"That he's glad I suck."

Despite the somber moment, she chuckled, and Daryl joined her, their brief laughter weaving in the cool, dark air.

"You do kind of suck," she teased before she thought better of it.

When she turned to Daryl, he was staring at her, regret swimming in his dark eyes. "I know you've never wanted to hear my apology before, Cassidy…"

When she started to rise, he held out a hand. "Please. Just this once, will you hear me out?"

Pain on pain. What was a bit more on this difficult day? Besides, they couldn't keep tiptoeing around the topic forever. "Okay."

"I'm sorry for betraying and hurting you."

"Forget it. I have."

Liar.

"I was a complete ass. I won't make any excuses. There are none. I destroyed your relationship with Leanne, as well."

"And now I'll never get to reconcile with her."

Daryl scrubbed a hand over his eyes. "Were you hoping to?"

"Not until it was too late. I should have forgiven her…and you." A dull ache flared behind her eyes. "You can't help who you fall in love with."

"But I didn't…"

Her heartbeat grew faster, heavier, a painful percussion. "Didn't what?"

"Love Leanne." Daryl's voice was so low she had to lean closer to hear it. "Not at first. She was a friend, a kind soul who let me ramble on about you, who listened and sympathized since she knew you as well as I did. When my letters went unanswered and one came back return to sender, I lost faith. I thought you'd made up your mind about not marrying me and were waiting to come home to tell me in person. The night Leanne and I—ah…" He cleared his throat. "I'd gotten drunk and…"

She shook her head. "I don't want to hear specifics."

He twisted her way and their knees bumped. "Her pregnancy resulted from a moment of extreme stupidity and weakness. Nothing drove me but my doubts. I'd regret it completely except we got Emma and I wouldn't change that."

"I wouldn't either." Their eyes locked for a breath-stealing moment. Some things were meant to be, especially the niece and nephew she adored with all her heart. She'd give up Daryl a hundred times to have them, as much as she loved him.

Had loved him.

Some of her old anger dissipated. Daryl and Leanne had been destined to create those beautiful little lives just as she'd been fated to uncover injustices and save lives, neither of which would have happened if Daryl had waited for her and she'd given up her career to help him on the ranch. In the end, everyone followed the right path after all.

Daryl shooed away a nagging mosquito. "I married Leanne to do right by her, but it was an obligation initially...not love. That came over time."

Cassidy strove not to read too much into Daryl's confession. It was like watching a door to a life she hadn't dared dream of slam shut in her face. "Either way, you chose her. And it was the right decision."

He angled his head and his dark eyes pierced hers through the dim light. "What would your answer have been if Leanne and I hadn't gotten together?"

A trickle of unease formed in her belly. She didn't like where this conversation was going. "What's it matter now?"

He stopped rocking and his stare lingered on her face with enough intensity to feel like a physical caress. "It shouldn't, but it does. It's always mattered."

Had she always mattered to him? For one night, she hadn't...

"I'd planned to move to Carbondale rather than lose you."

Daryl seemed to stop breathing and an unforgiving pang hit her in the chest at his stricken face. Counting to ten, she forced a casual shrug. "It all turned out for the best." She scrubbed the emotion from her voice. Daryl had enough pain without digging up old ones. "I love my career and Leanne was happy, an excellent wife and mother."

"Leanne wasn't happy." Three simple words, yet they seemed to tear out of Daryl, taking a part of him with it.

Pressure clamped down on her chest. "Is that what the kids meant when they said she wasn't around a lot? Was drinking?"

"We were having troubles."

She peered into his handsome, pain-filled face. His dark brown eyes were wide, the pupils dilated. His wavy brown hair, which he'd chopped off, lay flat against his skull, accentuating his cheekbones. His full lips were parted, his white teeth contrasting with his thick, trimmed beard. "Were you separated?"

"No. Yes." Daryl cleared his throat, but when he spoke, his voice was deeper and rougher than normal. "I don't know. She asked me to sleep at the main house on nights when she wasn't going out with friends."

Cassidy balled her hands and dug her fingernails into her palms to keep from reaching for him. Consoling him. "When did that start?"

"A year and a half ago."

"Were you arguing?"

His brows rose as he scrubbed his hand down his jaw. "We hadn't been until…"

She remained quiet, not wanting to push… not even sure if she wanted to know or get involved. The longer she stayed in Carbondale, the more entangled she became.

"I didn't like her going out," Daryl concluded.

"Ever?"

"No. Just not as much." He blew out a long breath as he shook his head. "And I wished sometimes it'd be with me. I—I couldn't make her happy anymore."

"Why?"

"She accused me of still caring for you."

"And what'd you say?" Despite herself, the huskiness in her voice exposed the growing ball of emotions filling her belly.

"No. That was over years ago."

"Right."

"Right."

Daryl stood. "I'd better go check on Emma…make sure she's really asleep."

"Daryl."

At her call, he stopped at the sliding door and turned. "You're a good father and you will get through this."

He nodded and trudged inside, leaving her alone once more. Did Daryl still care for her?

No takebacks, her sister's voice whispered in her head.

Leanne had taken Daryl from Cassidy when she'd left him for the Bosnia assignment. She wouldn't dishonor her deceased sister by taking him back again, regardless of possible residual feelings. She'd leave as soon as she opened the country store, regained her lost memories and found closure.

Daryl was reopening old wounds…feelings…and she suspected if she stayed long enough, she risked discovering she might still care for him, too.

DARYL SHIFTED HIS weight to ease his stiff back in the hard, upholstered hospital waiting room chair. He'd rather sit in a saddle for twelve hours than another minute in this torture device masquerading as a seat, but he'd accompanied his father to Joy's biopsy to support him and wouldn't be anywhere else. How much longer before they heard from Joy's surgeon again? His pa was gray-faced and tight-lipped. It wasn't the Loveland way to pry, yet his father's silent suffering left him unsettled and searching for a way to relieve it.

Stretching out his legs, Daryl crossed one boot over the other and eyed the outdated magazines littering the square table before him. Coffee rings and Magic Marker doodles covered its scarred surface. Across the room, ferns drooped from hanging pots in front of a trio of rain-coated windows. The stale scent of body odor, disinfectant and old coffee had him breathing shallowly through his mouth.

"Want some coffee?"

His father shook his head and sat with his arms folded across his chest, stiff and still as a statue.

"Ran into Neil Wharton at the cemetery yesterday."

Boyd swore under his breath. "I warned him not to approach you kids."

"We're not kids, Pa. Did the judge set a date for the hearing?"

Boyd drummed his nails on the chair's wooden arm. "My lawyer's working to get the request dismissed. No one's disturbing my pa's grave. He's got a right to rest in peace."

"Darn right. What about giving him a DNA sample?"

"No one's invading my privacy, taking my DNA, least of all some con artist."

They lapsed into silence. Boyd's knee jiggled up and down as he shifted in his seat. The large hand on the wall clock ticked forward another minute.

"Shouldn't be long now." Daryl pointed to the clock. They'd checked Joy into the outpatient surgery facility an hour ago.

Boyd limited his response to a brief nod.

It hadn't taken long for his new stepmother's upbeat, caring personality to endear her to her stepchildren, despite generations of feuding. She'd become the matriarch the Loveland clan hadn't known they'd needed until she stepped into the role. "Joy seemed in good spirits."

Another nod from Boyd.

"Doctor looked like she knew what she was talking about." In fact, the surgeon had talked so fast in her hurry to get to the operating room, Daryl caught only about every other word, but the ones he heard were reassuring. Joy would have only small scars and the biopsy results would take four to ten days.

This time a shrug answered Daryl's remark.

"Pa." Daryl angled his face until he made eye contact with Boyd. "It's going to be okay."

"Don't know that," Boyd said between clenched teeth. "Not for certain."

Daryl clapped his father on the back. The overhead PA system paged a doctor to Labor and Delivery. "Don't give up hope."

Boyd's brief laugh held little humor. "Been hoping for that woman all my life. Now that I've finally married her, I ain't aiming to lose her."

Daryl nodded. Boyd and Joy had been high school sweethearts until Joy's parents conspired to break them up. Falsely believing Boyd had left for the service to avoid her, she'd turned to another only to discover Boyd never stopped loving her when he'd returned home to find her pregnant and engaged. They'd reconnected at a bereavement support group a few years back and dated despite their feuding children's disapproval and schemes to end their relationship. They'd gotten hitched the summer before last and Pa had never been happier.

"You won't lose her." Daryl raised his voice over a wailing baby whose mother jiggled it beside the water dispenser.

"I waited too long…" Boyd lifted red-rimmed eyes to Daryl.

"To ask Joy out?"

Boyd raked a hand through his thick gray hair and nodded.

"When Ma passed, how come you didn't seek her out?" Daryl and his father stood to allow the young mother to slip between them and the coffee table on her way out the door.

Boyd dropped heavily back in his seat. "Joy was still married."

Daryl reached in his jacket's deep cargo pocket and produced the two ham and Swiss sandwiches Cassidy had thoughtfully prepared. Boyd shook his head and Daryl stowed one before unwrapping the other. He closed his eyes in appreciation when he bit into the thick sandwich made with tomato and sweet-and-sour pickles, surprised Cassidy remembered his favorite combination.

She was one heck of a cook, too. With her pinkie on the mend, she'd been whipping up increasingly complicated dishes from far-away places, each attached to a harrowing story that enthralled his children. Emma still wasn't eating nearly enough for his liking, and Noah's school grades continued to plummet, yet Cassidy kept everyone's spirits up with spontaneous activities and adventures.

Once they moved past their grief, would his family get back on track? He needed to provide them with a stable home and hid his grief as much as possible. He saved his darkest emotions for the sleepless nights he lay on the living room couch, staring at the ceiling, going over his marriage with Leanne, searching for the moment the fault lines appeared.

Or perhaps their foundation had never been strong. He'd married out of obligation, not love. Although he'd put Cassidy out of his mind and committed himself to Leanne, he saw now that she'd never completely left his heart. He found himself seeking her out after the children went to bed, her company like a balm he hadn't known he needed, the awkwardness and strain between them easing a bit more each day. He hadn't realized how lonely he'd been until Cassidy returned.

"Should have pursued her once she became single." Boyd picked up his hat from the seat beside him when a mother and child sidled by and requested to sit.

"Why'd you wait?"

The woman beside Boyd pointed to a parenting magazine and asked him to pass it over.

"I wanted to give you kids some stability." Boyd handed the woman the periodical. "Bringing someone else into the picture would have upset the apple cart."

"It was pretty much tipped over at that point." Daryl considered his adoptive mother's addiction and mental health issues. She'd had some good days, mostly bad. The real problem was never knowing which you were about to endure.

Boyd nodded. "I wanted to get things back to some kind of normalcy for you kids."

"But you denied yourself happiness in the process." Daryl studied his pa's hard-bitten face. He'd only really seen him cut loose and smile big when Joy entered the picture.

Boyd's mouth worked for a moment before he clamped it shut.

"She's going to be fine, Pa." Daryl nodded at the door that led back to the surgical rooms.

"I may have wasted years we could have had together." Boyd's blue eyes flashed up at Daryl. Hard. "Don't make that mistake, son."

"What do you mean?"

"I'll leave that for you to determine."

Just then, a nurse bustled into the waiting area and gestured for them to follow her. Outside a room labeled Recovery, the gowned surgeon met them, a surgical mask dangling around the neck of her scrubs.

"She did fine." The surgeon smiled into Boyd's relieved face. "She has a couple of small incisions that should heal nicely."

"Were you able to tell anything?" Boyd stood with his hands clasped behind his back, his feet planted apart, as if bracing for an oncoming storm.

The doctor's smile faded. "Not at this stage. The pathologist's report should be in later this week or early next and Joy's primary care doctor will call you with the results."

"We just wait till then," Boyd said heavily, almost to himself.

"Yes. Are there any further questions I can answer?" The surgeon's head swiveled between the two of them as the silence stretched. White appeared around Boyd's mouth.

"We're all set, thank you," Daryl answered, then turned to his father when the surgeon hurried to answer a beckoning nurse. "Pa? You okay?"

"Ain't me I'm worried about."

A nurse opened the swinging door to the recovery unit. "Mr. Loveland, if you'd like to follow me?"

Boyd lingered a moment. "'Man plans,

God laughs,'" Boyd quoted, his voice as gravelly and dark as day-old coffee. "Remember what I said. Happiness isn't meant to be postponed."

The door swung shut behind him, leaving Daryl staring at the laminate wood surface, turning over his father's parting advice.

He couldn't be encouraging Daryl to pursue Cassidy when he'd just lost Leanne...

Daryl's thoughtless actions forced Leanne into a life, a marriage, she may or may not have wanted. He'd already made one Fulton sister miserable and wouldn't do the same to another.

Besides, his situation with Cassidy was different from his father's with Joy. Boyd and Joy wanted the same traditional way of life and shared similar goals of family and community. Cassidy's dangerous, chaotic career, on the other hand, was at odds with the steady life he strove to provide his children. After barely surviving his early, preadoption years, he'd vowed to never put his children through the same kind of upheaval.

If God laughed while man made plans, he must be in stitches now. Cassidy had literally crashed back into his life, destroying it and the plans he'd laid. None of it made sense, least of all his growing feelings for the last person in the world he had any right to care about again.

CHAPTER SEVEN

CASSIDY PEERED DOWN at her sister's handwriting while standing at the country store's temporary particleboard countertop. She fought back a sneeze from the dust-filled air and tried to focus despite the whining sanders and varnish as Loveland men made the final tweaks on the remodeled barn. Two weeks had passed since she'd begun working on Leanne's store and seeing it near completion filled her with both pride and melancholy. The notepad shook in her trembling grip. Leanne's familiar script slanted neatly to the left, her lowercase *i*'s topped with circles, not dots. It was like looking at a ghost. Or hearing from one.

"It's always been too late!"

Cassidy flinched as her sister's voice returned to her, a bit of an argument they'd had in the white Jeep. Cassidy held her breath, waiting, hoping, straining for more, then released it in disappointment when Leanne's voice disappeared.

Are you happy with the store, Leanne? She cast her eyes out the window, to clouds chasing each other across an azure sky.

With me?

One page listed the vendors contracted to supply an array of products like local lavender honey, homemade canned preserves and tote bags made from recycled material with the words *Grow Love* on them. Another sheet detailed specialty baked products to be made on premise, such as apple cider doughnuts, apple fritters and caramel-apple crumb pie along with services like pumpkin patch and apple-picking wagon rides, the petting zoo and a corn maze with "Fright Night" thrills planned for Halloween week. A florist would be supplying mums for sale, a woodworker carved benches, picnic tables and wishing-well planters, and a holiday craft fair would showcase local talent.

"Is your head spinning yet?"

Cassidy glanced up at Joy's voice and returned her bright smile. "I think it's about to fall off. Leanne had big plans."

"She did indeed." Joy surveyed her hustling stepsons. "Boyd says the remodel will be completed on time, but you still have a lot to organize. Should we push back the opening date? We only have a week to go." Despite that converting the barn had been in the works for the past year, the final projects had come to a halt toward the end of summer, first with Leanne spending less time at home, then because of the accident. If it hadn't been for the Loveland men picking up the pace over the last couple of weeks, they may have had to open late.

"I've contacted everyone on her lists. Now it's just a matter of following through on the plans she left."

"All twenty pages' worth."

"Give or take," Cassidy laughed. "It'll be worth it to see this place come to life."

She eyed the cavernous space. The lofted, exposed beam ceilings, large windows and natural pine walls gave it a light, airy feel. Excitement mounted as she envisioned the built-in shelves filled with canned goods, bins overflowing with produce and a mini café where they'd serve smoked meat sandwiches and pumpkin soup. Leanne had loved fall. Cassidy planned on pulling out all the stops to keep her sister's legacy alive and make the country store a success for Loveland Hills Ranch. If she was going overboard then so be it.

Joy waved a hand before her flushed face. "Is there a place to sit down? I'm feeling a little…"

Cassidy raced around the counter, grabbed Joy's arm and guided her outside to one of the handcrafted rockers that'd arrived an hour ago. "How about some water?"

Joy nodded. "Thank you, honey."

When Cassidy returned with a couple of bottles, she passed one over and plunked down beside Joy. "How are you feeling?" Joy's biopsy results had indicated breast cancer, and she'd undergone lumpectomies last week to remove the tumors.

Joy sipped her water, then held the bottle against her forehead. "Fine. It was a straight-forward procedure, but you can't convince Boyd of that. He's been fussing like I had open-heart surgery. I would have come over sooner to help except he's been hovering non-stop. I finally had enough and threw him out!"

"Where's he now?"

"Still hovering." Joy rolled her eyes and pointed to a massive John Deere tractor where Boyd shouted up to Daryl.

Cassidy's breath caught when she spied her ex behind the wheel. He was ruggedly handsome in Wranglers, work boots and a red-and-navy plaid shirt that accentuated his broad shoulders and dark coloring. A red ball cap shaded his face against the bright sun. Boyd hollered something and backed away, waving, as Daryl restarted the engine with a deep rumble. He expertly reversed the heavy machine and headed back to the fields to retrieve more of the hay bales he'd been stacking along the rustic exterior. When the mums arrived, she'd place them on top along with straw scarecrows and autumn wreaths.

It'd been nearly two weeks since Daryl's apology, and despite her best intentions to keep her distance, she'd grown more comfortable around him as they spent time together sharing meals, catching fireflies with the kids or simply rocking on the front porch. The gruff cowboy's tender, solicitous care touched her deeply. But he was her brother-in-law, and recently widowed. Completely off-limits. Yet a part of her longed for physical closeness with him, a feeling she'd been battling out of respect for her sister.

Boyd turned on his heel and strode their way.

Joy sighed. "So much for freedom. Is there

anything I can do to help? Even if it's just making phone calls?"

"I'm fine." Cassidy smiled encouragingly. When Joy broke the news about her biopsy results, she'd asked for only two things: smiles and prayers. No sad faces, she'd warned, because she was going to beat cancer. Cassidy had been giving her both nonstop, her affection growing by the day for the courageous, warmhearted woman. "I'd rather you rest up."

"Now you sound like Boyd."

"You two talking about me?" Boyd's deep blue eyes twinkled beneath his brown Stetson.

"Complaining is more like it." Joy smiled affectionately at her husband and lifted her cheek when he leaned down for a kiss. "Cassidy needs my help, so shoo."

"Actually, Emma, Noah and I are heading to the town hall to file the paperwork for Leanne's charity."

"The hat and coat drive?" Boyd extended a hand and helped Joy to her feet.

Cassidy nodded. "I thought it'd be nice for the kids to honor their mother with something official."

Joy's face creased in concern. "I've been

worried about them. You haven't told them about my…"

"No. We're following your wishes."

Joy's features smoothed. "Good. How are they doing? I haven't been able to spend as much time with them as I wanted, but once I'm healed, I'll have them for sleepovers again."

Sleepovers? As in, she and Daryl would be left alone in the cabin? A fluttery sensation began in her belly and spread to her chest. Listening to him toss and turn on the couch beyond her bedroom each night, with only a door and her conscience to separate them, was tough. Often, she'd press her ear against it, listening to Daryl's private grief, battling the urge to comfort him. Without the children around, her resolve might disappear completely.

"Emma's still acting out and Noah's grades are borderline. I'm hoping if I get them involved helping others, it'll help them, too."

Joy beamed at her. "I don't know what this family would have done without you, Cassidy."

Her heart added an extra beat. No one had ever depended on her before, not personally.

The press corps maybe… "They're helping me, too."

"Take care, now." Boyd squeezed her shoulder and led Joy away.

"Aunt Cassidy!" Her head whipped around at Noah's call. He waved at her from the llama pens. "The smelly one keeps eating all the treats and I can't feed the baby."

"We're saving the treats for the customers," she hollered. "Remember?"

"Beuford paid." Noah pointed to the feed machine and waved a coin overhead.

"Aunt Cassidy!" Her head snapped toward the barn to spy Emma emerging with ink-covered hands. "The Magic Marker exploded and ruined my sign for the hat and coat drive. I don't want to do this anymore!"

"Don't give up," she responded, striving to keep her smile in place. It'd taken lots of encouragement to convince a reluctant and easily frustrated Emma to work on the charity.

Cassidy cupped her hands around her mouth. "Meet us inside, Noah!" She joined Emma, and they wandered into the back room's prep area, where the kids had been making signs for pricing.

Emma stopped at the large poster board she'd been agonizing over for days. Precise, rainbow-colored letters spelled out Hat and Coat Drive.

"I got my handprint on it and ruined it." Red splotches appeared in her cheeks and wet darkened her eyelashes. "Can I stop now?"

"You're doing a great job. In fact, your 'mistake' might be genius." She eyed the mark, opened a small bottle of bright red acrylic paint and poured its contents on one of the pieces of newspaper strewn about the wooden floor. "Watch."

Just then, Noah bounded inside, knocked into the table and sent the poster board skidding to the ground. Beuford, oblivious and panting heavily from the physical exertion of—well—simply moving, stepped into the paint and then onto the poster board, leaving bright red paw prints in his wake.

"Noah!" Emma pointed a paintbrush at her brother. "You ruin everything!"

"No, I didn't!" Noah grabbed a brush and brandished it. "Beuford did it!"

Beuford scuttled to a corner, snagged a dropped bread crust from their lunch and slumped to the floor, his eyes already closed.

"Kids!" Cassidy yelled, then lowered her voice once their eyes flashed her way. "What's the rule about arts and crafts?"

"You can never have too much glitter?" Emma supplied.

Cassidy held in a smile. "The other one."

Noah nodded at the empty Elmer's bottle. "Glue isn't a food group?"

"Paintbrushes aren't…" Cassidy prompted.

"Weapons," they chorused and dropped the tools to the table.

"The sign is ugly now." Emma folded her arms over her narrow chest and jutted her lower lip. "Can I get a soda at Grandpa's house?"

"Not yet." Cassidy placed the poster board back on the table and eyed it. "The paw prints look cute."

"They're awesome!" Noah raced over to pat the dozing dog. "Good work, Beuford."

Beuford's eyebrows twitched briefly in acknowledgment of the praise that was only his due, of course.

"See! Beuford likes it, too." Noah galloped back to the table, narrowly missing the newspaper holding the red paint puddle.

"He's not even looking," Emma griped. She lowered her arms and peered closer at the sign.

"Javi," Noah said, referring to their new stepcousin on the Cade side of the blended family, "said Beuford's superpower is seeing with his eyes closed because he never opens them." Noah's grin revealed the missing front tooth he'd lost at breakfast this morning.

"And farting," Emma added with a grudging smile.

"He's a champion at that, all right." Cassidy pointed to the red paint she'd poured. "How about we all dip our hands in it and then put them on the board to decorate?"

"Can I make one of mine a turkey?" Noah jumped up and down.

"If your sister agrees. She's in charge of the decorations for the drive."

"Maybe…" Emma angled her head and surveyed her brother, relishing her power.

"Please!" he wheedled.

"Okay."

"And I'm in charge of the animals with Pa, right?" Noah asked.

"Right. Have you thought of a name for the charity yet, Emma?" Cassidy dipped her hand in the paint and pressed it on the board.

Emma placed her red-coated hands in a fan position, applying it beneath her lettering. "What would Mama want?"

"What do you think?"

Emma's face crumbled. "I don't know. All

she cared about was her computer and friends and this stupid store."

Cassidy caught Emma in a tight hug, then staggered back when Noah flung himself in the mix. They toppled to the floor in a tangle of limbs. She smoothed the damp strands from Emma's wet cheeks with her paint-free hand. "Honey, I don't know what was going on with your ma, but I can say for certain that she loved you, very, very much."

"How do you know? You don't remember anything."

Cassidy hid her wince. Disjointed pieces of memory had been returning, snippets of an argument she seemed to have been having with her sister in the Jeep. She couldn't hear the words clearly, but she saw Leanne's livid face. Why had her sister summoned her home to quarrel? It made no sense. Worse, a nagging feeling that Cassidy had caused the accident grew.

Why had she come back to Carbondale?

It was a mystery she desperately wished to solve, not just for herself but for a grieving Daryl. She wanted to help her sister's family pick up the pieces—an altruistic wish, nothing more. So why did her eyes follow handsome Daryl, then? "I know what a big heart your mama had." Cassidy rubbed Emma's arm. "How could she help but love you?"

Cassidy had come to love them as her own these past few weeks.

"I'm too messy and I forget to put my clothes in the hamper," Emma whispered, breaking Cassidy's heart. "And one time I ruined Mama's makeup when I borrowed it to put on my Barbie."

"And I'm too loud and I don't clean behind my ears," Noah sniffled.

"You're right," Cassidy announced, sitting up and taking the children with her. She wrapped an arm tightly around each, the paint on her hand now dry and flaking. "None of us are perfect and sometimes we annoy each other, right?"

Emma and Noah nodded.

"But we still love each other, don't we?"

Emma shrugged. "I guess."

Noah heaved out a long-suffering sigh. "Girls are gross, but Emma's okay. Sometimes."

"See. You love each other. Just like I love you." She showered their faces with kisses until they giggled and shoved her away.

"Hey! What's this?" boomed a deep voice from the doorway.

Emma and Noah leaped to their feet and raced to their father, catching him around the waist. "Aunt Cassidy was just telling us we're annoying," Emma informed him.

Cassidy's heart lurched when Daryl's brown eyes landed on her, a teasing light in them. "Oh, she did, did she?"

"But she still loves us because we're lovable," Noah added, hanging on to his father and bending backward until his hair swept the floor. "And she gave us slobbery kisses. Do you love Pa, too, Aunt Cassidy? He's not perfect because he still can't make mac-n-cheese and he burns stuff but that's okay, right?"

"Oh—ah…" Cassidy shuffled her feet, her face aflame.

"Are you gonna kiss him?" Noah dragged his father closer.

Cassidy's heart thrummed as Daryl's gaze dipped to her mouth, then rose. He cleared his throat and dragged his eyes from hers. "How's the sign for the clothing drive coming?"

"Want to add your handprint, Pa?" Emma pointed to the paint.

Daryl crouched, dunked his hands in the red fluid and eyed the poster board. "Mine are too big—there isn't space."

"Put them over ours!" Emma pushed his hands down so they crossed over the other prints. "Then we're all holding hands."

Noah pointed to the paw prints. "Even Beuford helped."

"Many hands, doing good," Emma murmured, stepping back and cocking her head as she assessed the sign.

"What did you say?" Daryl placed another handprint directly over Cassidy's.

"Many Hands, Doing Good." Emma's voice rose in excitement. "That's the name of Mama's charity."

Cassidy's breath caught. "That's perfect!"

"But even if it wasn't, you'd still love it, right?" Emma asked, peering up beneath her lashes.

"Yes, I would. We all would," Cassidy said stoutly.

Noah caught her hand and dragged her to Emma and Daryl. "Family hug!"

When she attempted to back away, Daryl clasped her firmly around the waist and, in an instant, she was engulfed in a Loveland hug that both shattered her already fractured heart and began mending it, too.

"Are we a family?" Noah asked, voice

quavering. His gaze swung between her and Daryl.

"Yes," affirmed Daryl. She lost herself, momentarily, in his thick-lashed, brown eyes. "We're family."

Incapable of speech, she simply nodded. She'd been solo for so long. To be included, wanted, by this tight-knit group filled her with unexpected joy. Simple. Pure. Sweet. Was she worthy of their affection if she wasn't the best, the most successful? Perfect? She'd assured Emma of that truth and she needed to begin heeding it herself.

Then her cell phone buzzed, interrupting the tender moment. She wasn't sure if she felt disappointed, relieved or both.

She moved a distance away. "Brenda?"

"Hello?" her editor shouted.

Cassidy wandered to the edge of the open back door for a better signal, her eyes on Daryl and the kids as they resumed decorating the sign. "Brenda?" she repeated, louder.

"I thought calling you in Uganda was tough… Glad to finally get a signal."

"You'd better hurry because it probably won't last long."

"How are you feeling?"

Her gaze lingered on Daryl as he lifted his

son to the sink and washed the red from his hands.

Happy. Peaceful. Fulfilled.

"Better. My vision's back and the ribs and pinkie are just about healed."

"Watch the boom!" called her editor to someone.

"Are you sailing?"

"We're on the Long Island Sound, but I had to reach you right away. We just got a lead on the missing Sudanese girls."

Cassidy's pulse picked up speed. A couple of years ago, seventy-three girls had been kidnapped from school, never to be seen or heard from again. "Are they with the National Islamic Front?"

"No. That's the kicker. The tipster claims the Sudanese government is behind the kidnapping to turn public sentiment against the militant group."

"Where are they holding them?" Cassidy gasped. Her heartbeat drummed in her ears. If true, this was the scoop of the year…possibly the decade.

"That's for you to find out once you chase down the lead. Charlie's still on the Syrian gas attacks and Je'nai is getting married next week. I could hand this off to Pradeep—he's champing at the bit for a chance at a story like this—but you're my senior writer and I wanted to give you first crack. Besides, if anyone can find those girls, it's you."

It had everything Cassidy loved about investigative reporting: danger, mystery and a chance to change the world.

But what if she wanted to change the world in her own backyard instead?

"I—I—" Cassidy eyed Daryl and the kids rinsing the brushes in the sink. Emma flicked water at Noah, who returned the favor, the water fight escalating until Daryl hauled them back from the sink, drenched. He yanked off his cap and droplets flew from his hair as he shook it at the squealing children.

"When would you need me to leave?"

At her question, the children's laughter died. Daryl's grin disappeared. Their concerned eyes slammed into her and they all seemed to hold their breath.

"Lara's been checking flights," her editor said, referencing her secretary, "There's a United flight to Abuja leaving at ten thirty-five."

"Tonight?"

Noah's mouth dropped open and quivered while Emma buried her face in her father's side. Daryl's anguished eyes nearly ripped her heart from her chest. How could she leave them? They were just growing accustomed to life without Leanne. It'd be cruel to upend their lives again.

On the other hand, the missing Sudanese girls needed her help, too. Plus, if she found them, she'd be hailed a hero and reach heights in her career she'd only dreamed of before now.

Who needed her more?

"If it's too soon, there's also a nine fifteen leaving tomorrow morning, but we can't delay much longer. We've got to reach the girls before our lead dries up and they move them again."

"I understand," Cassidy murmured, thinking fast.

As she watched, Daryl directed the children's attention back to the sign, his shoulders hunched. They half-heartedly added embellishments to the poster board while casting sidelong glances her way. None spoke.

"So which flight should I have Lara book?"

An involuntary smile crossed Cassidy's face when Beuford lurched himself to his feet, lumbered across the room, then plopped his hind end onto the red-soaked newspaper.

At Emma's squeal, he scooted forward on his front legs, dragging his butt in a messy smear.

"Beuford!" Emma shouted. "Bad dog!"

"He's not bad." Noah grabbed a can of green paint and held it over the poster board. "Take it back!"

"Kids!" Daryl roared.

"What's that ruckus?" Brenda asked. "Sounds like World War III..."

"Just about."

Daryl dived to snatch the green paint can in midair, then face-planted on the red-smeared ground.

"Which flight, Cassidy?" Brenda prompted as Daryl rose, staggering, temporarily blinded by the paint dripping in his eyes. He swiped it away as the kids giggled, shaking a finger at them, his teeth white against his rainbow-colored beard.

She'd never seen him more attractive.

"Better ask Pradeep," she replied, hoping she wouldn't regret this decision the rest of her life. "I'm not going."

"Are you sure?" Brenda gasped, incredulous. "You never pass up a story, let alone the scoop of the century."

Daryl bowed to his now laughing children, adding an extravagant flourish, Clumsy the

Clown style. When his gaze swerved to her, a question in it, her lips curved into an involuntary smile. "I'm sure."

She ended the call, pocketed the phone and joined the group.

For the first time, she chose family over her job.

Her family, according to the kids and Daryl.

Did she dare become a part of it? And if she did, would she ever be able to leave them when the time came?

CHAPTER EIGHT

"CAN WE PICK up the apples on the ground?" Noah tugged Daryl's coat and pointed to the golden-hued, oblong fruit littering the orchard's grassy floor.

After eating a last-minute picnic supper, he, the kids and Cassidy had fanned out along a row of old trees to pick the ripe apples for cobbler. Tripod-shaped wooden ladders leaned against laden boughs while woven baskets rested beneath them. The gnarled branches crossed overhead and protected them from the brisk breeze blowing a distant storm in from the west.

Daryl plucked a Colorado Orange, one of the heirloom apple varieties grown on Loveland Hills, and carefully placed it in his basket to avoid bruising. "Those are for cider, not eating."

"Can we bring them home and make some?"

Daryl opened his mouth to refuse, caught Cassidy's subtle nod and agreed instead. They didn't have a press and would probably create mush, not cider, but the kids would have fun.

Daryl peered down at his son as the daylight faded, relieved to see Noah smiling more this past week. While Daryl's grief for Leanne hadn't lessened, he and the children were growing accustomed to her loss and returning to regular life. Cassidy was critical in helping them. When Noah bragged about standing up to the bullies and proudly showed the A he'd earned on his recent book report, his first good grade in weeks, Cassidy organized this impromptu outing to celebrate.

Not following the usual evening routine, per se...

But a little spontaneity lifted the children's spirits, and his.

No denying he galloped home faster than ever from the range, climbed his cabin stairs two at a time, wrenched open the door and breathed a sigh of relief when he spied Cassidy, not Joy, whipping up some unpronounceable but delicious meal with the kids. He'd stopped expecting Leanne, which filled him with guilt, followed by hope they'd eventually move on. Heal. Together, they helped Noah and Emma deal with their grief. He and Cassidy had always made a good team on college assignments, and they worked just as well in real life. She was becoming a part of the stable life he'd desired but didn't receive from his biological parents. The kind of family he'd wanted for his children.

And himself.

Daryl admired Cassidy's spontaneity, her adventurous side, her willingness to throw caution to the wind, and he worried over it, too. How much longer before she decided she'd had enough and took the next assignment her editor offered? Alongside his regrets over Leanne, his dread of losing Cassidy also kept him up at night. Often, he heard her pacing in his old bedroom while he stared at his living room ceiling, wondering if she hurt and needed someone to talk to like he did.

Pa was preoccupied by the legal battle with his supposed half brother, Neil, as well as Joy's health. Sierra's wildlife vet practice recently rescued an orphaned bear cub, a cattle rustling outbreak consumed Travis's sheriff's department and Heath had recorded one of his songs in Nashville. Except for Maverick, who'd left his pro bull-riding tour to rehab his shoulder injury, the rest of his brothers were as busy as he laboring to bring in the hay before the first frost while spending their free time remodeling the country store. Since Lovelands didn't pry, they hadn't been pressuring him to talk...and he appreciated the solitude of his work. Yet the weight of his questions about his future and past only grew the longer he went without an outlet.

"Can we try the corn maze yet?" Emma pointed at the mowed, patterned field he'd completed for the country store's grand opening on Saturday. A gust lifted her braid and the air grew damp and heavy.

"We haven't picked our bushel." He tugged another apple from its branch and tucked it into his bag.

"Please, Pa," Noah wheedled. "We want to try the treasure hunt."

"Yeah." Emma pulled out the punch card meant to track the designated stopping points and provide directions to the next spot. "What if it's a dud?"

He mock-gasped, clasped his heart and staggered as he pulled the pretend arrow Emma had just fired at him. "You got me," he choked out.

"No, Clumsy the Clown!" Emma and Noah groaned, giggling, and Cassidy knocked the wind out of him when her beautiful mouth curved into an amused smile.

He did his best Butch Cassidy imitation, turning in a slow circle before collapsing into the yellowing grass with a groan.

"Pa!" Emma and Noah hollered, racing to his side.

At the last minute, he reared up and they scrambled backward, squealing. He chased them in circles, darting through the apple trees, hollering, "You ungrateful kids! I'll teach you!"

Even Beuford hauled himself to his feet and woofed. After a few minutes, he sniffed the air and lumbered into the maze.

"Beuford!" Noah broke away and sprinted after the dog, Emma hot on his heels.

Daryl leaned against one of the trees, slightly winded. The scent of Cassidy's exotic, floral perfume reached his nose before he sensed her presence.

"Should we go after them?" Her green eyes shimmered up at him, clear and deep, the color of a hidden lagoon in a forest glade.

"Let's give them a minute." Emma and Noah had had few moments to cut loose and just be kids since Leanne's passing. He hated to take it from them, despite the approaching storm.

"Ten should be enough for us to finish

picking the apples." Cassidy cocked her head at the children's exuberant shouts rising from the maze. An occasional bark signaled they'd located Beuford. "We'll go after them if they don't come out by then."

"They might not want to leave." Unable to resist, he tucked a soft wave that had escaped her clip around her ear, then stuffed his hand in his pocket. "You did an excellent job with the clues and treasure spots."

"You designed the pattern," she said, a slight catch in her voice.

He caught her eye and held it. "We make a good team."

An attractive pink bloomed in her cheeks. With her honey-brown hair pulled from her makeup-free face, her lithe frame clothed in a white down jacket, laced-up work boots and jeans showcasing her shapely legs, she looked exactly the way she had the day they'd met. Petite, brunette, flashing green eyes, a small heart-shaped mouth…a very beautiful young woman who could just about bring a man to his knees in simple boots and jeans. In fact, the way she looked in a pair of slacks should be downright illegal…he'd thought… still thought.

They'd reached for the same book at the

college store, realized they both came from the Carbondale area, discovered they had a course together and grabbed some coffee before heading to the lecture hall. He couldn't remember the class, but he'd never forgotten their first conversation—a debate about whether postproduction photography editing was cheating. Both were purists. Both were dreamers. Both had ambitions to document the world someday.

He'd been fascinated by the way her magnetic eyes went from introspective to feisty, her quick, lopsided smile, her exuberantly gesturing hands, and the way her belly laugh shook her shoulders, too. His heart had tumbled, tripping, falling over itself, hard, and he'd thought, *I'm going to marry you*.

Cassidy squeezed his arm, dragging him back to the present. "Daryl? You okay? You have a funny look on your face."

His muscle tensed beneath her grip, and he forced himself to back away. "Fine."

A partly true answer. Cassidy eased Daryl's heavy heart and confounded it, too. She'd regained her strength and recovered her assertive nature these past few weeks. She was as willing to speak her mind as ever and argue with him directly rather than seethe in silence like Leanne. It was wrong to compare the two women, yet Cassidy drew him, along with unwanted feelings he struggled to keep under wraps. He was a grieving widower, not a single guy hoping to win Cassidy's hand.

Besides, even if he could pursue her, their lives were complete opposites. Soon she'd grow tired of this small town, stop taking pity on him and his children and grab the next flight to parts unknown. His heart was already broken having lost Leanne, and he wouldn't risk opening himself up to mourning the loss of another Fulton sister.

"You don't look fine." Cassidy closed the distance between them again. This close he noticed the familiar smattering of freckles crossing the bridge of her nose.

"Are you happy?" The question left him too fast to stop.

Her brows flew up. "Why do you ask?"

He studied the grass as he flattened it with his boot tip. "You said you'd planned to stay in Carbondale with me ten years ago... Would you have been happy here?"

When he chanced a glance at her, he saw her pained eyes filled with the same confusion he felt. "I don't know. I'd like to think so. Look, maybe we should go find the kids."

"Not yet." Against his better judgment, he couldn't let her, or this moment, go.

She stopped and turned slowly. "Daryl, what do you want?"

"To know if you're happy now."

Happy enough to stay? he added silently, knowing he had no right to ask it. Or think it, even.

Her teeth worried her bottom lip. "Most times. Especially with the kids." She cleared her throat. "And you."

Their gazes tangled. Clung. His heartbeat thundered in his ears. They swayed close enough for their fingers to brush, and the sweet peppermint of her breath reached his nose.

"I don't hear the kids anymore," Cassidy whispered.

He gave himself a shake, tore his eyes from her beautiful face and listened. "I don't either." Could they be lost?

With the light fading, they might wander from the maze into the greater cornfield and lose their bearings. The predicted storm was rain to freezing rain tonight. If Emma and Noah got caught in it overnight, they'd be exposed to the elements, suffer hypothermia…

Without thinking, he laced his fingers in Cassidy's and sprinted for the entrance.

Just as they plunged into the dense foliage, she yanked him to a stop. "How about we split up? You start at the other end and I'll begin here. We'll meet in the middle."

He nodded. In the distance, thunder boomed, signaling the storm's arrival. The wind picked up and bent the swaying corn. "We'd better hurry!" He released her hand. "Be careful!" he shouted over his shoulder before racing to the exit.

His heart hammered as he called, "Emma! Noah!"

A faint drizzle fell from the darkening clouds. He turned left, then right, then right again, following the pattern to each stopping point. The last two hadn't been touched, suggesting Emma and Noah hadn't gotten this far at least.

His breath rasped harshly in his throat as he sprinted down one row, then across the next. He backtracked at times, in case they'd gone the wrong way. Lightning split the purpling air and thunder crashed hard on its heels.

"Emma!" called Cassidy's voice in the distance. "Noah!"

They were both getting closer to the middle; where were the children? The rain pelted from the sky now in hard, driving sheets. His body shook beneath his soaked clothes.

"Pa!"

His heart quit beating when he heard his little girl. "Emma!"

"Noah!" Cassidy cried just around the corner.

He rounded the bend and his knees went weak with relief at the sight of the three people he loved most in the world, along with one smelly but endearing dog.

Love.

The thought karate chopped his solar plexus and knocked the wind from him. He didn't still love Cassidy. Impossible. But he was in danger of falling for her again if he wasn't more careful.

"We were trying to find Beuford because he went in the cornfield," Emma babbled, nearly strangling him as she clung to his neck. "Then we got lost."

"But I heard Aunt Cassidy calling us," Noah said, crawling onto Cassidy's lap where she knelt in the mud, oblivious to the torrent flattening her hair to her skull. "And Emma heard Pa, so we knew how to get back."

"I love you," he whispered in Emma's ear,

fierce, then set her back on her feet. Then—
"Let's go!"

Cassidy skidded in a wet patch on their
race back and smacked the ground, hard. His
pulse jetted faster still as he helped her to her
feet, running shaking hands over her to check
for injuries.

"I'm okay." She stepped back, and her
ankle gave way. "Maybe not... Ouch!"

"You hurt your ankle." Daryl slid his arm
around her waist.

"Is the bone sticking out?" Noah leaned
close, eyes wide.

"Call 911!" Emma pulled his cell phone
from his jacket pocket.

"We won't get reception out here." The
pummeling rain transitioned into a driving
hail. It tapped on the ground and slid like peb-
bles beneath their feet. "Hold on, Cassidy,"
he warned, then scooped her up and cradled
her gently against his chest. Lightning split
the air and a thunderous boom broke overhead. "Hold on to me!" he hollered to the
kids, who slid their fingers through his belt
loops. "Run!"

Together, they slipped and skidded their
way back to the truck. One family, working
together. He wrenched open the passenger

door just as the hail transitioned into freezing rain. Relieved, he watched his kids and dog scramble inside to safety. Yet he hesitated to release Cassidy, reluctant to let her go when she fit perfectly in his arms, her heart beating against his, her head tucked beneath his jaw like it belonged there.

They made a good team, all right…only he didn't expect to win this rematch with her. In fact, he suspected he might lose his heart again in the process.

CASSIDY BLEW A strand of hair from her flushed faced and ignored the ache in her shoulders as she rolled out another piecrust. Behind her, the country store's industrial ovens radiated enough heat to beat back the chill seeping around the doorjambs as night descended on Loveland Hills. She sprinkled a dusting of flour over the sticky dough and ran the rolling pin over it, spreading it thinner and thinner. The sweet, fruity scent of the fifty pies she, Sierra and Joy had baked earlier teased her nose. Along with the crumb pies, the apple fritters and cider doughnuts, would they have enough baked goods for tomorrow's grand opening?

Concerned, she'd stayed on after Joy departed to make supper at Loveland Hills' main house. She'd offered to feed the kids and Daryl so Cassidy could continue baking.

Daryl...

All day, she'd relived the security of his strong arms as he'd carried her to the truck, the scent of his soapy-clean skin, the thud of his heart against hers. When he'd set her down on the passenger seat, her arms had remained clasped around his neck and she'd had to practically drag them off before she'd given in to temptation to bury her fingers in his thick hair and nestle into his warm, hard body again.

All while his children—*Leanne's children*—watched from the back seat.

A groan ripped from her throat. She should have taken the Sudan assignment. Instead of being embroiled in foreign violence and political unrest, living with Daryl posed an ever-increasing threat. With her old resentment for him lessened, her admiration grew more each day. The spontaneous boyfriend of her college years had been replaced by a responsible family man who drew her more. She admired his devotion to his children, his acceptance of them, imperfections and all, and his ability to give unconditional love.

Her father had loved her, too, but *he'd*

expected great things from her and nothing less. Growing up the eldest child, she'd sometimes felt it was her responsibility to make it big and take care of the family. This wasn't expected of Leanne, not that Cassidy wanted her younger sister to feel the same pressure in that regard. Whether her father intended it or not, she'd always felt as though she had to earn his love, to be worthy of his sacrifices…something she couldn't do if she spun her wheels in Carbondale and didn't return to the job of her dreams.

Only she wasn't certain it was her dream anymore given how frequently she woke with Daryl's name on her lips.

Was it okay to stay in one place and work less? She'd always believed the marker of a successful life was reaching the highest professional standards. Yet the simple, homey satisfaction of watching Leanne's country store come to fruition shook her view of life.

She carefully picked up the piecrust, draped it inside a baking tin and scooped seasoned sliced apples into it. The scent of cinnamon stung her nose, and her face contorted as she held in a sneeze.

"Feeling okay?"

Her head jerked up and her breath caught

at the sight of Daryl leaning in the doorway holding a sack of flour. She took in his strong jaw, straight nose, heavy brows. Under the weight of the flour, his biceps strained against his blue denim shirt, the width of his shoulders accentuating a narrow waist. A little light brown chest hair peeked out of his opened collar and he lifted his chin in greeting as he sauntered inside. Then his lips curved in a smile and a fluttery sensation filled her belly.

"Cat got your tongue?" he teased, coming up behind her. "How's the ankle?"

She inhaled a deep breath of the crisp, cotton smell of his freshly laundered shirt and the clean masculine scent of his skin. "Better. Why are you here?"

"Came to lend a hand. Joy mentioned you were still baking and I didn't want you putting too much pressure on your ankle by standing and making pies till all hours." When he stooped to place the flour sack on a shelf beneath the counter, she noticed a broad, muscular back and tree-trunk-sized thighs. Men around here must get a pretty good workout just getting through the rugged days of ranch living.

She forced her attention back to her task,

measured ingredients into her mixer and attached a dough hook. "You can bake?"

He rolled up his sleeves, revealing muscular forearms. "Why not? I'm an enlightened kind of guy."

True. Which was exactly the problem. She liked that about him.

Too much.

"Really?" She arched a brow. "Reliable sources say your baked macaroni and cheese stinks."

He rubbed his jaw as if she'd socked him. "We should have a bake-off… We'll see who's the better mac-n-cheeser."

"I'll call my manager," she said, trying and failing to keep herself from smiling. "In the meantime, get some rest. I'll need you all day for the opening tomorrow and you must be exhausted getting in the last of the hay. I've only got a few more pies to go."

"And you're not tired from working all day? How about we make an assembly line?" He ambled around the counter to face her. "One of us makes the dough and rolls it out while the other chops the apples and seasons them."

"That'll work." She gave in with a sigh,

happier than she ought to be with him near. "I'll take the apples."

"Good." He tied on a green chef's apron. "I feel like beating up on some dough."

"Why?" She slipped an apple on the peeler and corer and cranked the handle. "What's going on?"

"The judge ruled against Pa's motion to dismiss Neil's complaint. He agreed Neil had satisfactory cause and is allowing Neil's case to proceed." Daryl dumped ingredients into the industrial-sized mixer and flicked on the switch. He raised his voice as it whirred, the hook cutting through the shortening and flour. "We go to trial next month."

"I'm so sorry," she called over the noise.

Daryl stopped the mixer and scraped the shortening clinging to its sides. "He won't win."

"I hope not. The ranch has already faced enough struggles." Her voice grew husky as she recalled Daryl's reasoning for why he'd chosen to return to Loveland Hills rather than join her as a photojournalist.

"We'll manage. We always do."

They lapsed into silence, both immersed in their work. Yet she couldn't help but be hyperaware of the brawny man working a hand's length across from her. There was something about a guy—at least six feet two inches, and two hundred pounds of rock-hard muscle—working in a kitchen with deftness and skill. It melted her resistance faster than butter on a roasted cob of corn.

When he caught her stare, he smiled and reached across the counter, lifting a lock of her hair off her shoulder. "You have flour in your hair. And…butter?"

"Probably. I forgot to put the shield on the mixer the first go-round, right after I'd dropped two dozen eggs on the floor and burned the grease for the fritters."

"Oh, man," he said, surprising her with a rich, deep chuckle. "Could you have had a worse day?"

"I've had a few," she said out of the corner of her mouth, thinking of her recent accident and the danger-filled job awaiting her, its appeal waning exponentially by the amount of time spent around one ruggedly handsome cowboy… "Occupational hazard."

"How'd you get the gunshot wound in your left arm?" He sprinkled flour on the countertop before transferring the dough. "I saw the bandage when you were in the hospital."

Her hand rose to the now healed scrape

and her mind flashed back to the Philippines. "Running from Duterte's goons."

He leaned toward her, bracing his hands on the counter, brows lowered. "They were shooting at you?"

She fit another apple on the slicer. "Best way to stop an unflattering story from getting out."

Daryl slapped the dough into a ball. "You could try not being a dictator and, I don't know, give democracy a chance?"

"Now, where's the fun in that?" After a last crank, she pulled off the peeled sliced apple.

"You love your job, don't you?" Daryl shoved the marble roller into the dough, rotating the ball as he flattened it with brisk, efficient strokes.

"Most of the time." Her knife flashed as she cut the slices in half and dropped them into a stainless-steel mixing bowl.

"What about the rest of the time?"

"I'm lonely. It's a pretty solitary job."

He looked up, dark eyes peering at her from beneath hooded brows. "So's ranching."

"But you have the kids and…" Her voice trailed off, swallowing back her sister's name as she cranked the apple peeler. He'd never see his wife, his partner, again.

He trimmed the ends of the crust, transferred the dough and pressed it into the tin pie dish. "You never want to have children?"

"No time."

"You're not working now."

"No."

He smiled with a strange mixture of relief and approval. It made her instantly think, *Don't get any ideas, buster. I've got my own life. Just because I'm here doesn't mean I'm necessarily staying.*

But she was tempted to. More so with each passing day.

She couldn't deny the attractive appeal in his dark eyes, strong jaw, the small cleft in his chin and the gracious, laid-back manner that suggested he didn't know he was good-looking. He never had. She'd thwarted more than one would-be rival in college only to have him insist "Ashley" must have lost track of time when she stopped by to borrow a book at 2:00 a.m. or "Tara" must have expected someone else when she'd answered the door to their study session wearing lingerie.

Perfectly innocent…

And clueless…

But she'd loved that humbleness about Daryl, his good, old-fashioned cowboy courtesy and humility. When she thought about it, he'd become exactly the kind of father she'd imagined he'd be...loving but firm, playful and a good role model. Most important, he loved them unconditionally and didn't lay his expectations on them as her well-meaning father had. Somehow, she'd interpreted her dad's insistence on her success as an unspoken understanding that just being herself wasn't good enough, not when compared with all he'd done to help her be better than "good," to be "great."

If she'd had children, she would have wanted Daryl to be the father. She'd planned on it, in fact, when she returned from Bosnia, never imagining her biggest rival would be her sister.

"Thank you for doing this." He passed her the pie tin.

She dumped the syrupy apple mix into the pan. Daryl strode to her side and dropped the top crust over it.

"It's nothing." She pinched the edges of the crusts with her thumb and index finger.

Daryl joined her, tenting the dough. "It's not nothing. The kids are excited for opening day tomorrow. I doubt they'll sleep. It's the first thing they've been excited about in a long, long time."

"I'm sure Leanne…"

Their fingers tangled over the last inch of uncrimped dough and neither of them moved. Breathed. She felt his calluses as he gently squeezed her hand; he was a man who did hard, physical work, and it appealed to her more than any of the desk jockeys she'd met in her line of work. "I'm talking about you, Cassidy. *You* make them happy."

"I'm not doing anything special."

"You just can't help it." His eyes searched hers, a muscle jumping in his jaw as if he held back some strong emotion.

"Help what?"

He cupped her cheek and leaned his forehead against hers. "Being special."

She caught herself as she swayed toward him, yanking back so fast she stumbled. He caught her elbow and steadied her. "I shouldn't have said that."

"No."

"It's disrespectful of Leanne and you."

"Let's just forget it."

"That's the problem. I can't forget it. Can't forget you."

"Maybe I should go."

"No!" He ran a hand over his hair, leaving a trail of white. "I'm out of line." His grave eyes landed briefly on her face.

"I'm sending you to the penalty box, buddy," she declared, and her shoulders loosened when Daryl's face lost its intensity. Knowing he shared her mixed-up emotions filled her with a strange sense of joy and trepidation.

"We'd better get moving if we're going to finish up before the kids' bedtime," he said gruffly, returning to the opposite side of the counter. "I want to hear how you got out of that Bengal coal mining cave-in."

"Spoiler alert, I made it."

"For the record, you need to pause after saying 'spoiler alert,' so you don't actually spoil it." His eyes twinkled at her and he started up the mixer again.

She cranked the apple slicer. "I thought it was fairly obvious."

He scooped out the dough when it finished combining and plopped it on the counter. "This could all be just a dream…"

"Do you ever wish it was and you'll wake up, life back to normal?"

His hands stilled, and his eyes lifted to meet hers. "Then you wouldn't be here."

"But Leanne would."

"Would she? There's something I didn't tell you."

Cassidy stopped turning the handle and pulled off the cored apple. "What?"

"Leanne's suitcase was in the Jeep, too."

The apple thudded to the counter. "Where was she going?"

Daryl shrugged his shoulders slowly, as though they carried an enormous weight. "I don't know."

"Was she leaving you?"

"She must have been." His voice broke.

"I wish I could remember, Daryl." She rubbed her temples, tears pricking the backs of her eyelids. "This must be so difficult."

Strong hands cupped her shoulders and she opened her eyes to stare into Daryl's set face. "There's nothing harder, but we'll figure this out, Cassidy."

Would they? she wondered when Daryl returned to dough making. Her new cell phone hadn't recovered any text messages between her and Leanne, nor had her email account shown any exchanges between them.

Leanne's final days remained an unsolvable mystery… Cassidy's jaw firmed…yet she wasn't one of the best investigative reporters for nothing. She'd find Daryl the answers he needed and leave once the country store was established, Joy strong enough to run it.

What about the answers you need? asked a voice from within.

Daryl swore they'd figure everything out, but perhaps some mysteries were better left unsolved after all…especially when it came to her and Daryl.

CHAPTER NINE

"WE'RE ALMOST OUT of pies!"

Cassidy glanced up at Sofia's ominous news, her stomach rollicking. The raven-haired woman whose husband, James Cade, managed Cade Ranch, waved at Cassidy from farther down the glass bakery display case. Above her, late-morning sunshine glinted on glitter-glue letters spelling out Grand Opening. Joy had deemed the sign homey and colorful to her worried grandchildren. Who cared if it wasn't professional? Perfect?

It had heart, which was most important when it came to their family-run business.

"I'll help make more once things die down." Cassidy boxed up a caramel-topped crumb pie, inhaling the sweet, buttery scent wafting from the kitchen behind her.

"That's not happening anytime soon." Sofia pointed to the long checkout line, then at the crowd thronging the country store's aisles.

"You're getting one of the last crumb pies."

Cassidy handed change to her customer and smiled. They'd opened their doors just four hours ago and were already down to only six dozen doughnuts, eighteen fritters and six pies.

Beneath her green-checked smock, her sticky skin reflected her nerves and the humid air fogging the windows. She surveyed the packed space, alternately thrilled and terrified by the store's instant success. They'd quadrupled the amount they baked to keep up with demand.

Jewel Cade sauntered in through a side door, poured herself a cup of the free lemon water at the end of the bakery section and leaned against the glass display. Her fiery-red hair was tamed into a braid hanging beneath her tall black Stetson, and the skin visible beneath her freckled face glowed red. "I'm giving the pony a fifteen-minute break."

"Have you had a lot of riders?" Cassidy followed the next customers' orders and filled a bag with fritters and doughnuts.

"A lot?" Jewel sputtered on her drink. "At one point, we had a one-hour wait time. We're down to twenty minutes, so I thought I'd give Twilight Sparkle a breather."

The waxy paper bag crinkled in her grasp

as Cassidy passed it to the waiting patron. "Isn't Twilight Sparkle one of the My Little Ponies?"

Jewel's fringed suede jacket swung with her shrug. "She doesn't let fame go to her head." With a wink, the cowgirl ambled away after snagging the sample plate of a cut-up doughnut and dumping its contents in her cupped hand. "Thank you kindly." She tipped her hat with a grin and disappeared outside.

Cassidy held in a chuckle, not the least bit offended, and brushed sugar from her gloved fingers. Seeing the Loveland and Cade blended-family members labor together, all focused on the store's success, was deeply gratifying. Growing up, she'd carried the responsibility of her family's accomplishments solely on her shoulders. Her father's struggles leveled enormous pressure on her to be their success story. Yet the hustling Cade-Loveland clan proved triumph was better when shared.

A young mother stepped to the front of the bakery line. She jiggled a fussing toddler on one hip. "Do you have chocolate chip cookies?"

Cassidy shook her head and made a mental note to add cookies to their bakery offerings.

They'd had multiple requests. "How about an apple-cider doughnut?"

"What's cider?" A towheaded boy peeped around his mother's knees. He wore only a T-shirt and jeans, despite the forty-five-degree day. One toe poked through a hole in his ragged sneakers.

"It's like apple juice. Want to try a doughnut sample?" Cassidy chopped up another one and extended the paper plate.

"Go ahead." The mother gently nudged her son. "It's free."

Eyes as big as saucers, he took the smallest piece and popped it in his mouth. An instant smile revealed a row of tiny teeth and deep dimples.

"Good?" Cassidy prompted.

"You can have one to split with your sister." The mother smoothed a hand over her daughter's wispy hair. "Okay?"

When the little boy nodded, Cassidy passed him a doughnut wrapped in wax paper and another to his mother, waving away her crumpled bills. "It's on the house."

"Oh, no. I couldn't. We always pay our way." The mother attempted to give back the doughnuts, but Cassidy shook her head.

"Once you touch it, I can't serve it, so it'll

go in the garbage anyway. Besides, these are getting old. You're doing me a favor by taking them."

The mother eyed her skeptically. "Well… if you're sure…"

Cassidy recognized the same pride her family and their neighbors possessed, despite their money troubles. Pride didn't cost anything and sometimes, besides love, it was all you had. Funny how she'd traveled the world documenting social injustice and forgot the dire straits in her own backyard. Western folks suffered because of weather afflicting crops, cattle falling prey to drought and jobs relocating to other countries, like the ones her father lost before his injury. She could document their plight while in Carbondale, another way to honor her sister and draw attention to an important issue.

"Please. Take them," she assured the woman. "And check out our clothing drive." She gestured to a doorway. Above it hung the Many Hands, Doing Good poster. Inside was a small room where they'd organized a slew of donated clothing that'd exceeded her expectations. Carbondale was a generous, caring community. "We have so many coats and shoes, we're out of room. Just ask for Joy or

Emma. They'll be thrilled to give you whatever you need."

"Can I get new shoes?" The hope in the little boy's eyes made Cassidy swallow hard. She remembered what it felt like to want, to need and to do without.

"Thank you, ma'am," the mother said with a tremulous smile. She broke off a bit of doughnut for her toddler, passed it over and hurried to the clothing drive.

Cassidy held in a sigh as she helped the next customer. If only Leanne was here to see her plans come together...better than Cassidy had dared hope. Traipsing around the globe, she'd felt fortunate to have escaped Western America. Now she saw Leanne had been the lucky one after all, with a supportive and loving family and community surrounding her.

Why had Leanne been leaving them, her suitcase alongside Cassidy's in the Jeep? Given his grief, Daryl seemed devoted to his wife. Yet somewhere along the way he'd stopped making Leanne happy and thus far, Cassidy had turned up nothing to explain it. In fact, the more time she spent with Daryl, the harder it was to understand how someone could *not* love him.

Once, he'd been the love of her life and she'd never loved anyone since.

Her cheeks heated as she remembered their near kiss in the kitchen the other night. Old feelings mixed with new for the mature, caring widower. She'd thought she'd loved him in college, yet her feelings now seemed more complex, tested by life's realities. A reflection of the complicated situation? Undoubtedly. So much had changed; so much time had passed. But even though her sister was gone, Cassidy wouldn't cross the line and explore her feelings no matter how tempted.

Around Daryl, Emma and Noah, her loneliness disappeared. She was part of a real family with lasting relationships, something impossible for her to achieve, given her demanding career, her crazy travel schedule, the danger she placed herself in and her workaholic life. Since she rarely had time to enjoy her successes, however, what was the point of them?

"Well, this place sure is nice." Neil Wharton stepped to the counter. Blue eyes, similar in color to Boyd's, gleamed behind his dark-framed glasses.

"You shouldn't be here," she said beneath her breath, grateful Boyd and Daryl were driving wagons filled with customers to distant apple orchards and pumpkin patches.

Neil's teeth flashed in a wide smile. "Why not? Half of it will belong to me someday."

Her heart sank. "You're a long way from proving that. Please leave."

"Now!" Sofia ordered, joining Cassidy. She planted her balled hands on her hips and glared.

"Fine." He settled a rancher's hat over his cropped, silver hair. "But only if you agree to pass a message on to Boyd."

"We're not doing you any favors," Sofia hissed.

"Excuse me." Neil cocked his head and stared at Sofia. "Are you a relative?"

"I'm Boyd's daughter-in-law." Sofia tossed her hair, the color high in her cheeks. "And Cades and Lovelands stick together."

Cassidy glanced nervously at the rest of the preoccupied Lovelands and Cades, grateful they'd thus far missed this exchange. The fledgling store couldn't afford a brawl on opening day. "What's the message?"

Neil's smile reappeared. "Tell him I'll agree not to exhume our father's body if he'll settle with me out of court. My lawyer will prepare a document with my demands."

Sofia snorted. "Over my dead body!"

"Outta here!" Maverick, Daryl's older brother, appeared. He dumped fresh peas into a depleted bin and stomped their way. So much for keeping the peace… He glowered down at Neil. "Trespassers will be shot on sight."

Neil's smile fell. "This is a place of business."

"It's still our private property."

"Fifty percent of it. The rest will be mine." Neil lifted his squared-off chin. "Too bad this place will be demolished when I sell to the fracking company."

"Keep dreaming." Maverick grabbed Neil's elbow and hustled him outside before the other Lovelands noticed the argument. Cassidy flattened her hands against the countertop, faint with relief to have the situation handled quickly.

Neil would not destroy Leanne's store, or Loveland Hills, she vowed; this family's fight was now her own.

"Do we have any more jalapeño jelly?" called Sierra as she emerged from the preserves aisle.

Before Cassidy could answer, Sofia's son, Javi, who'd been overseeing coloring in the children's play area, jumped up. "I'll check!"

"Have someone carry it back for you!" she shouted after Javi, then turned to her next customer.

"I'll supervise," Maverick called, looking none the worse for wear, thankfully, after escorting Neil off the property.

As Cassidy loaded another bag with doughnuts, the deep rumble of a tractor engine filled her ears. Daryl's easy smile flashed when he stopped the vehicle outside a nearby window, hopped down and helped passengers off the attached wagon, depositing the pumpkins they'd picked onto green metal carts. Another wagon pulled up alongside it, Boyd behind the wheel. When he cut the engine, she caught the faint sounds of the sing-along Heath led outside for those waiting for the next wagon ride.

She hummed the melody to "This Land Is Your Land" along with him and rung up her next customer. Heath had invited her to hear him and his band, Outlaw Cowboys, gig at Silver Spurs tonight, a local honky-tonk. It'd been a long time since she'd heard live country music, and she wanted to kick up her boots, let loose and celebrate the store's successful opening once she finished baking for tomorrow.

"Here's ten more," Travis said behind her. He bore a metal tray crammed with fragrant pies. "Where would you like them?"

She shot him a grateful smile and pointed to a lower shelf in the glass cabinet. How kind of him to help while in the middle of an intense cattle rustling investigation. How thoughtful of all of them. Even Amberley Cade, Jared Cade's wife, canceled a barrel-racing tour date to bake alongside her husband. Cole Loveland's wife, Katlynn, had flown in from LA between show tapings to babysit the Cade and Loveland little ones while Cole and Noah manned the petting zoo. On the opposite side of the store, recently married and newly pregnant Brielle Cade, Justin's wife and the head of a local mental health and rehab facility, checked out customers purchasing dry goods and produce while Justin hovered protectively.

It was a far cry from the tropical forests of the Philippines and the arid landscapes of Sudan…but it fulfilled another of her needs, one she hadn't fully realized she wanted— no, needed—until now…family, community and… She glanced out the window again and returned Daryl's wave before he restarted the tractor engine…

…love.

Was she falling *in love* with him again? Her head throbbed along with her heart. Daryl offered the kind of family she wished for but was incapable of having. She eyed the bustling Cades and Lovelands, who exchanged smiles and good-natured barbs in equal measure. What would they think of Daryl if he moved on so soon after losing Leanne…? If he *was* ready to move on…

Either way, she didn't dare go further with her feelings. Instead, she'd help Daryl recover his old self, rather than their old relationship, and leave Loveland Hills, leave Daryl and his children stronger than when she'd arrived. Seeing her work pay off was a start. If the store stayed as busy, it'd help the Lovelands gain even more financial stability—or at least pay for their recent legal fees and medical costs.

If only she felt as stable with the rest of her life, her traitorous heart and the mystery surrounding the crash. She was falling for this loving family. Was she in danger of heartbreak again if she lingered too long?

THE INSTANT DARYL ducked inside Silver Spurs later that night, his eyes automatically scanned the packed crowd for Cassidy. Perspiration gathered at the base of his throat and slicked his body beneath his button-down shirt. He peered through the gloom, listening to Heath's deep voice pouring through wall-mounted speakers. When Daryl spotted Cassidy, his heart shifted into another gear.

Standing on the dance floor's edge between Sierra and Jewel, she looked stunning in a deep rose, off-the-shoulder dress revealing her creamy shoulders and curvy legs. The stage's bright lights picked up the honey-colored strands in her wavy hair and illuminated her beautiful face and sparkling eyes. He barely heard the song Heath belted out. The room, the world—heck, even the universe—shrank down to this one incredible woman.

Cassidy had been a blur of action today as she'd labored to bring Leanne's vision to life, creating a legacy for his children. When he'd left them with Joy for a sleepover, they'd barely had time to hug him good-night in their excitement to chatter on about their exciting day with Javi, who'd also been invited to the impromptu get-together. Emma, especially, had bragged about how many coats they'd distributed. Many Hands, Doing Good gave her a purpose, a direction, an outlet for her grief. He couldn't be more grateful to

Cassidy, yet deep down, gratitude vied with other, stronger emotions he refused to examine too closely.

"Hey," he said by way of greeting when he joined the women.

Jewel nodded without taking her eyes from Heath. Her engagement ring sparkled as she pumped her fist while her fiancé ripped through a guitar solo. Sierra moved aside, making room for him to stand beside Cassidy, and her fetching smile sent his pulse zipping through his veins.

"Where are the kids?" she shouted in his ear.

Her exotic floral scent curled beneath his nose and his body tightened in awareness. "Joy invited them for a sleepover."

Her eyes widened. "You mean they're gone...all night?"

"That's usually how it works."

Her heart-shaped mouth dropped open and the temptation to sample it seized him. Hard. Did she still taste as sweet? The urge to kick himself followed. He turned to leave, but Sierra blocked his exit.

She cupped her hands around his ear and hollered, "Where are you going?"

"Anywhere else."

Sierra followed his gaze to Cassidy, then swerved back to his face. "I warned you what would happen if you moved her in."

"And I promised I wouldn't get attached."

Sierra's eyes narrowed, and she sniffed his neck. "Then why are you wearing cologne? And an ironed shirt?"

Warmth flushed his face. He tugged at his restrictive collar. "No reason."

"Uh-huh." She pursed her mouth, skeptical. "Be careful."

"I know."

"No, you don't." Sierra followed his gaze to Cassidy, who, like Jewel, applauded wildly when the Outlaw Cowboys ended their song. "I just hope no one gets hurt."

"Too late for that," he said darkly.

Sierra rose on her toes, kissed his cheek and hugged him. "Forgive your overprotective sister?"

"Always."

Sierra and Jewel headed to the ladies' room, leaving him alone beside Cassidy.

"Thanks for your help today." She smiled up at him. "I didn't expect such a big turnout."

"Driving a tractor wasn't much. You deserve all the credit."

Her eyes widened and so did her smile,

sending his heart careening in his chest. "It was a group effort."

"You look beautiful," he said as the band struck up the opening notes to the next song.

"What?"

"Nothing. Would you like a drink?"

Before she could answer, Heath shouted, "I need everyone on the dance floor for this next song I wrote. I'm debuting it here and it's called 'Loved You First.'" Heath pointed at Daryl. "Come on out. Don't make me insecure about this one, now."

Jewel returned, alone, and shoved Daryl onto the dance floor. "You heard my man. Get dancing, you two."

"People will talk." Cassidy raised her voice as Heath began to sing.

Jewel shrugged. "If they're pathetic enough to gossip about two people dancing, then who cares what their itty, bitty brains are thinking? Or not thinking since, you know, they only have about three brain cells to rub together."

Daryl grinned and extended a hand to Cassidy. "Shall we?"

"I guess we must," she said breathlessly as he swept her into his arms and slowly danced her around the crowded floor.

She smelled so good. He closed his eyes and breathed in the sweet scent rising from her neck. The way her small hand wrapped around his, the other resting on his shoulder, stirred his blood. His heart lifted. His spirit soared.

Euphoria.

Then reality slammed him back down to earth. It didn't matter that she fit in his arms like she belonged there. He knew better. She belonged to journalism, to the career she loved, and he had no place in that world, even if he was free to pursue her. As for him, he was a single father with two kids, a cowboy with a modest life, a widower still grieving the woman he'd come to love and had somehow driven away.

Was it possible to love two women at once, in two different ways?

Until Leanne pulled away from him and the kids, he'd felt content with the quiet life they'd built together. Cassidy, on the other hand, left him unsettled, on tenterhooks, never knowing what came next, but excited to discover it nonetheless. She was exuberant. Unrestrained. A migrating butterfly you were lucky to see and wrong to capture.

His hand slid up from her tiny waist to her back, pressing her closer as he swept her in slow circles. He didn't want to think about the future or their past. All he wanted to do was savor this sweet, blissful now. He accepted this was the most he could ever hope for.

The most he deserved.

And in that acceptance, he found an odd kind of peace. He felt as if he was floating, drifting on the high of the moment. Tomorrow didn't exist. For this brief span of time, she was his and they were one. He gazed down at her rosy mouth and wanted to kiss her more than he wanted to breathe.

"Heath's really good," Cassidy said directly in his ear as he rocked her back and forth. "When did he start writing songs?"

His muscles clenched at the delicious feel of her lips whispering across his ear. "He always has, but he signed a studio contract a year ago."

"So Travis is the county sheriff, Maverick is a professional bull rider, Heath is a songwriter and Sierra is a wildlife veterinarian, right?"

He pulled back to stare down into her flushed face. "Right."

"Everyone pursued their own dreams but you and Cole."

His shoulder lifted and fell beneath her hand. "Cole always wanted to be a rancher."

"And you?"

"It's not important."

She angled her head to catch his eye again. "Yes, it is. You always wanted to be a photographer."

"And a husband and a father." His hand slid farther up her back to bury itself in her glossy waves. "I got what I wanted."

"Not all of it." She brushed the back of his neck with her fingertips. His heartbeat thudded loud in his eardrums.

"No one gets everything they want." His voice was husky now. Her touch was messing with him. Bad. "I'm lucky to even have this much."

"Why do you think that?" Her hand stilled, and a line formed between her brows. "You deserve to be as happy as your siblings."

He looked away.

"Don't you?"

When the music ended, he led her to a small table in the corner of the bar. "What would you like to drink?"

"Why won't you answer the question?"

Air rushed between his clamped teeth. "Because I'm not like them."

"How?"

He whisked the empties from the table and

placed them on an empty booth nearby. "I'm adopted."

She gasped. "You never said… Why didn't you… I don't understand."

He clenched his hands as an uncomfortable feeling knotted up inside his chest. "It's not something I talk about."

"I can't believe you never told me." Her betrayed expression cut him straight through.

"It's not important."

"Yes, it is," she fired back, indignant now. "You said it's the reason you don't deserve to be as happy as your siblings."

Daryl frowned. "I am happy. Or I was, before…"

"You didn't go to college to be a rancher," Cassidy cut in.

"I went to college because Pa was able to spare me those four years." He signaled to a waitress carrying a laden tray.

"Why go at all if you intended to stay on the ranch?"

"Because I wanted to…I don't know… experience more."

"So did I," she said simply and their gazes snapped together. They'd both wanted to mold their lives into something different then.

In that moment of awareness, he felt the

click—the reconnecting of the bond that had once been severed. Something shared. They were connected in a way he'd never connected with anyone else. Not even his wife, much as it pained him to even think it.

Cassidy tapped her chin, a faraway look in her eyes. "What if I had a way for you to experience more, without leaving the area?"

"What do you mean?"

"Do you trust me?"

"Yes" came the instant answer; it shook him that he didn't even have to think about it.

Her smile was big and bright. It electrified him. "Do you still have your Canon?"

"What are you planning?"

She lifted a brow. "Let's just say it's time I reminded you of who else you are...besides dad, sibling, son, rancher."

"That's who I am. There's no one else."

"Oh, yes, there is," she countered. "I knew him once. I'd like to know him again."

The waitress stopped by their table, took their order and hustled away. He opened his mouth to ask for more details, intrigued, when one of his friends shuffled up to their table.

"Stopped by your country store." Dan Cooke yanked his red ball cap off his perspiring, shaved head, then resettled it, cupping the brim. "Couldn't find where you were selling your moonshine."

"We don't have our liquor license yet," Daryl drawled, sarcastic.

Dan hooted, slapping Daryl on the back. "Let me know when you do."

When he ambled away, Cassidy shot Daryl a quizzical look. "What's he talking about? You don't drink hard liquor."

"I didn't used to. A lot's changed in ten years. I've changed." He expected to see disapproval on her face, or the very least, disappointment. But when Cassidy's eyes met his, that wasn't what he saw.

She looked sympathetic. Understanding. It took him aback. "Why haven't I seen you drinking it now?"

He thought back over the past several weeks, realizing he hadn't even thought of the flask tucked in his saddle bag. "I don't need it anymore."

"Oh," she said quietly, and her eyes swerved to the waitress delivering their drinks. "Then maybe you haven't changed as much as you think. And I have a plan to remind you."

He clamped his mouth shut to keep from saying more. The Daryl who'd fallen in love with her wasn't the same man sitting across from her now. He'd experienced too many dis-appointments, made too many compromises, suffered through too much loss. Besides, he knew better than to drop his emotional armor around Cassidy. To allow her inside his for-tress. They'd damaged each other once upon a time, and he was still leery.

Yet she captivated him. Not only because of her stunning uniqueness but also by the way she made him feel unique. Special. "Cho-sen," not "adopted." Around her, he wasn't just an unwanted child, a brother, son, father, rancher… She made him want to know himself again, the man whose dreams he'd forgotten.

He was falling for Cassidy, he realized as he wrapped his hand around his sweaty soda can…

…while acknowledging at the same time she might break him all over again. Would he be content with his insular life, his old self when she inevitably left him again?

CHAPTER TEN

CASSIDY LIFTED HER Canon Rebel T5i, sighted through its viewfinder and snapped pictures of worn garments swaying from a clothesline stretched between abandoned factory buildings. Despite the frigid morning temperature, shouting children played keep-away with a can. Some didn't wear coats, others were missing hats and gloves. A couple were in stocking feet. Her throat swelled at the juxtaposition of innocence and desperation, joy and despair.

It'd been two weeks before she'd been able to coordinate a date for her and Daryl to document struggling Westerners left behind by relocating manufacturing plants. Her blood fired, despite the chill in the air. She sensed the deeper story: proud workers stuck in the industrial past, unable to find their place in the technological present.

She blinked stinging eyes. So much for staying detached…but among her own people, she felt more connected than ever to her subjects and their suffering. The need to tell their story clenched her belly and gripped her heart. America had the second-highest poverty rate among rich countries. A living example of a wrong in need of being made right stood before her.

"This isn't legal," Daryl cautioned beside her, clicking away on his old college Canon.

Despite his warning, his voice crackled with energy. Fire. This was the Daryl she remembered, intense, focused, passionate. He was as affected by this human tragedy as she. Yet the new, mature Daryl, who admitted his imperfections and accepted them in himself and others, drew her just as much. He balanced his work with his family, something she'd never been able to do.

"Trespassing? Since when has that ever stopped us?" Cassidy trained her camera on a group of men hunched around a rusted barrel. They held their hands over the dancing flames inside it, their lined faces gray with exhaustion and poor health. The stench of burning rubber and garbage stung her nose. "Besides, don't we have connections with the county sheriff?"

"Travis doesn't have jurisdiction here."

Daryl swapped his lens for a wider angle and began firing off shots of the entire tableau, the playing children in the foreground, their weary parents watching in the background, the wasteland of the factory looming over them all.

"We can handle ourselves." She clicked a photo of the building's crumbling brick exterior and the inlaid granite sign reading Great Western Sugar Co.

"Let's talk to them." Daryl lowered his camera and nodded at the men who'd been casting wary glances their way. "We need to hear their story."

She nodded, pleased by his zeal. "You sound like a photojournalist, not a rancher."

"I'm a human being." Daryl stowed his camera. "No one should live in these conditions. Especially children."

"Agreed."

He stopped her. "Thank you for bringing me. For showing me what I've been missing."

A lump clogged her throat. "And what's that?"

"Life," he said simply.

Together they approached the adults and a sense of déjà vu overwhelmed her.

On their first assignment for their college

newspaper, she and Daryl had teamed up. They'd planned to investigate rumors of un-documented workers who'd been falsely promised good jobs in America, then been forced to work without pay or risk deportation. When Daryl discovered children working alongside their parents with dangerous equipment, he'd transformed from laid-back cowboy to avenging citizen. He called Border Patrol and the American Civil Liberties Union, confronted the owner, then restrained the man when he tried escaping.

Throughout the ordeal, Daryl remained calm, cheering up the petrified kids while agents and lawyers spoke to their parents. Watching him clown around for the children, pulling smiles from them, had been endearing and one of the most beautiful acts of humanity she'd ever witnessed. In that instant, she'd thought: *You'll be the father of my children someday.*

How wrong she'd been.

"Howdy," Daryl said to the men, pulling her from her thoughts. "I'm Daryl Loveland and this is Cassidy Fulton. Can we trouble you for a few minutes of your time?"

"We'd like to ask you a few questions," Cassidy added.

"Are you cops?" One of them was quite young, Cassidy realized. Weary eyes said he was eighteen going on a hundred.

"No." Daryl blew on his hands, then extended them over the fire.

"CPS?" asked another man, referring to Child Protective Services.

"We're investigative journalists." White plumed the air as Cassidy spoke.

"You're what?" A man with grayish teeth curled his lip.

Daryl removed a flask from his coat pocket and passed it to Gray Teeth. "She writes stories for magazines."

"Him, too," Cassidy hurried to add, referencing Daryl's past. He shot her a surprised glance.

"I'm just a rancher," he deflected.

"More than that," she countered. *Remember who you used to be*, she urged silently.

"Hey. This ain't bad," one of the men said, tipping back the flask. "How much of this you got?"

"Enough." Daryl glanced over his shoulder at his truck and she recalled the large jug in its bed… He'd brought along a bribe. Impressive.

"Well." Another man rubbed his hands together. "Now we're talking."

"I hope so." Cassidy fished out her cell phone, indicating the recording app. "Do you mind?" After a few hesitant nods, she hit the record button. "Can you tell us how you came to live here?"

"Don't have no other place to go." An older woman joined them. She had salt-and-pepper hair in a low bun and a stern chin. "My husband used to work here till they shut down the place in '98. Couldn't find any other work. When we lost our home, we came out here."

The rest repeated a version of the same story, their tongues loosening as the flask wove through the group.

"Why not go to a shelter? Apply for social services?" Cassidy asked.

"We don't take handouts." A man with a faded John Deere cap shoved his shoulders back. "We want work, that's all."

The group nodded, their expressions fierce. Proud.

The John Deere cap guy handed over the flask and Cassidy accepted it in solidarity. She tipped it back, then gasped, choking when liquid fire hit the back of her throat. Daryl thumped her on the back, grinning. A round of guffaws rang in the chilly air. "But if there're no jobs," she wheezed once her eyes stopped watering, "then why not relocate to another state?"

"I was born here," the woman said simply. "This is my home. My people."

Cassidy nodded. Their jobs may have abandoned them, but they wouldn't abandon this place. Misplaced loyalty? Fear of the unknown? Or something more primal she understood the longer she stayed in Carbondale? You didn't put down roots. They wove into the fabric of your soul and connected you to your home, wherever you traveled.

"What about health care? Education for the children?" Daryl accepted his flask and pocketed it.

"We take care of our kids," the man with gray teeth said flatly.

"Darn right, Russ," the older woman said.

"Are they immunized?" Cassidy pressed.

"Thought you said you weren't with CPS?" The woman's jaw squared.

"We're not, though we'd like to help."

The woman threw up her hands. "You think we don't want what every parent wants for their kids? We may not have fancy clothes or computers or such, but we're doing the best we can."

"I drive 'em to the bus stop every day," supplied another man. On closer inspection, he wore an auto body shop uniform.

"Tori, the redheaded one over there—" the woman pointed to one of the children "—she just won the school spelling bee and all our kids get attendance awards every year."

"And they've been immunized at the clinic." A young mother joined them carrying a baby on her hip.

"What do you do for money? Food?"

"Sell scrap metal from buildings like this, odd jobs, anything we can get." The man named Russ pointed at the auto body guy. "Jack keeps our old generator going so we can run the stove, refrigerator and heat."

Cassidy eyed young Jack. "Ever thought about getting your own place? You've got a steady job."

"My family's here. I couldn't afford a place and help out."

"We don't want much," said John Deere cap guy. "Just jobs and community."

"Ever worked in an apple orchard?" Cassidy mused out loud, earning her a surprised, and approving, look from Daryl.

The man pulled off his cap and scratched his balding head. "Picking apples?"

"And other crops for a country store. Plus, we need help driving wagons and making cider." They'd been struggling to keep up with the greater-than-expected flow of customers. The Lovelands and Cades, busy with ranching, were exhausted from splitting their time. The store made enough to hire a few employees, and this hard-hit group looked deserving and capable.

They exchanged long looks, and cautious smiles crept across their faces. "We're not afraid to get our hands dirty."

"We've got an old pickup we could loan you to drive back and forth," Daryl offered.

"Thank you kindly," said Russ. "This calls for a celebration! Where's some more of that moonshine?"

A growling engine approached and cut off their cheers. Car doors creaked open followed by thudding boots. When Cassidy turned, she spied a group of young men with shaved hair and facial scruff storming their way.

"Who the hell are these two?" demanded what appeared to be their leader. He sported a strip of hair that began at his low brow line and ended midway down his neck.

"What's it to you?" Daryl growled. His massive hands balled at his sides. He stepped between the new arrivals and the factory residents.

The leader cast a wary eye over Daryl's large frame. "This is our turf and we've come to collect the rent."

"We don't have all of it yet," said Russ, his face ashen. "But Jack here's getting paid next week and—"

The leader signaled his two goons, who strode to Russ. Without preamble, they punched him hard enough to drop him, then hauled back their heavy work boots to kick him.

The children's noisy play ceased; everyone held their collective breath.

The sound of a gun being cocked split the quiet. "Back off, now!" rasped Daryl.

To her shock, he trained a handgun on the two sidekicks. Colorado was a concealed carry state, and she supposed she should have guessed Daryl would have brought his gun along... She certainly was glad he had.

The men scuttled away, and Russ gasped on the ground, spitting up blood.

Cassidy stumbled when someone grabbed a fistful of her hair and yanked her backward. The group's leader pressed the cold tip of a knife to her temple. "Drop the gun or this pretty lady won't be so pretty anymore."

Daryl's stormy eyes met hers, then rose to the man holding her captive. His expression promised death. "If you hurt her, I will kill you."

His calm tone only made his words more lethal. Her heart skittered in her chest. She'd never been in a hostage situation like this before, but she'd witnessed enough. A positive outcome wasn't a guarantee by any stretch. Why had she dragged Daryl into this? He had two children at home already missing one parent. If anything happened to him...

The leader tightened his grip, and she bit her cheek to keep from crying out. "Drop the gun," he snarled. "Or we'll take this little honey back to our place for some fun."

His accomplices guffawed, a harsh, grating sound. Crows over a kill.

Daryl's gaze bored into her and he seemed to communicate something... Not so much words as a feeling, an assurance to trust him...which she did, despite his past betrayal.

She trusted him with her life.

Daryl slowly lowered the gun to the ground, then dived forward and knocked her captor off his feet. Instinctively, she lunged, snatched up the gun and trained it on the two goons. They halted their headlong rush to help their struggling leader.

He and Daryl grappled on the ground, the knife flashing between them. In a blur of movement, Daryl swatted the knife away and punched the leader out cold. Cassidy nearly cried with relief when Daryl stood, unharmed, and hustled her way. He'd defended her, reacting as quickly and efficiently as a military person in a foreign country, putting his life on the line.

"Call 911." He retrieved his gun and pointed it at the thugs. "On the ground," he barked.

A couple of hours later, after finishing their witness statements, Daryl and Cassidy strode from the sheriff's office.

"Thank you, Daryl," she said once they hopped in his truck. "You saved my life."

He cupped the side of her face, leaned close and brushed her lips with a heart-stopping kiss so brief she could have imagined it. Dreamed it. Maybe she had. If so, she didn't want to wake from this adrenaline-fueled moment. Or lose it.

She slid her mouth over his before he moved away, savoring the mint of his breath. It was irresistible; he was irresistible. With a groan, he thrust his fingers in her hair, then dropped them to her shoulders, pressing her close. A whimper emerged from her throat, a wordless plea. In answer, he kissed her back, slowly at first, as if rediscovering a once-familiar place, its shape and texture, the old rhythms returning. Then he opened her lips, and the caress grew more intense, ardent. It consumed her deliciously. She thought of nothing but the kiss and the strength of the arms holding her. They made her feel safe. Comforted. Her heart beat faster. Her breath quickened, and she wanted the moment to never end. It was easy to become lost in his tenderness, in his humble heart, his sensitive soul.

She ignored the worry teasing the back of her mind, warning her that this was a mistake. She was here, she was happy for once, and his mouth felt as natural to hers as if she'd been kissing him for years, without a decade apart, without her sister, her career, life coming between them.

She let the kiss continue a little longer and deeper before catching herself. By kissing him, she revealed her returning emotions, feelings best kept to herself. She pulled back, trembling, realizing his body shook just as hard. When their mouths came apart, he leaned his forehead against hers and his chest rose and fell, fast and hard.

"No need for thanks," he said quietly, his words little more than a ragged breath. "You've saved my life, too."

"PA'S FAMOUS!" EMMA twirled through the living room holding the local newspaper aloft. Pictures Daryl had taken of the factory residents filled the top half of the front page with Cassidy's freelance article running beneath it. Happiness burst inside him, bright as fireworks, when Cassidy turned wearing an approving smile. Since their mind-blowing kiss last week, he'd been unable to stop thinking, wanting, hungering to repeat it, despite the fact he shouldn't have given in to the adrenaline-fueled impulse in the first darn place.

"I don't know about famous." Daryl returned his attention to his macaroni and cheese casserole and spooned cooked elbows into a buttered baking dish. Cassidy had challenged him to a cook-off for tonight's supper and he was determined to win.

"Daryl Loveland and Cassidy Fulton." Emma squinted down at the paper. "Your names are in the paper. That makes you stars."

"You and Noah are the stars." Cassidy poured milk into a saucepan on the cooktop, added shredded cheddar cheese and stirred it with a wooden spoon. "You're expanding Many Hands, Doing Good to help."

Since the article's publication yesterday, their phone had been ringing off the hook, the community spurred to action.

"It's what Mama would want." Emma laid the paper on the kitchen island and carefully smoothed the center crease.

"She'd be very proud." Daryl set down the milk he'd been pouring over the pasta and swept Noah and Emma into a bear hug. It pulled them off their feet, squealing, and his heart swelled with pride at how they'd stepped up to lend a hand.

Emma and Noah eagerly assisted him and Cassidy in coordinating with other ranches to bring fresh produce to the struggling families. They were even planning a Halloween-themed fund-raiser event to raise money for their housing. Cassidy raised their social conscience and opened his eyes in other ways, too. Life was an adventure to her, not just something endured. She made him want to make a difference rather than mark time as he had with Leanne. He felt like a traitor for thinking it, but he couldn't deny the truth.

Cassidy challenged him by breaking him from his comfort zone. With her, he stretched in new directions and wanted to take chances with his life—and maybe even his heart. Cassidy hadn't mentioned returning to her job lately, and her revelation about deciding to choose him over her career years ago still rocked him.

Perhaps not everyone he loved would leave him…although, the reason for Leanne's abandonment kept him up nights. They'd stayed together but had grown apart, proving that leaving your partner could be emotional distance, not just physical.

"I bet you my allowance Aunt Cassidy's mac-n-cheese will win, Noah." Emma peered up at Cassidy as she dumped butter into the saucepan.

"No fair!" Noah kicked a couple of fallen noodles in Beuford's direction. The dog snapped them up without bothering to open his eyes. "Pa always puts in too much butter and milk."

"No, I don't," Daryl protested, assessing his macaroni-to-cheese-to-milk ratio. The noodles clung to the wooden spoon as he swirled it through the mix, and he added more liquid.

"See!" Noah hopped on a stool and spun himself in a circle. "He just did it."

"You should follow a recipe like Aunt Cassidy." Emma picked up the cookbook beside the stove.

"I'd rather eyeball it." *Yes. Definitely more milk*, Daryl assessed, adding another quick pour.

"Then you'd better check your vision because I'm—" Cassidy dumped her cheesy milk mixture over her noodles "—going to beat your butt."

"Er," Daryl interjected, "you're going to beat my butter."

"Nuh-uh!" Emma grabbed the swear jar. "Aunt Cassidy said *butt*, so she owes a quarter."

"So do you for saying *butt*, butthead." Noah giggled so hard he snorted.

"I've got this." Cassidy deposited five quarters, grinning. "Buttheads."

Noah crashed to the floor in a convulsion of laughter loud enough to rouse Beuford. He lifted his head, woofed, then hauled himself to his feet.

"I love you, Aunt Cassidy." Emma flung

her arms around Cassidy's waist. "Please don't leave us."

"Yeah!" Noah piled on and Beuford sniffed around Cassidy's ankles.

"Oh—I—uh…" Her eyes met Daryl's, a plea in them, and he banged his wooden spoon against the side of the casserole dish.

"Time's up. All entries in the first-ever Loveland Mac-N-Cheese Bake-Off must be in the oven or be disqualified."

"Hurry, Aunt Cassidy!" Emma grabbed one end of the dish.

"I want to help!" Noah gripped the opposite handle, and to Beuford's everlasting delight the contents tipped to the kitchen floor in a lumpy mess.

"Ohhhhhhh…noooooo," howled Noah. "Sorry, Aunt Cassidy."

Beuford slurped up the cheesy noodles in noisy gulps.

"Now we're going to have to eat Pa's icky mac-n-cheese." Emma cast a hasty look his way. "Sorry, Pa. And sorry, Aunt Cassidy, for making you lose."

"It's okay. You were only trying to help." Cassidy hurried to the broom closet and returned with a mop.

"Beuford's got it!" Noah pointed to the already half-cleared floor. "Pa says he's better than a garbage disposal."

"Aunt Cassidy doesn't have to lose." Daryl eyed his casserole. "She can help with mine... even though it's already perfect."

"Ha!" His pulse sped at Cassidy's teasing smile. She ambled closer and peered down at his mix. "Are you making macaroni soup?"

"I beg your pardon," he replied, mock-offended.

Emma and Noah giggled.

"Emma and Noah," Cassidy ordered. "Start spooning out the excess fluid." She grabbed a cereal bowl from a cabinet and set it next to the baking dish. "Daryl, grate more cheese."

"Yes, ma'am," they chorused and labored as Cassidy cleaned the floor. Within minutes, they had the proportions to her liking. Daryl pretended to stumble carrying it to the oven.

"Pa!" Emma squealed, biffing his arm once he'd safely deposited it in the oven. "No more Clumsy the Clown. We're not little kids any-more."

For some reason, his eyes stung at the comment. He wrapped his arms around them both, pulling them close. Someday they'd grow up and leave him...and he'd be on his own. Alone. "No matter how big you get, you'll always be my kids."

Noah and Emma squirmed away, and he caught Cassidy's tender stare. Not a word was spoken, but he sensed she understood him and in that understanding, he felt less alone. The children's pleas returned to him as he set the oven timer. He added his own silent one.

Please don't leave us, Cassidy.

Three hours later, he and Cassidy stood beside Emma's bed, the sound soother set to ocean waves, the clock projecting the time on her ceiling.

"That was your best mac-n-cheese, Pa," she murmured sleepily.

"That's because we did it together." He grabbed the empty water glass on her nightstand. "Everything's better when you do it together."

Cassidy nodded and the light in her green eyes melted his heart.

"Can you tuck me in like a mermaid?" Emma asked without opening her eyes.

"Ariel or Madison?" he clarified. *Splash* and *The Little Mermaid* were Emma's favorite movies.

"Madison," she sighed.

He tucked the blankets around her legs and stepped back. "Night, Madison."

"Sea you later." Emma cracked open one eye. "Get it? *Sea?*"

"I *sea* what you did there." Daryl ruffled her hair. "And I still love you, despite your horrible puns."

"Same, even Clumsy the Clown." Emma's lashes fell to her cheeks, and he and Cassidy quietly let themselves out of her room.

"I used to love *Splash* when I was a kid," Cassidy said when she dropped onto the couch. "I loved the idea of being able to become someone else."

"You weren't happy with who you were?"

"It's more like my father wasn't satisfied unless I was successful, achieving great things."

"All parents want the best for their children."

"True. And I never really thought about it until now…but seeing you with Emma and Noah, I think I missed out on something important."

"What?"

"Unconditional love."

I loved you, he thought. *Unconditionally.*

"I wanted so much to please him, to live up

to his expectations and pay him back for the sacrifices he made to get me to college." Cassidy fingered the sofa throw blanket's fringe.

"You felt like you owed him."

"I do owe him." Her hands bunched the fabric. "If not for my father, I wouldn't be successful."

"Who defines success for you?" he challenged. "Your father or you?"

She opened her mouth but remained silent, processing. "I—I never thought about it before."

"Maybe you should," he said, finally understanding what drove Cassidy, why she'd never be satisfied with an ordinary life.

He'd been naive to expect her to be happy settling down with him. It was just as stupid to expect anything more from her now. Cassidy was who she was. An adventurer. And he was who he was—rooted, traditional, a family man.

How she found it in her big heart to have not only forgiven him, but to stay and help his family grieve, he'd never understand, though it didn't surprise him. She'd always put others ahead of herself and she would have done the same ten years ago by putting aside her dream to settle in Carbondale with him. He was no one's sacrifice, though. She'd said she might have been happy here, but what if she hadn't? He would have made her as miserable as he'd made Leanne.

Cassidy screwed up her features in a thoughtful expression. "Maybe I should consider it," she agreed slowly.

As they stared into the fireplace's glowing embers, he listened to her quiet breathing, felt the soft brush of her arm against his, inhaled the delicate floral scent of her shampoo. He wanted to gather her in his arms and kiss her again. Hold her. Lose himself in her as he had last week, but his wedding picture above the mantel caught his eye. He could not betray Leanne. Other than her unexplained suitcase in the Jeep and her frequent girls' nights, she'd been loyal to him, even if they'd been unhappy.

"Why didn't you ever tell me you were adopted?"

He turned at Cassidy's question and their noses brushed. For a long moment he considered possible answers and went with the truth. "I wanted you to think I was a Loveland."

"You are a Loveland."

"Not always. I used to be Daryl Clemmons."

She ran a hand down his arm, her face pinched with concern. "When did your parents pass away?"

"They didn't."

Cassidy drew back, eyes round. "I'm sorry. I just assumed…"

"It's okay. Most people don't expect parents to not want their children."

"Daryl… How could they not want you?"

A weight settled on his chest, heavy enough to crush his breath. "They cared more about drugs. They were always on the move, looking for the next fix."

"How awful. Were you glad to leave them?"

"Mostly I was just glad to be rescued."

"Rescued?"

He stared down at his clasped hands. "When I was seven, they drove to a house and left me inside the car. They said they'd be right back. It was night and I must have fallen asleep. When I woke up, snow covered the car. There must have been a blizzard because I couldn't open the door. When I tried to break the window with a hammer, it recoiled and hit me here." He pointed to the C-shaped scar at his temple.

"That's terrifying!" Cassidy exclaimed.

"I was bleeding and didn't have anything

to eat. There was half a bottle of water, but I finished it by the end of the first day."

"First day?" Her voice rose. "How long were you trapped?"

"When the sheriff found me, he said I'd been in there for three days."

"I can't believe you didn't freeze to death."

"We had an old wool blanket in the back seat. And I had a coat. Plus, the snow kept the windchill from having an effect."

"And where were your parents all that time?"

"In jail, strung out. My mother had overdosed, and my father was passed out when neighbors called the cops. They couldn't remember their names let alone that they had a son."

"Monsters," Cassidy whispered. "They should never have had children."

"Child Protective Services agreed. The sheriff at the time, Emmitt Loveland, had me stitched up, then asked his cousin Boyd to put me up until they found a place for me. When a spot opened in foster care, Boyd decided to keep me instead and that's how I became a Loveland."

"You went through so much."

"I only ever wanted to stay in one place. To

have parents who came home every night. A stable family, which is why…"

"Why?" she prompted when he paused.

It felt like he swallowed crushed glass, his throat raw and scraped. "When I found out Leanne was pregnant, I had to do the right thing. I wanted to give my child the stable family I always wanted, even if it meant letting go of the only person in my life I'd ever loved…unconditionally."

She closed her eyes, as if she took his words into her heart to keep, then slowly opened them again. Tears dripped down her cheeks. When he brushed the wet away with his thumbs, Cassidy caught his hand and pressed a kiss to his palm.

Her lips moved against his skin as she said, "I loved you, too. Unconditionally. But you made the right choice. If you hadn't, I would have made it for you. But stability doesn't guarantee happiness… You and Leanne were having issues."

They looked into each other's eyes and Daryl felt the earth shift. He wanted to tell her how much he'd missed her. That he was happy to have her back in his life again, despite his devastating loss, but he was too afraid of ruining things to voice that thought. Hell, he was too afraid to even have that thought. "I still don't know what happened."

"But you weren't happy. Or Leanne. Were the children?"

He shook his head, mute, thinking back to the year and a half leading up to the accident, the uncertainty of Leanne's whereabouts, her withdrawal, the kids' questions: Where's Mama? Is she coming home? Does she love us? Are we bad?

Cassidy threaded her fingers through his hair, and his breath caught at her touch. A deep yearning gripped him. A need to pour himself into her. "I'm sorry, Daryl."

"Don't pity me," he whispered, his voice hoarse.

"I don't. I admire you." Her green eyes burned into his. "Despite everything you've gone through, you're an incredible father and you're giving your children a strong foundation."

"I drove Leanne away."

"We don't know that."

"I couldn't make her happy...not as long as I still loved you."

"But those feelings changed. Ended."

"I wanted them to," he blurted, the words base-jumping off his tongue without a safety net, his heart overruling his brain. "I did everything I could to forget you, but I couldn't. There's a hole in me where you used to be. Every day since you left, I've walked around it and fallen into it each night. I've missed you like hell."

"Don't." She leaped to her feet and backed away, her expression stricken. "Don't say anything else."

"Why?" he asked when she reached the bedroom door, though he knew the answer. He just wasn't ready to let her go.

Same story, different time.

"Because I'm afraid of what I might say back," she whispered before slipping through the door.

He stared at the dying fire's embers, his heart beating erratically as he mulled her words. Cassidy was right. Stability didn't guarantee happiness. Love did. And even then, it only made life's struggles worth battling.

The question was—how long did you keep fighting?

CHAPTER ELEVEN

CASSIDY TUGGED DOWN the hem of her saloon girl Halloween costume, then frowned at the cleavage the move revealed. With a sigh, she hauled up the neckline again. How had she let Sierra talk her into wearing this revealing outfit? She spied Daryl's sprite-like sister line dancing in the cat costume she'd offered as well and shuddered. No way would she have squeezed her curves into that scrap of cloth with a tail. She was lucky to breathe in this costume as it was.

Cassidy backed farther into the shadows of the converted barn Sofia Cade used in her event planning business and let the cool autumn air pouring through an open window wash over her heated skin. Excited chatter, stomping boots and an Outlaw Cowboys' rollicking song filled the crammed space. Line dancers twirled and clapped in time to the music.

Attendance at the fund-raiser party, thrown

by Many Hands, Doing Good to raise money for the ex-factory workers, exceeded their expectations. Excitement bubbled. If they reached their financial goal, they'd begin renovating foreclosed homes next month for the families now working at Loveland Orchards to rent.

"You look beautiful."

Cassidy jumped slightly at the deep rumble of Daryl's voice near her ear. Perspiration broke across her brow. He offered a glass of punch and she shivered when their fingers brushed. Since the night by the fire, she'd avoided being alone with him. Her heart played his confession about missing her on a continuous loop. She'd never stopped missing him, too, and with each day she lingered in Carbondale, her fear of acting on her growing feelings intensified.

She raised the cup and sipped the strawberry concoction. "You don't look half-bad yourself."

Which was a huge understatement.

Wearing a low-slung gun belt around his narrow hips, a fitted black Western shirt revealing his broad chest and shoulders and a wide-brimmed hat pulled low over his deep brown eyes, he was the handsomest outlaw she'd ever seen.

"Not *half*-bad?" His white teeth flashed in a dangerous smile. "So what's the other half?"

Gorgeous.

"Can't tell you all my secrets," she said, offhandedly, though she was dead serious. What would he say—do—if he knew her thoughts? Her lips still tingled with the remembered feel of his mouth, the soft tickle of his beard and how he'd simultaneously taken control of their heated moment, all while making her feel freer than ever before.

Her reaction when he'd shared his feelings terrified her. She'd leave the ranch, ASAP, if the country goods store no longer needed her oversight. Deeper still, her connection to her niece, nephew and Daryl fulfilled her in ways she'd never anticipated. A life without them became harder to imagine.

"How about a dance?" Daryl brushed back the damp tendrils sticking to her cheek. The tenderness in his touch matched the expression in his warm brown eyes. Butterflies took flight in her belly.

"I don't remember how to do that one." She nodded to the dancers' synchronized moves.

"Boot-Scootin' Boogie?" Daryl raised a dark brow. "Westerners come out of the womb knowing that one."

She laughed.

Daryl's lips twisted. "This doesn't have to be so serious."

"What doesn't?"

"Us."

"Oh. Uh—" Flustered, she downed the rest of her drink and set the cup on a high-topped table.

"Let's forget everything and just have fun tonight." He tipped up her chin until her eyes rose to meet his. His lighthearted expression momentarily dazzled her. She hadn't realized just how haunted he'd looked until now. It was like the first warm spring day after a bitter winter. "We've been working hard. We deserve it."

"Do we?" she asked a bit breathlessly. Given her traitorous thoughts, she doubted she deserved anything but a swift kick out of this lovely family. It belonged to Leanne. Not her.

No takebacks.

Daryl cupped her shoulder, then slid his calloused fingers down her arms to grip her hands. "Yes. We do. I did the investigation piece because you wanted to remind me of who I used to be. Dance with me. Let me remind you of your old self, too."

She nodded, trying and failing to ignore the heat exploding from their linked fingers. It rose up her arm to suffuse her body.

Holding tight, she followed as he shouldered through the crowd and found a tiny space on the dance floor. The band lit into "Cotton Eye Joe" and Daryl, as comfortable in his own skin as ever, began slapping his pumping knees.

"Yeee-haaaw!" he hollered with a wink. He linked arms with her and twirled them in a fast circle that got her giggling. Technically, this was a round dance, not line dance, but the moves were still synchronized. Her body somehow remembered the steps, claps, lassos and turns, nevertheless, moving in time alongside Daryl until they hit the chorus again and he swung her around and around.

"I'm going to fall!" she laughed, flushed and slightly off-balance.

"Not a chance." Daryl's grip tightened, and he lifted her off her feet, spinning them.

"You're terrible." Shoving at his chest was like pushing a mountain, but he released her instantly. They resumed the heart-pounding dance until its breathless conclusion, raising several eyebrows and conversations behind lifted hands.

"Thank you!" Heath shouted into the microphone. "We're taking a break for the costume contest judging. Please line up behind my lovely fiancée, Jewel, to enter, and good luck!"

"You're pouting." Daryl briefly pressed a finger to her mouth, and she fought the urge to close her lips around it.

"I'm not…" She caught his arch stare and gave up. "Fine. I wish they weren't taking a break. That was fun."

"There's not much line dancing in the Philippines, huh?"

She rolled her eyes. "The only scootin' I'm doing is out of the way of bullets."

His smile faded. "It's a dangerous job."

"Somebody's got to do it." She forced a laugh, hating the concern in his eyes, knowing she'd put it there.

"You do it well." He wrapped an arm around her and led her from the dance floor.

"Thank you." She waited for him to say more but he only stared up at the sky when they stepped outside. A quarter-moon rose over Mount Sopris and stars dazzled, brilliant against the velvet black. She'd traveled the world and seen more than her share of beautiful spots, but none moved her more than the Rocky Mountains in her own backyard, standing next to her first love.

Her only love.

Would she ever give her heart to another the way she had with Daryl? Doubtful. It hadn't been the same since he'd walked into her hospital room.

"Pa!" Emma charged up to them in a sparkling pink ballerina costume and cowboy boots. "Grandma Joy says we can come over for a sleepover with Javi. Can we?"

"Please!" wheedled Noah. He wore an orange T-shirt, shorts and socks with cardboard-painted "flames" attached to his back.

"Did anyone guess your costume yet?" Cassidy asked.

Noah crossed his arms. "Just Beuford. He licked me."

"Can't fool a dog." Cassidy fussed with the costume she and Noah labored over last night. "He knew you were a Flamin' Cheeto."

"Pa." Emma bounced in her boots. "We have to hurry because Grandma Joy is leaving soon. She said she's tired."

"Tired?" Daryl frowned. "Let me talk to

your grandma and then we'll see about you going over." He turned to Cassidy. "I'll be right back."

"I'll go with you," she offered.

"No. Stay. I…" He peered up at the sky, then at her again with a toe-curling intensity. "I don't want to waste this night. I'll be right back."

"Okay." Goose bumps rose on her arms. No denying she wanted to stargaze with Daryl. As she watched the trio disappear through the door, someone called her name.

"Hey, Sierra." Cassidy wandered over to the picnic table where Daryl's sister sat half in shadow. "What are you doing out here by your lonesome?"

"Getting some air." Sierra waved a hand before her flushed face. "Too many people in there."

"I think it's starting to thin out." Cassidy slid onto the bench seat opposite Sierra.

Sierra shrugged. "I'm more comfortable around the four-legged kind of company anyway."

Cassidy dropped an elbow to the table and leaned her cheek into her palm. "How's the orphaned bear cub doing?"

"Forest?" Sierra smiled. "He's getting big.

It's hard not to get attached since I'll be letting him go in a few months."

"I bet."

"What about you?" Sierra asked.

"Me?" Cassidy straightened in surprise.

"Are you getting attached?"

Cassidy's heart momentarily stilled. "I've always been attached to Noah and Emma."

Sierra brushed back her long blond bangs and studied Cassidy. "What about my brother?"

Cassidy's mouth opened, then closed as she worked out a response. "I'm doing my best not to," she confessed after an awkward beat of silence.

"It might be too late for Daryl." Over Sierra's shoulder a spruce tree's bow shook when a barn owl swooped in and perched.

"W-what do you mean?"

"I've seen the way he looks at you." Sierra reached across the table and briefly squeezed Cassidy's cold hands. "I'd wager he's as much in love with you as he's ever been."

"No. He loved my sister." Cassidy cleared her clogged throat. "Loves."

"Do you love Daryl?" The barn owl swiveled its heart-shaped face in every direction, as if looking for the elusive answer Cassidy sought.

She massaged her now throbbing temples. "I care about him. I don't know if I'm in love with him."

"Would it matter if you were?" Sierra pulled off her cat-ear headband and dropped it to the table. "Either way, you're not planning to stay here, right?"

Cassidy shook her head slowly. It seemed to weigh a thousand pounds, nearly as much as her heart.

Sierra's hopeful expression faded. "Will you promise me one thing?"

"Yes."

"If you truly care for him, go before you hurt him. He's already had his heart broken. Let us help put it back together before you shatter it again."

Cassidy stared into Sierra's anguished eyes, understanding a protective sister. She'd been one once, too…until she'd turned her back on Leanne without hearing her out…before she'd tried to understand…forgive.

If she'd chosen Daryl over Bosnia in the first place, and moved to Carbondale right after graduation, none of this mess would have happened. She would have been happy here…at least in the short term. Still, the chance existed her restless spirit could have been stifled.

Sierra was right. To protect Daryl and the children's hearts she had to avoid getting too attached. After the harvest season, she'd take the next story assignment on offer and leave. "I promise," she whispered, glancing at the doorway. "Can I ask a favor?"

Sierra nodded.

"Will you drive me to your place? I'd like to see Forest."

"I have to be up early for the animals. Would you mind staying over and I'll bring you home after my first feedings?"

Daryl emerged through the door, craning his neck, searching for Cassidy. The naked hope on his face, the yearning, mirrored her own.

Cassidy shoved away from the picnic table and linked arms with Sierra, her chest tight. "I think it's for the best."

"WHERE'S CASSIDY?"

Daryl turned and spied Maverick leaning in the doorway to the Halloween party. "She's spending the night with Sierra," he told his brother.

"Why?"

"Something about wanting to see the bear cub."

"It's something to see," Maverick said mildly, striding to a discarded, empty soda can. After picking it up, he dropped it, along with a few others, into a recycle bin. Typical Maverick. He'd always been a caretaker, the family "fixer" who'd cleaned up the messes Daryl's adoptive mother created when she spiraled, as opposed to Heath, who'd been their mom's whisperer, soothing her erratic moods. Now that Maverick's shoulder injury sidelined him from professional bull riding, and the ranch's usual catastrophes had largely abated, he seemed a bit lost lately. Was Daryl his next "project"?

"I'd better go in and see if Jewel needs help with the costume contest judging."

"Wonder Woman won." Maverick dropped into one of the slatted rocking chairs grouped on the back patio and pointed to the empty seat beside him.

Yep. Daryl was Maverick's next "fixer-upper."

He smothered a sigh and sat. "Good for Amberley," he said, referring to his legally blind stepsister-in-law.

Maverick nodded. "She's a superhero, all

right. One of the tour's best barrel racers. You'd never know she had any kind of challenge."

"Jared's a lucky man."

"Luck had nothing to do with it. He knew what he had to do to win her heart."

Daryl nodded. "Don't know many who'd walk away from a pro football comeback."

"What about Cassidy?"

Daryl slid Maverick a side-eyed glance. Unlike most Lovelands, Maverick hit issues with blunt force. All the better to fix them, he claimed.

"What about her?" Daryl stalled.

"When's she going back to her job?"

"She hasn't said." Just speaking those words released some of the hope locked away in his heart. Maybe she considered staying… *One of these days,* he said to himself, *I'm going to tell her. Tell her I love her more than I could love any woman. Tell her that my life started when she walked into the college bookstore.* But not yet. He didn't want to back her into a corner and make her feel she had to either say she loved him, too, or run.

"Have you asked?"

Daryl shrugged.

Maverick's chair creaked as he rocked it faster. "You're afraid to."

Daryl's tongue suffered momentary paralysis. He gaped at his brother, mute.

"You're afraid to ask because you don't want her to go." Maverick nodded without tearing his eyes off the distant moon. "Deny it. Go on. See if you can."

Daryl's nostrils flared with the force of his exhale. "Leave it, Maverick."

"If I spotted you behind the wheel of a truck headed over a cliff, shouldn't I try to stop you?" Maverick quit rocking. In the quiet, wings flapped as a barn owl soared from a nearby spruce.

"That's what you think I'm doing?" Daryl's fingertips dented his black slacks.

Maverick's blue eyes, a deep cobalt unique to their family, pierced Daryl's. "And your kids are in the back seat."

An ache flared along Daryl's clamped jaw. "Low, Mav."

"Truth hurts, dude."

"Haven't done much but hurt since Leanne's passing."

Maverick's thick eyebrows drew together. "Why add on more, then?"

"I'm not," Daryl denied, though Maverick had a point. Spending time alone with Cassidy was playing with fire, yet he'd been hurrying back to see her when he darn well knew better.

"You don't have feelings for Cassidy?" Maverick's voice rose, skeptical.

Daryl hung his head. "She's just going to leave anyway."

"If you care for her, then convince her to stay," Maverick surprised Daryl by saying.

Daryl's head snapped up. "Tried that once."

"All I remember is you letting her go, then hooking up with her sister." Maverick peered steadily at Daryl from beneath the brim of his rancher's hat.

Daryl flinched. The truth didn't just hurt. It cut to the bone.

"You want something, you go after it and you don't quit until you get it."

"We're not right for each other, even if I was free to woo her."

"Last I checked, you're single. Second, you two didn't look wrong for each other on the dance floor."

"You weren't the only one watching us. I don't want people talking."

"Who cares? Besides, if you're giving them

a little joy in their boring lives, then you're doing them a favor."

"That's one way to look at it." Daryl chuckled.

"Are you in love with Cassidy?"

"I don't know."

"Then convince her to stay long enough to find out. Show her all she has to gain with you."

"I can't offer her fame. Glory."

"But you give love. Trust me. I've had fame. Glory. It's not all it's cracked up to be."

Daryl nodded slowly. Maverick slapped his knee and they rose. "Your life with Leanne is over. Don't lose this chance to start a new one with Cassidy."

"It's not that simple."

"Then you weren't listening. It isn't easy. It's necessary. Take her out on her own or with the kids, on the town, in the wilderness… make her see that love is the greatest achievement."

Daryl eyed his brother, the handsome face and brawny build that buckle bunnies flocked to see from show to show. Beneath his toughness beat a romantic's heart. "How about you? Anyone special caught your eye?"

"Me?" Maverick scoffed, putting his

brother in a headlock that transitioned into a bro hug. "Maybe once I've fixed all of y'alls' lives, I might have time for one of my own. Right now, I gotta get rid of Neil, our wannabe uncle, and figure out why Joy's taking afternoon naps again."

"Do you think the cancer's back?"

"Only one way to find out, but Joy's being stubborn about seeing the doctor. Claims she always gets tired this time of year on account of losing her son Jesse."

Daryl thought about Jesse, the Cade son who'd broken his family's heart with his addiction and resulting death. "Could be true, but better safe than sorry. She's made Pa the happiest I've ever seen him."

Maverick rubbed his large hands together. "I'm calling a family meeting about it, and Neil, next week."

"What are your plans for Neil?"

"If Travis will agree to look the other way, murder."

Daryl laughed. "Can't see him bending the law that far."

"Sad but true. I'm thinking we can hire a PI to investigate Neil."

Daryl turned with his brother and headed back to the party. An infectious beat pulsed from the open doorway. "I'd be on board with that."

Maverick stopped Daryl with a hand on his shoulder. "What about the rest of my advice? You going to wimp out and let other people's opinions, or your doubts, stop you from going after what you want?"

Daryl shrugged, noncommittal. "Better put your attention on Pa and Joy. They need your help more than me."

Maverick leveled him with a penetrating stare. "Not true, but I won't stick my nose in where it's not wanted."

"Since when's that ever stopped you?" Daryl chuckled, and Maverick joined him.

"True." He thumped Daryl on the back before disappearing into the party crowd.

Daryl stared after Maverick, grateful for his family. Yet they didn't help him feel less alone. Only one person chased the emptiness inside away—Cassidy. Her spontaneity, her boldness, her crackling energy got his heart beating fast. Her passion, when he'd kissed her the other night, blew him away. He felt more for her than he'd ever felt for Leanne, and it scared him.

The side-eye looks he was getting from the townsfolk who noticed their closeness, however, reminded him not to stray from the straight-and-narrow path he'd followed to avoid being like his biological parents. He wasn't born a Loveland, but he'd be the best one possible, a credit to the name they'd given him when he'd needed it most. It carried an expectation of high moral principles, strength of convictions, emotional fortitude.

Sacrifice.

Did that have to include his happiness? He'd given up Cassidy once to right the wrong he'd done. Now he had a second chance to have a relationship based on love, not obligation. How could he pursue a future relationship, though, when he still hadn't figured out what went wrong in the past with his marriage? He'd failed Leanne somehow and until he understood why, he might repeat the same mistake with Cassidy.

And this time, he was determined to get it right. Maverick was right. Time to fight for what he wanted, and what he wanted was Cassidy.

CHAPTER TWELVE

CASSIDY IGNORED HER screaming muscles, rose on her toes and tiredly swished the duster over the kitchen ceiling fan. Late-afternoon sun streamed sluggishly through a nearby window. It cast a golden glow over the lemon-cleanser-scented room and illuminated minute particles suspended in its warm light. A sneeze built in her head.

"Achoo!"

"Bless you." Daryl's muffled voice carried from the walk-in pantry, where he organized dry goods. "Hanging in there?"

"Barely." She rubbed her aching neck. "Fall cleaning is no joke. I'm never in one place long enough to make a mess, let alone picking up one this big."

"Hey," Daryl protested. "Are you dissing my housekeeping?"

"Not the parts that show."

"I heard that." He ducked his head around

the frame and twinkling brown eyes belied his mock-frown.

"You were meant to," she laughed. Her stomach did a funny little twist, a familiar reaction when it came to spending time alone with Daryl. Yet despite the unsettled feeling, she enjoyed their new ease with each other, their chemistry and connection even when doing the most mundane tasks.

"Found another crayon." Daryl emerged holding a green piece in his palm.

"In *there*?"

She watched him, askance, as he dropped it into the heaping bucket containing crayons they'd begun collecting this morning. They'd decided to give the cabin a thorough scrub before the holidays hit. The kids had school and Daryl had the day off since Travis worked the range while on vacation to give his siblings a break. It'd seemed like a good plan... six hours ago.

"Where haven't we found one? At this point, I think they're reproducing." Daryl hooked his thumbs in his worn Wranglers, and the move drew attention to his broad chest and lean abdomen beneath his white T-shirt. A flush raced across her cheeks. He looked handsome in that rugged, down-to-earth way of his: mussed dark hair and a beard shadowing his square jaw, brown eyes lit with a mix of intelligence, humor and tenderness and an easy smile that tumbled her heart.

"Should we leave to pick up the kids from the bus stop?" It was located on the main road, a long walk from the tucked-away cabin.

"Boyd's getting them, so we'd have more time *alone*." The layers of unspoken meaning infused in the innocuous comment dried her mouth for a wild second.

Since the Halloween fund-raiser a couple of weeks ago, Cassidy's resolve to keep her distance had met with resistance. Daryl seemed to be launching a campaign to win her over to Carbondale, to Loveland Ranch, his family and him. Every day, he surprised her with thoughtful gestures, some small, like semiprecious stones he'd collected on the range. Others were bigger, like organizing family hikes and teaching the children how to take photos.

Each activity strengthened their bond and it scared her to death. Her editor promised a new assignment soon and it couldn't come fast enough. Much longer with Daryl and the family she'd begun to think of as hers, and she'd never leave.

If only she could be sure she'd be happy here forever.

"Let's take a break." Daryl threaded his fingers in hers, led her to the living room and tugged her down beside him on the couch. "Turn," he ordered.

Despite her resolve, she presented her sore back and melted when he began kneading the kinks in her neck. Her eyes closed in bliss. A gal could get used to this. His fingers were strong. Sure. Gentle. The deft touch of a man used to working with his hands. They found the knots and eliminated them as effortlessly as he anesthetized her worries. A dangerous ability.

Her lids flew open, and she skirted to the opposite end of the sofa. "Are we still going to eat—"

"Steak for dinner?" Daryl interrupted. "Yes." Were they finishing each other's sentences now? "Did you get the—"

"Potatoes?" she supplied, then bit back a dismayed laugh. Yep. They were at that stage. Lord help them.

She grabbed a pillow and clutched it, needing the barrier. "Joy dropped some off on her way to the country store when you brought the kids to the bus stop."

"How'd she look?" Daryl's eyes darkened with concern.

"Pale. I hated leaving her to run the store today."

Daryl blew out his cheeks as he nodded. "Sierra planned to help once she fed and dosed her animals."

Cassidy plucked at the pillow's tassel. "Has anyone brought up her going in for testing again?"

"Maverick's been on her and Pa's case, but Joy says she wants to get through the holidays before looking for trouble."

Worry furrowed Daryl's brow and Cassidy's fingers tightened on the pillow to keep from reaching for him. "How will you and the kids do?"

"As far as getting through the holidays?"

"It'll be their first without Leanne." Silence thrummed between them. While they hadn't consciously avoided saying Leanne's name, it'd been a while since either had spoken it.

Daryl glanced out the living room's large front window, his face impassive. When she squeezed his tense arm, he swallowed suddenly, audibly, then straightened and folded his forearms across his chest. "Technically, Leanne spent the day with your parents last year…so they only had me. This Christmas, they'll have both of us." His gaze swung back to her.

"Daryl." Her voice cracked as she stared into his hopeful eyes. "There's a good chance I'll have my next assignment before Thanksgiving."

There was a barely perceptible release of breath. "Not if you turn it down."

"I can't keep postponing."

"Why not?" He brushed a thumb over her knuckles.

A fine shiver coursed throughout her body. "That's my life." Despite herself, she laced her fingers in his, hating herself for giving him mixed signals…all the more reason to leave. What was more, she wasn't convinced he knew what he wanted, fully, either.

Help with the children? A substitute wife? She wasn't Leanne's replacement. Even if Cassidy could carve out a life with Daryl and the children, it'd be vastly different from the one he'd had, and preferred, given his need for stability and her unsafe career.

"You could have a new life here." He leaned closer still, bracing himself on the couch cushion with his free hand. Something inside her fluttered like captive wings. Would he kiss her again?

Then an odd expression crossed his face. His brows scrunched together as he thrust his hand farther into the space between the cushion and the couch's frame.

"What is it? Another crayon?"

"Not sure. Thought I felt the edge of something." After some wriggling, he produced an old flip phone. "This used to be Leanne's." His voice lifted in wonder. "She thought she'd lost it, so we got another and…"

A different kind of excitement seized Cassidy. "Is it password protected?"

Daryl flicked open the cell and gazed at the blank screen. "Yes, but I know it. When we set up the phone, she used the kids' names."

"Do you still have the charger for it?" Urgency sped her words so they slid into each other. Had they finally uncovered their first real lead in solving Leanne's mysterious last months? The phone's age ruled it out as the one used to call Cassidy, but it might hold other important clues.

"I tossed an old charger that could be it when I cleaned the junk drawer." Daryl leaped to his feet, and they raced to the black garbage bag beside the rear door.

Moments later they'd located the cord, plugged it into a free wall jack beside the bedroom's desk and hovered over it. The cell screen glowed to life. He typed in the password and tapped the enter key, and the time and date appeared over a background of lavender fields.

Cassidy's throat tightened. She recognized the image. Provence... Leanne had always wanted to see it. Now, this picture was the closest she'd ever get.

"I'm in." Daryl's gaze tangled with hers, then fell to the apps filling the screen.

"Look through her files."

Only one appeared, titled Passwords.

He accessed it, and Cassidy's knees went weak when the number and letter combinations to Leanne's email and social media accounts appeared.

"She'd always had trouble remembering all her different passwords," Daryl said huskily. "I told her once it could be dangerous to keep this on her phone where people could find it... Maybe it's a good thing she didn't listen?"

Cassidy met his eyes and placed a reassuring hand on his arm. She nearly cried with relief as they opened the accounts. The breaks in her memory might finally be filled.

"Who's Robyn?" Cassidy frowned down at Leanne's numerous email exchanges with the unknown woman.

"Her hairdresser. She's been battling cancer and passed away a few weeks ago." Daryl's index finger hovered over the emails.

"What's wrong?"

"Sounds stupid, but I don't feel right invading her privacy." A muscle thrummed along his jaw.

Daryl. He always tried to do what was right, even when it ran counter to his own interests. How strange that a quality you could find irritating about someone might also be why you loved the person.

Was she falling in love with him again?

"We need answers," she urged. "Neither of us will have closure without them."

Their eyes clicked before he tapped on Leanne's last sent email.

Hey, girl. Call me! I'm not having such a good day today. Daryl knows something's off with me and he keeps trying to do nice things like offering to take those ballroom dance lessons I wanted to do a few years ago. Today, he had my saddle retooled with our wedding date. I didn't want to cry in front of him— since we know what a sham that date was— so I jumped in the shower and stayed there until I stopped crying. He doesn't love me. I'm not good enough and no matter what he gives me, it's not what I really want. His heart.

An exclamation of air blew from Daryl's clamped teeth.

"I can go through these on my own." Cassidy ached at the hurt turning his face ashen.

Daryl shook his head. "I need to know. Even if it's tough to read."

They scanned several mundane emails going back further in time. One said,

Thanks again for letting me crash last night, Robyn, especially when I know you're not feeling well. Sometimes it's just too hard to be part of a life you know isn't supposed to belong to you...or where you're not really wanted. Daryl thinks the worst, that I'm going out to bars every night, and at this point, it's better if he hates me rather than just tolerates me. His sense of duty means he'd never let me go unless I do something drastic. I just have to figure out what that is...

"I was devoted to her," Daryl choked out. "The kids loved her. Why did she feel like she didn't belong?"

"When did you say she started acting differently?" Cassidy scrolled back farther in the emails.

"Eighteen months ago." They went through more exchanges that seemed upbeat until they found the first message in a much graver tone.

Robyn— Can I come stay at your house tonight? I can't even think about Daryl right now without crying and I don't want to see him when he comes home. When I was cleaning out his old sock drawer, I discovered a small box wedged in the back. At first, I thought it was a surprise anniversary gift for me, so I was going to put it back. But then I had this weird feeling. I can't describe it, but I just felt like I needed to see what was inside and I wish I hadn't. It was the original engagement ring he'd intended to give Cassidy before she put him off. I stared at it forever, thinking about the last eight years together and how it'd all been a lie. He kept that ring because he still loves Cassidy. He always has and always will. What is wrong with me? Why am I never good enough?

Stupid me for thinking I was better for Daryl than Cassidy. She wanted to travel and have a career. I wanted to stay in Carbondale and be a wife and mother, which Daryl said he wanted, too. I figured once I convinced him to want those things with me, he'd forget about Cassidy. I thought he had…only I was wrong, stupid me.

I shouldn't have made him my world when he really didn't want to share it with me. I need to let Daryl go and not hold him back. From now on, I'm making my own way and proving I don't need anyone. The country store will show I'm able to be successful, in my own small way…maybe everyone will believe in me then.

At a muffled choking sound, Cassidy whipped her head around to spy Daryl's eyes mashed shut, his balled hands at his sides, his shoulders stiff and high. She flung her arms around his tense body. It was like hugging marble. Cold and hard.

She stroked his whiskered cheek. "Daryl," she breathed. "Look at me."

His nostrils flared, but he otherwise remained immobile, his stoic grief moving Cassidy powerfully. "Please," she pleaded. "I'm here for you."

"I shouldn't have kept the ring," he said, his voice raw and rough.

"Why did you?"

"It wasn't a conscious decision. I'd like to think I forgot it was there, but I'd be lying. I wanted to hold on to that last piece of us. If I'd gotten rid of it, it meant I'd really lost you, and as long as I still had that small connection, I'd get by. Except I didn't consider that by not letting you go, I never let Leanne in."

"You did everything you could to make her happy."

"I didn't give her what she wanted most," he ground out, all emotion scrubbed from his voice. "I was a terrible husband. A horrible boyfriend to you. No good, just like my parents."

"You made mistakes, like everyone, but it doesn't mean you're a bad person," she said to ease the pain rolling off him. She touched his tight jaw, drawing his face toward hers. "Especially to me." His lids flew open and he shifted his eyes away, but not before she registered the haunted look in them. She'd seen it when she'd put off accepting his proposal in college. Had glimpsed it when he'd described his parents' abandonment. He wasn't just hurting over Leanne's words, but over every other person he'd let down and been disappointed by in return...including her.

"You should hate me worst of all." He shoved to his feet, snapped shut the flip phone and strode to the door.

She caught up to him and wrapped her arms around him from behind. She pressed her cheek to his back and held him. It'd been Leanne's choice to go after Daryl when he'd loved another, despite her misguided rationale. Daryl had done his best to be a devoted husband and father to his and Leanne's children. She hated knowing he blamed himself for Leanne's unhappiness, but Cassidy didn't know how to make it better any more than she knew how to quell her own grief when it came on so strong she could barely push past it.

She felt his tension ease as he turned and silently wrapped his arms around her. Somehow, even though she was in his arms, his body felt heavy against hers. As if his sadness were weighing him down. She wanted to take away his hurt. They shared the loss of her sister, the anguish for a woman who'd been an important part of both their lives.

The naked pain in his expression was mixed with the same yearning firing inside her. A tear dripped down his cheek and when he ducked his head to hide it, the last of her restraint evaporated. She didn't analyze her actions as she drew his face toward hers. It felt right when she pressed her mouth to his. His lips were warm and moist, softer than any lips she'd ever kissed.

Daryl tried to pull away, but she kept her grip on the back of his neck, keeping him close. Cassidy wasn't experienced with being the aggressor, but with Daryl it felt natural to slide her tongue along the seam of his lips and urge them open. She felt the slightest apprehension in his breathing seconds before his mouth opened to hers. The first slide of his tongue sent shocks through her chest, and when he tightened his grip on her and took control of the kiss, deepening it, claiming her, possessing her mouth like no one else ever had, she felt as if he were pouring his soul right into her.

She gripped the sides of his head, meeting every needy stroke of his mouth with her own. Their kiss intensified, became more passionate than any kiss they'd shared before.

Daryl groaned as he tore his lips from hers, leaving her breathless and craving more.

His eyes were wet, dark, and he almost looked angry, but she knew it wasn't anger in his intense gaze. It was the same hunger gripping her. She wanted to feel more of it. More of him. She rose on her tiptoes to kiss him again.

"Cassidy," he warned.

"Kiss me, Daryl. Just kiss me."

He groaned again, and it was the most delicious sound she'd ever heard. Their mouths crashed together. His hand slid up her back to bury in her hair, sending a teasing heat to coil in her belly. He moved his lips to her jaw, and—oh, Lord—her neck. Oh, she liked his mouth, his teeth, on her neck best of all. He drew on her skin gently as he kissed her there, sending shivers down her spine.

She couldn't think, could only feel, and want, and crave. She brought his mouth back to hers. He was better than chocolate, better than a summer swim, better than breathing. She wanted to live in his arms and lose herself in that talented mouth of his forever. She didn't loosen her grip on his head as he tried to pull back again. She didn't want him to move away. He made all the longing for those she'd lost, including him, go away, erasing the feeling of being alone.

She was in Daryl's arms. *Daryl.* The man who'd once meant the world to her, the one she'd nearly given up everything to have, the guy who'd morphed into the most incredible man she'd ever known—more amazing than she'd imagined he'd be as a father, a sibling and son. Despite his efforts to block Leanne from his heart, he'd still cared for her in his own way. How else to explain the depth of his hurt? The betrayal?

Of course, the irony was she comforted the man who'd betrayed her…but she was beyond caring now. Before returning to Carbondale, she'd put him from her mind, if not her heart, loving him the way you loved a favorite toy you'd lost, with a sense of nostalgia and regret. Since living with him and the children, she'd been trying to deny the newer, deeper, more meaningful feelings she'd developed.

She'd been blind to think she could push him away.

This wasn't how you loved a memory. A college boyfriend.

This was how you loved a man.

And Daryl Loveland was 100 percent man.

Could he be her man?

He tore his mouth away and shook his head. "Cassidy. Stop."

She froze.

"Don't kiss me like that. Not because you feel sorry for me." His glistening eyes conveyed the anguish and the want warring within him.

Goodness.

What had she done?

He was breathing as hard as she. He'd kissed her like he couldn't get enough, and right now she didn't want to deny him when he'd discovered his role in his and Leanne's estrangement.

"I feel sorry for this horrible situation." She stroked the sides of his wet face. "And yes, that's a part of it, but I'm also kissing you because I want to…because I'm—I'm falling for you again. And it makes me want to run from you—from us—as fast as I can. As far as I can." The words tumbled quickly from her lips. When she finally paused long enough to look at him, the muscles in his jaw were clenched again. "But at the same time, I never want to leave you. I don't want to give you the wrong impression. But I—"

He cupped the nape of her neck and sealed his mouth over hers again, kissing her deeply, passionately, like he'd been waiting his whole life to kiss her. His tongue moved slowly over hers as he backed her against the wall beside the door. His strong arms enveloped her, keeping her close, pressing their bodies together. Oh, he felt good.

He drew back, slowly, as if he were savoring every second their lips touched. "But you've given me hope. I'm falling for you again, too." With a crooked smile, he brought their mouths together again. Bliss loosened her muscles. Was there anything like a kiss that began with a smile? It tasted like sunshine. Promise. Hope. It was softer this time. When they parted, she opened her mouth to speak, and he pressed his lips to hers again.

She tried to talk, he kissed.

She was starting to like this routine.

When he pulled away again, she could barely breathe, much less speak.

He touched his forehead to hers, shaking slightly.

"Cassidy," he whispered, dampness spiking his lashes. "Stop talking. I just want to feel you right now and nothing else. Just this. Us."

She smiled through her tears.

He kissed her again. And again.

She marveled at the way her body flamed

inside. All these years she'd wondered if there was something wrong with her for not feeling terribly attracted when other men kissed her. And now, kissing Daryl, feeling his need for her, his affection, she knew it was because her heart had always belonged to him.

"I'm home!" yelled Noah from the kitchen as the side door banged open.

She and Daryl jerked apart, eyes wide, chests heaving.

"Anyone here?" hollered Boyd. His boot steps grew louder as he crossed the living room.

"Just looking up something on my phone," Daryl called. He glanced at the cell, then at Cassidy, his eyes falling to her mouth, lingering in a way that melted her inside. "To be continued?" he murmured, low.

They had a lot to work out, and uncover, about the past and the future, but today had been a start. She listened to Boyd helping the kids off with their coats. What would he and the rest of the family think of Daryl moving on…if he could move on? She wouldn't be a rebound or a means for him to get through his grief. Had he changed enough to handle a wife who wanted him, a family and a job that put everything, including her, at risk?

She wanted to achieve greatness, in all aspects of her life, including her personal one. The uncertainty ahead terrified her, but there was only one way to find out, and it wouldn't be by running away.

"'To be continued," she agreed, her heart overflowing with hope and trepidation.

CHAPTER THIRTEEN

"ATTENTION! ATTENTION!"

The babble of voices continued unchecked, despite Maverick's shout. Both the chattering Cade and Loveland clans were crammed into the Loveland main house's kitchen. Oversize cowboys and their partners occupied every inch of space, the temperature rising with the noise. The aroma of pot roast and homemade rolls lingered in the thick air despite being cleared with the last of the supper dishes twenty minutes ago. Outside, the children played tag in the early fall evening while awaiting dessert.

Glancing out the window, Daryl spied the growing number of grandkids speeding through the dim, his own two in the mix. Noah's bray caught Daryl's ear and he smiled at Emma's wagging finger and sassy grin as she tagged Javi. They were happy, and so was he since discovering the truth about his and Leanne's troubled past.

He slid his gaze to Cassidy, then bit back a chuckle when she crossed her eyes at him, briefly, before assuming her serious expression again.

He loved her playful side.

Loved the way she made him, and his children, laugh again.

She'd expanded their world with bold adventures while making them feel accepted and cared for in their own skins. Especially him. With Cassidy, he didn't have to prove himself or overcompensate for feeling like an outsider.

A few days ago, when they'd uncovered Leanne's emails, his heart had split in two. He'd suspected he'd disappointed Leanne for not loving her the way she deserved. He'd never known the catalyst for destroying their marriage had been his selfishness in keeping Cassidy's ring, though. Because of it, Leanne had meant to leave him. Understanding his role in their estrangement hurt with a near physical ache, yet Daryl's grief had eased as the days passed and his heart opened further to Cassidy.

She'd been willing, once, to give up her career and settle down with him. Would she again? She'd had her dream career for a decade. It might not be as easy to walk away now. He'd been giving her room to think, but he needed to broach the topic and settle things between them with Thanksgiving so near and Christmas fast on its heels. Beyond stolen kisses and surreptitious hand-holding, they'd steered clear of serious talk this past week.

A loud whistle erupted, stunning everyone into temporary silence. Jewel stood on a chair. Her red hair flamed along with her freckled cheeks. She lowered her fingers from her mouth and pointed at the group. "Y'all are acting like naughty schoolkids. Pay attention to Maverick or I'll take you behind the shed." She tapped the leather belt holding up her Wranglers and jumped down with a wink, Heath's hands going to her tiny waist. "It's taken forever for all of us to square our busy schedules and meet and we have to make the most of it."

"Thank you, Jewel." Maverick's deep blue eyes resembled the sea before a storm. Calm with a hint of trouble ahead. "First off, thank you, ladies, for the fine meal."

"I didn't do anything," scoffed Jewel.

"Exactly why I'm including you in the thanks," Maverick drawled with a grin. The Cade brothers guffawed loudly in approval.

Heath dropped a quick hand to Jewel's arm, checking her before she executed one of her trademark shoulder jabs.

"So funny I forgot to laugh," Jewel jeered, but good-naturedly.

"You're welcome for the meal." Joy rose slowly to her feet. "Nothing makes me happier than being surrounded by family. We should have dessert before the pies get cold."

"If you don't mind, I'd like to talk over a couple of things first."

At Maverick's request, Joy dropped back in her chair and cast a wary glance Boyd's way.

"What do we know about this Neil fellow besides him being a conniving cheat out to steal our ranch?" Maverick produced his cell phone and tapped on its screen. "He's nowhere online. Might as well be a ghost."

Cole linked his fingers and cracked his knuckles. "I'd like to turn him into one."

"Those are some fighting words," Heath murmured near Daryl's ear.

"It's time we get rid of this guy before Pa's blood pressure goes up any higher." Daryl kept his voice low since only he and Heath knew their father's doctor advised hypertension medication if his numbers remained high.

"Neil's taking care of a stray dog," Sierra

volunteered, surprising them. "He brought it to my practice thinking I'm a regular vet."

A blip of silence passed before Maverick spoke again. "He's got a place in town? Not a hotel room?"

Sierra nodded. "Not sure where, though."

"That means he's here for the long haul," Travis muttered.

"I might have an idea where he's staying." Cole shifted in his seat, his arms crossed. "Stopped by Aunt Suzanna's place and spied a rental car in the driveway. Now that I think of it, I saw the same blue sedan in the country store's parking lot when he came skulking around."

"You think she'd take him in?" gasped Sierra. She scooped up their tabby, kissed its nose, then settled it in her lap.

"Makes no sense," Heath mused, and Daryl nodded. Their great-great-aunt, an eccentric and former hoarder, had lived a solitary life, rarely leaving her house save for Sunday services.

"Why would she take in company, especially one intent on upending our family?" Travis propped a shoulder against the wall and stared off into space. He wore the same inward expression he assumed when mulling over clues in his cases. Lately he'd been wearing it more often as cattle rustling escalated in their sleepy community.

"Could be he's charmed her." Cassidy tapped a fingernail on the side of her water glass. "Made himself helpful to Aunt Suzanna in some way."

"She wanted me to replace her screens with storm windows," Cole said slowly. "But when I arrived, someone had already done it."

"Neil!" Boyd's face flushed red. "If he gets her to testify on his behalf, he might persuade the judge to exhume my father."

"She'd never!" Sierra exclaimed, then turned to Cole, who knew Aunt Suzanna best. "Would she?" The cat's loud purr rose as she stroked its arching back.

"She likes historical intrigue." Cole glanced at the living room, where the TV played a Broncos game. Later tonight, they'd planned to watch the season finale of his wife Katlynn's show, *Scandalous History*. Aunt Suzanna had helped Cole and Katlynn solve the century-old mystery of the events causing the Cade-Loveland feud. If not for their work, the families wouldn't have reconciled, and Boyd and Joy's marriage might not have occurred.

"She was the local historian for years," Daryl reminded the group, then clamped a hand on his jiggling knee. Beneath the table, Cassidy's soft hand slid into his and squeezed. His heart rate settled. It felt good to have someone on his side, a partner. But for how long? "She might have some insights to Grandpa's past that we don't."

"I'd know if Pa had another son." Boyd's frown eased when Joy patted his arm.

"Could be Grandpa didn't know." Travis rocked back on his heels. "I'll swing by Aunt Suzanna's tomorrow. I've got another report of missing cattle at Fuller's place, so it's on the way."

"Can you arrest Neil?" Jewel asked hopefully. "And can I help?"

"Likely to get yourself arrested in the process," Heath said affectionately. He smoothed down one of Jewel's cowlicks before pressing a brief kiss to her nose.

She glared but made no move away from her fiancé.

"Can't bring any charges unless Aunt Suzanna says he's trespassing..." Travis's fingers drummed on his gun belt's empty holster. He'd driven straight from the county sheriff's office for the family meal and had locked his firearm in Pa's gun safe.

"Cassidy and I will pay Aunt Suzanna a visit," Daryl offered. "She always liked Cassidy. Plus, Cassidy's an investigative journalist. She'll get to the bottom of what's going on."

His mouth curled at Cassidy's pleased smile. Maverick arched a brow, Sierra pursed her lips and the family shot Daryl and Cassidy assessing looks.

Would they approve of his pursuing Cassidy so soon after losing Leanne? Would they expect him to wait? But he'd already waited too long for Cassidy and let her go without a fight—a mistake he would not repeat.

"Sounds like a plan, and if we're all agreed..." Maverick's gaze circled the table. "I'd like to hire a private investigator to look into Neil and his mother."

"Can't ask you to put out that much cash," Boyd protested. While he appreciated his children's physical help, he refused their monetary aid.

"You're not," Maverick countered, firm. His cleft chin jutted. "I'm offering. In fact, I'm insisting unless anyone has an objection.

The more dirt we can get on this guy before the trial, the better. Agreed?"

A rousing chorus of "yes" filled the room.

"Now that's settled, let's get dessert." Joy bustled to the counter, retrieved a stack of dessert plates and turned. Without warning, the color in her face faded and the dishes crashed to the tiled floor.

They all leaped to their feet, overturning chairs in their hurry to help. Boyd rushed around the table and led Joy back to her seat while Jewel pushed a glass of water into her mother's trembling hand. Within minutes, they'd disposed of the broken pottery and wiped down the floor.

"How about paper plates?" Joy laughed shakily. "Guess we don't need to be fancy since it's just family."

"Ma. Enough." James Cade, Joy's second-oldest son, squatted beside his mother's chair. "Maverick and I've been talking."

"That sounds bad," Jewel wisecracked, then sobered when she spied James's subtle head shake.

Silently, Daryl agreed with Jewel. James's siblings complained about his controlling ways and Maverick prided himself on sticking his nose into others' problems, whether he was asked or not. Growing up, each of his siblings turned to him with their troubles, to keep from adding on to their overworked Pa's worries. However, once the family returned to stable ground, Maverick never relinquished his role as "fixer" or understood they didn't need or want his help anymore.

"We're worried about you." Maverick paced the length of the kitchen with enormous strides. "And want you to see the doctor and get tested now versus after the holidays."

Joy's mouth dropped open. Her silver bob swished when she snapped her head to face Boyd. "Did you know about this?"

Pa shook his head. The dark pouches beneath his eyes and the extra groove in his forehead showed he was as concerned as their combined offspring. "Not opposed to the intention, though Joy has the final say. And I would have appreciated a heads-up." His dark blue eyes pinned each of his children in turn.

"Every time I've scheduled a family meeting, it's gotten postponed." Maverick shoved a large hand through his clipped hair, making it stand at odd angles.

Boyd's face scrunched. "No one's mentioned them."

"I kept them from you," Joy admitted,

stunning the group. No one took so much as a breath. "I guessed Maverick's intention and didn't want to hear what the group had to say. Not before the holidays."

"What good's saving this holiday if we end up not having you at the next one?" growled Justin Cade, the reformed black sheep of the Cade clan.

"Don't be harsh with Ma." Jared Cade's chair scraped the floor when he stood and strode to his mother. He dropped a protective hand to her shoulder.

"I love you, Ma, but your head's in the sand." Jewel banged the side of her balled hand on the table. "Talking loud's the only way you'll hear us." The prickly cowgirl jerked her arm free of Heath's hold and dashed the shine from her eyes.

"Children, please," protested Joy. "Don't argue. The whole point of waiting was to give us peace during the season."

"It ain't peaceful not knowing where things stand." Boyd caressed the side of Joy's face. "If the cancer's back, the sooner we treat it, the better."

"But if it's back, then…" Joy's mouth trembled.

Sierra reached across the table and grabbed

Joy's hand. "Then you'll get the right medical treatment and beat it. With all of us by your side."

Murmurs of agreement circled the table and Jewel added her hand atop Sierra's and Joy's.

Joy's lips lifted in a tremulous smile. "I don't want to ruin Christmas. Thanksgiving."

"You think that means anything to us compared to you?" Boyd exclaimed. He blinked hard up at the ceiling, his jaw clenched.

"We love you more than Santa, Grandma!" Javi flung himself across the room and landed heavily on Joy's and Boyd's laps.

Joy's face fell when she observed Emma's and Noah's stricken faces. Daryl's heart dropped with it. They'd been so intent on the conversation they'd missed the children's entry.

Noah covered his face with his hands and asked through his fingers, "Grandma Joy? Are you going to die?"

"Honey." Joy lowered his hands to give him a reassuring look. "I'm going to be just fine. I already beat cancer. This little tiredness is nothing to worry about."

"Will you go to the doctor so he makes you better?" Noah's lower lip trembled.

"I promise."

The group breathed a collective sigh of relief.

"Pa didn't say anything about cancer! He never tells us what's going on!" Emma yelled, then dashed back outside.

With a muttered oath, Daryl tore after her, Cassidy hot on his heels. He caught up to Emma on the steps of the gazebo, where dried mums wilted in box planters.

Daryl sat beside his tense daughter and gathered her close. When she pushed him away, he tightened his grip until her body eased against his and she released sob after sob. "Why do I always lose people I love?" she cried.

Daryl's chest tightened. He'd grown up worrying about the same thing. Still agonized over it. Leanne was gone and, if he didn't move fast, possibly Cassidy, too.

"You haven't lost Grandma Joy." Cassidy brushed a hand over Emma's hair and her concerned eyes met Daryl's. The depth of her feelings for his children touched him. How would Noah and Emma handle it if she left them? Another loved one gone. His jaw clamped. He couldn't let that happen.

"She has cancer!" Emma lifted a tearstained face. "Everybody knew but me and Noah."

"I thought you had enough to handle after losing your ma."

"I could have made her a card," Noah spoke up behind them. Cassidy opened her arms and he crept onto her lap and buried his head on her shoulder. "Grandma Joy needed us."

"You always keep secrets," Emma sniffled, accusing Daryl. "I'm not a baby."

"I tell you everything I can."

"You never said where Mama went all those nights. Or why she was in the car with Aunt Cassidy."

"We still don't know the answer to that last one, sweetheart." He tucked her head into his shoulder and stroked a hand down her back.

"Will Aunt Cassidy ever get her memory back?" Noah wrapped one of Cassidy's locks around his finger.

"I hope so, honey," Cassidy vowed. "I'm trying very hard to remember."

"Are you going away?" Noah said, his voice muffled against Cassidy's neck. "I want you to stay forever and ever."

"Me, too!" Emma straightened in Daryl's arms. "What about you, Pa? Do you want Aunt Cassidy to stay?"

"I do," he declared, his gaze locked on Cassidy. Seeing his father gray with fear over possibly losing Joy shook Daryl. Life was unpredictable and the time you had with the one you loved wasn't to be squandered. Tonight's dinner made him even more determined to convince Cassidy to remain in Carbondale, to give her enough good reasons to never leave him again.

"Forever and ever."

"AUNT SUZANNA?" DARYL shaded his eyes against the midmorning glare and peered at his great-great-aunt's white-sided cottage. It'd come a long way from the run-down, debris-filled house he and his brothers helped her organize a while back. In fact, it looked a tad too neat, he mused, as he assessed the meticulously raked lawn despite a copse of leafless oak trees. Was Neil helping her with yard work—a duty usually shared by the Loveland siblings? A rough wind rattled the tree bows and chilled the tips of his ears as he pulled his hat lower. A dog's low bark sounded from inside the home.

Neil's stray?

"Maybe she's not home." Cassidy huddled beside him. Wearing a red knit cap and a white parka, she looked pink-cheeked and utterly kissable with her face tipped up to his. Between comforting Emma and Noah last night, and his early-morning barn work, they hadn't had a real moment to hash out their future. He'd wanted to give her space to make up her mind but chafed at the delay.

A humming engine grew louder and a blue sedan pulled to a stop beside the house. Neil Wharton exited the car. He wore a dressy black wool coat over gray dress slacks and black dress shoes so shiny the sun reflected off them.

"Howdy." Smiling, he sauntered their way. "Did you come here to see me or Aunt Suzanna?"

Daryl ignored his outstretched hand and scowled. "Why would I come here to see you?"

"As I'm staying here, I thought, perhaps, you'd come to make amends," Neil said smoothly. "Family shouldn't be fighting."

"You're not family," Daryl ground out. "Whatever you've conned my aunt into thinking."

Neil's smile faltered. "She's the one who reached out to me."

"Now, that's a flat-out lie!"

Neil scrambled backward at Daryl's advance.

"Boys!" Aunt Suzanna waved from the front door. "I won't have you brawling like a pack of jackals. Inside. Now!"

"Forgot how feisty she is," Cassidy murmured in his ear as they traipsed inside.

"She's a firecracker." Daryl held the door and breathed deep as Cassidy passed by him inside, leaving the tantalizing scent of exotic flowers in her wake. Inside, a hairless dog wearing a plastic cone collar wagged its way toward them. Its ribs stuck through its blotchy skin and a bandage wound around one of its back legs. Neil dropped to one knee and the dog bounded into his outstretched arms.

"How are you, Aunt Suzanna?" Daryl kissed her creased cheek.

Her scowl softened slightly. "Still kicking."

"I can see," he replied, dryly, then turned to Cassidy. "You remember Cassidy Fulton, Leanne's sister?"

Aunt Suzanna's eyes narrowed behind bifocals perched on the tip of her short nose. "Isn't this the gal you were supposed to marry the first go-round?"

From the corner of his eye, Daryl glimpsed Neil's shocked expression as he gave the dog a final pat and straightened. What a hypocrite. He'd come to Carbondale with false accusations and he had the audacity to look offended. Daryl shoved his clenched hands in his pockets. "We were never engaged, but yes, Cassidy and I dated."

Cassidy stuck out her hand. "It's nice to see you again."

Aunt Suzanna took it, a smile replacing her frown. "Good to see you, honey. Always thought you were a smart little thing. Reminded me of myself. Curious. Ambitious. Hardworking. I liked digging in the past, but you write stories about nowadays."

"I do." Cassidy ruffled the curious stray's ears when he sniffed her legs.

"Don't ever give that up," Aunt Suzanna cautioned, much to Daryl's chagrin. "It's good for a woman to be independent. The world needs more like you."

"Thank you." The pleasure in Cassidy's voice set off a warning bell in Daryl's head. He had nothing against Cassidy working… just not a job that'd expose her to the kind of danger she described in her nightly bedtime stories. The kids ate them up, shivering under their covers as she described her life-or-death encounters.

It would become too real, however, if Cassidy resumed her hazardous career. She'd break their hearts by coming in and out of their lives irregularly, her life in constant jeopardy. They'd already suffered enough upheaval. Cassidy had found a local story to investigate. There had to be more in the area to keep her fulfilled professionally…

"Heard you lost some of your memory." Aunt Suzanna waved them to a floral-patterned sofa before heading to the kitchen. "What can I get you two?"

"I've regained a bit." Cassidy unzipped her jacket, shrugged it off and sat. He followed suit and glowered at Neil, who stretched his frame into an armchair, crossing his legs and folding his hands, totally at ease…as if he belonged here. The dog flopped across his feet with a contented sigh. "And I'll have sweet tea if you've got it."

"Daryl?" Aunt Suzanna called.

"Same."

In the tense quiet, a grandfather clock chimed eleven o'clock and he held back a yawn. Before dawn, Cassidy had woken him when snippets of memory returned to her. His mind drifted back to her gentle hand shaking him from sleep.

"She begged me to return to Carbondale to take care of Emma and Noah," Cassidy whispered, her hair mussed, her eyes wild. "I remember it! She'd wanted to escape for a little while and think about her future with you."

His mind sharpened and he sat up, understanding now how Leanne persuaded Cassidy to come home, her concern for her niece and nephew a powerful motivator.

Cassidy's eyes searched his, her disquiet clear, as she relayed her phone call with Leanne. But hearing his wife's intentions hurt less than he'd imagined. She'd been ready to move on and so was he, with the woman who'd cared enough about his family to drop everything and come home to safeguard it.

Aunt Suzanna returned with refreshments, pulling him back to the present.

"You got your clock fixed." Daryl accepted her offered glass.

She passed another cup to Cassidy, then hustled back to the kitchen. "Neil helped me."

"W-what?" Daryl sputtered on his first sip and set his tea down on a coffee table.

"My grandfather was a watchmaker in Kaiserslautern." The dog's tail thumped at his new master's voice.

"He's been handy to have around," Aunt Suzanna crowed as she returned, another glass of tea in hand for Neil. "And he speaks English so well."

"Thank you, Aunt Suzanna." Neil stood and waved a hand at the chair. "Please sit. I don't mind standing."

"You're a dear." She patted his cheek and sank into the tufted cushioned seat. The dog scrambled up onto gangly legs. It trailed Neil across the room to the front window.

"So how did you meet Neil?" Cassidy asked after another gulp of tea.

"I found him is what I did," Aunt Suzanna announced. The lines around her eyes crinkled, deep with pleasure. "After I got the place organized, I began going through the boxes of family memorabilia I'd saved and came across Clarence's war correspondence."

"How come Pa didn't have it?" Daryl watched Neil as he stared outside, his jaw and nose similar to Pa's…

"Your father thought it best to store family items here to safeguard them from…" She stopped and cleared her throat. Daryl knew she thought of his erratic adoptive mother. During her bouts of anger, she'd destroyed many items in the house.

"And you found something that piqued

your interest," Cassidy interjected, smoothing over the awkward moment.

Aunt Suzanna shot her a relieved smile. "Yes. He'd written home about a girl he'd met in Germany. Seemed quite taken with her. He asked if we still had his grandmother, my sister's, engagement ring. I knew it must have been serious, but we never heard more of her and I got to wondering why."

"I would have been curious, too."

Daryl shot Cassidy a surprised glance. *Whose side are you on?* he silently communicated. She wasn't seriously going along with this farce.

She arched a brow, her expression as neutral as Switzerland. "Do you have the letters?"

Aunt Suzanna shook her head. "Turned them over to Neil's attorney. When he's finished with them, he'll hand everything off to Boyd's lawyer."

"Would have been kind of you to let Pa in on everything first," Daryl said as mildly as possible considering he seethed inside.

Aunt Suzanna gazed at him over the top of her bifocals. "Boyd wouldn't have believed any of it, let alone agreed to find out more."

"Did you search for the girl Clarence mentioned?" Cassidy asked, cutting the tension thickening the air between him and his aunt.

Aunt Suzanna nodded, eyes aglow. "Found her and her son, who was born eight months after Clarence returned to the States. Neil and I spoke on the phone. When he described the watch Clarence had sent him, along with correspondence his mother had, I offered to put him up, so he could meet his kin. Neil here doesn't have one bit of family over there in Germany. Now, that's a darn shame."

"The shame is him going after our ranch." Daryl shot to his feet and paced to Neil.

"It's my inheritance," Neil said calmly.

"Then how come you never contacted our family before?"

"I didn't know if I'd be welcome until Aunt Suzanna reached out."

Daryl stared Neil dead in the eye. "You're not welcome."

Neil reached down to stroke his dog's head. "That might change. I'm hoping so."

"Not as long as you're demanding we dig up our family."

Neil's mouth tugged down in the corners. "A completely unnecessary step if Boyd would consent to a DNA test to establish our connection."

Daryl glowered at him. It was a reasonable request, but he'd never go against his pa by siding with Neil on this point. "Either way," he forged ahead, "we can't just give you half the ranch. We're struggling as it is."

"I'm not trying to burden anyone," Neil insisted. "I only want what's fair."

"What's fair is you getting on the next plane and leaving America, buddy."

Cassidy wedged herself between them and gently pressed on Daryl's chest until he stepped back. "Let's not lose our heads. Did you bring your birth certificate, Neil?"

He shook his head. "I forgot it in my excitement at Aunt Suzanna's invitation. I only needed a passport to travel."

"Is Clarence listed on the certificate?"

"No."

Cassidy cocked her head and her green eyes sharpened. "Who's listed as the father?"

"A friend of my mother's who wanted to help her out and avoid me being tainted with illegitimacy."

"And that was?"

Neil shifted his weight. "Frank Sterholdt. He died over twenty years ago."

"What a shame," Cassidy murmured. "Did he and your mother marry?"

Neil pulled a handkerchief from his pocket and dabbed at his glistening forehead. The dog woofed, as if sensing Neil's unease. "Frank was already married."

"Yet he consented to having his name on the certificate…" Cassidy tapped her chin.

"He was a very good friend." Neil's voice rose, defensive. Adrenaline zipped in Daryl's veins. Cassidy was onto something, her journalistic instincts zeroing in on a topic Neil didn't want to discuss…possibly his real father. He'd share Frank's name with Maverick's private investigator. It might be the answer they needed to avoid the trial altogether.

"Indeed…" Cassidy's phone vibrated in her pocket. When she pulled it out, she glanced at the screen and stood. "I'm afraid I have to take this. Thank you for the refreshment, Aunt Suzanna, and it was a pleasure getting to know you, Neil."

She shot a warning look at Daryl, as if cautioning him to behave, donned her jacket and headed outside.

"Don't you think he has the Loveland blue eyes?" Aunt Suzanna smiled affectionately at Neil.

"No," Daryl said curtly and shoved his arms through his jacket sleeves.

"I suppose you don't have them either." Neil tucked his handkerchief away, composed once more. "But I believe you aren't genetically related, yes?"

Daryl strove to keep the fury from his face at the reminder of his adoptive status. "I'm still more Loveland than you." He softened his tone when he turned to face his relative. "Will you be standing with us or with Neil at the trial?"

"I'll be on the side of truth," she tutted, rising. "If Neil is a Loveland, we need to know and welcome him with open arms. It's our family's way, as you should understand better than anyone."

She lifted her cheek, and he grazed it with an obliging kiss. "I'll let Pa know. Take care now and call us if you need anything. Hear?" He donned his hat, scowled at Neil, then tipped its brim at his aunt before exiting.

Outside, he took several deep, bracing breaths of crisp air, processing his relative's admonishment. He'd been accepted into the Loveland fold, no questions asked. Was he being too hard on Neil? He knew what it felt like to be alone in the world without a family.

Then again, family didn't—or shouldn't—turn on each other like Neil.

"Will I have mercenaries with me?"

He whipped around at Cassidy's voice and spied her a short distance away beside his truck, her back to him. His heart picked up speed. Had her editor called with an assignment?

"How soon would you need me in Nuevo León?"

His body clenched at the name. Nuevo León was ground central in Mexico's violent drug war. Hired guns or not, Cassidy's life would be in grave danger if she traveled there.

A dark throb of pain rose from his clamped jaw and exploded behind his eyes. His family might lose Loveland ranch if Neil proved his case, but it didn't compare to losing Cassidy a second time.

He had to convince her to stay.

Tonight.

CHAPTER FOURTEEN

"WHERE ARE WE GOING?" Cassidy peered at the blur of orange and red trees as Daryl drove along an unfamiliar back road. A brilliant sunset exploded on the horizon, the light turning soft and purple. He'd been oddly quiet since visiting Aunt Suzanna, but the hand gripping hers was firm and the familiar rough, calloused skin reassuring.

"It's a surprise." His fingers tightened around hers. When he glanced her way, a smile played on his full lips.

"What kind of surprise?" Hardly anything stunned Cassidy given her career, but her jittery stomach and fast-beating heart had her on edge since her editor's phone call.

"If I told you, it wouldn't be a surprise," Daryl drawled. His warm, teasing tone settled her nerves a bit, and she dropped her head back to rest on her seat.

Brenda's assignment filled Cassidy with both dread and anticipation. A deep dive into the Mexican drug war, and the Nuevo León families caught in the crossfire, was the kind of story she loved best. Lots to expose about the suffering citizens held hostage by vicious cartels more powerful than the agencies protecting them. As happened often, the story's outline formed in her mind, a plan to interview clergy, police, families, politicians and even, if possible, ex–cartel members or current ones willing to talk on condition of anonymity.

She'd have to leave Carbondale, Emma, Noah and—oh, Lord—Daryl, however, to do it. The country store was on secure ground now with the new hires proving themselves more than up to the task, yet she'd miss it, too.

A tearing sensation sheared her heart; it pulled in two directions. Her connection to Carbondale had deepened with new relationships, and no small part of that was Daryl's patient acceptance and encouragement. While she'd begun a follow-up story to her displaced manufacturing workers piece, an in-depth look at the effect of automation on small, family-operated ranches, she wasn't sure it'd challenge her. She couldn't reach the pinnacle of her career reporting on small-town Westerners, let alone win a Pulitzer Prize.

Although in some way that kind of success had started as her father's dream for her, it'd become hers. She couldn't imagine coming this far and giving it up.

Could she still have a fulfilling and meaningful life if she stayed in one place and dialed back her schedule? Despite her happiness at Loveland Hills, the answer still eluded her.

Daryl's blinker clicked on and they turned down a rutted dirt road. Her teeth bumped together as they bounced down the narrowing lane until it ended on an open field littered with scarlet leaves, some drifting lazily from the surrounding trees.

"Pretty!" she exclaimed, taken with the juxtaposition of red and green, the sky deepening to twilight.

"You haven't seen anything yet." With a wink, Daryl ducked from the truck and disappeared around back. The tailgate opened, then closed with a metallic clang.

Excitement pebbled the skin on her arms. If she returned to her job full-time, this might be one of her last nights with Daryl. She'd make the most of it. As she reached for the handle, the passenger door opened to reveal a beaming Daryl.

"Right this way, darlin'." He helped her

down, then led her across the meadow, her hand tucked inside his. A large picnic basket hung from his opposite arm.

The air was clear and sharp; the afternoon rain was gone, and the huge trees were washed clean. Soggy leaves gave way underfoot. Roosting birds called from a copse of pine trees. Nearby, water rushed over stone, the sound like tinkling crystal in the evergreen-scented air. It filled her with peace.

"I've never been here before." Her voice emerged hushed. Deferential. As if they'd entered a grand cathedral and witnessed a miracle.

"I came across this spring last year when searching out more watering holes." In the growing dim, Daryl's even white teeth glimmered.

"I hear it, but I don't see it. Oh—" Her exclamation fell from her rounded mouth as the ground dropped off ahead. A natural spring tucked in a narrow ravine materialized. "How beautiful," she breathed. The first stars glimmered on its dark surface, diamonds on velvet.

"Not nearly as beautiful as you." He stopped at the ravine's edge, leaned close and captured her lips in a brief, heart-stopping kiss. Her hand crept around to the back of his neck to pull him closer, craving nearness, but he shook his head. "Not yet. Follow me."

Carefully, he led her down the embankment, across the spring's shallowest spot and up over the other side where the mountain protruded in a rocky ledge jutting over Carbondale. She gasped at the stunning, panoramic view. Ranch lands rolled out to the horizon, the distant town lights glowing softly in the early night, and emerging stars burst overhead in infinite numbers. Her soaring spirit expanded and shrank, as if she could touch the rising moon despite being just a speck on life's canvas.

Daryl retrieved a blanket from the basket. He laid it on the ground, then tugged her down beside him. Her eyes widened as he retrieved a bottle of sparkling cider, a platter of cheeses, crackers and sliced apples, and dark chocolate brownies he must have picked up from the country store's bakery.

He poured cider into champagne glasses, handed her one, then clinked his rim to hers. "Here's to lovers everywhere—the have-beens, the are-nows and the may-bes."

"And what are we?" She sipped the bubbling, slightly tart drink.

He ran the back of his knuckle against her cheek. "Are-nows, I'm hoping."

"We should add a fourth category. 'Always have-beens.'"

"Forever." He fed her a piece of sweet apple with sharp cheddar.

Her mouth exploded with flavor, her heart with love. Daryl was a skilled rancher, a rugged cowboy and a doting, playful father. This romantic side, though, was one she hadn't seen since college and the nostalgia of first love, forever love, burned in her chest.

"We believed in 'always' once before." She broke off a piece of brownie and dropped it in his mouth. Warmth coiled inside when his lips closed around her fingers, the contact electric.

He rose over her and looked into her eyes. "We were kids then."

"True." She stared up into his beautiful face. "Some things haven't changed, though."

"Not this." He threaded his fingers through her hair, tugging it slightly, and brushed his mouth against hers. The world spun as he intensified the pressure, kissing her all the way down to the blanket until his body rested against hers, shoulder to shoulder, hip to hip, feet tangling.

She gasped when his lips slid off her mouth to trace her jawline. "No one's ever made me feel the way you do."

"Don't go to Mexico," he said hoarsely, his voice a mere whisper against her ear. She shivered at the vibration followed by the sensation of his mouth teasing her sensitive earlobe.

"You overheard my call with Brenda." She eased away.

His hands were gentle on her cheeks. "It's a dangerous assignment."

Her lips twisted. "Don't worry, cowboy. It's not my first rodeo."

He chuckled, but there was a morose tone to his laugh. "I don't want you at risk."

"Is this about starting a new life together or keeping me safe?"

He buried his face in her hair and breathed deep. "Both."

"Now *that* actually does scare me."

He drew back. "You're afraid to walk away from a high-stakes job, of not being 'someone.'"

Air rushed from her. "Maybe."

Definitely.

He gathered her close. "You'll be Emma's and Noah's 'someone' and my everything."

Her resistance crumbled and it seemed like her heart leaped from her chest into Daryl's. That was how fully she gave it to him. Tears stung her eyes. She pressed a hand to his bearded cheek. "I want to."

With a whoop, he swept her up and twirled her around before setting her back on her feet. "You'll call Brenda and turn down the assignment? Ask her for one less dangerous?"

"Is that the only way we—" she gestured between them, backing away "—can work?"

The look on his face was desperate and he took a pleading step toward her, arms wide, palms out. "It's not just about me. Emma, Noah... They've already lost one mother. I don't want them suffering again."

"You don't think I can look after myself?"

"There's no one I believe in more, but you can't control every situation."

"How about a compromise? You come with me if Joy's strong enough to watch the kids. You're a great photographer. And bodyguard... I saw your moves at the factory with those thugs."

He reached out and grabbed her hand. "I'm committed to the ranch."

"Not to me?" She swallowed down the old hurt, the memory of their last parting.

"To you, too." He drew her hand to his lips and pressed a soft kiss into her palm. "Just not your riskier assignments. How about doing local stories, or less dangerous ones? You don't have to be the most daring journalist in the world."

Didn't she, though?

She'd been raised to fly as high and as far as possible, and Daryl's protectiveness could be suffocating in the future. She might end up hurting him again by leaving if he couldn't come to grips with his issues about stability. Security. She loved him but didn't want his fears to limit her career.

On the other hand, she might have been drawn to those assignments as an excuse not to get stuck in one place, going nowhere like her father. He'd sacrificed to guarantee she wouldn't repeat his grim life. But this was her life, not his. Maybe she should give Daryl and life in Carbondale a chance.

"I—I—" She hesitated. She loved Daryl and Emma and Noah. Even smelly old Beuford… "I don't know if I can give up all of what I do, who I am, for you." Her throat tightened. "I'm an adventurer who seeks the unknown, truth, justice. Hazards come with it."

"And knowing your day before it starts,

your community and family comes with me, along with my heart if you'll accept it."

The rising moon spun in his dark eyes and she glimpsed their peaceful future together. She'd pushed him away once before and regretted it. Would she again? "It's a lot to decide."

"It's up to you." He lowered his face to hers and their lashes tangled. "It's always up to you."

"I wish it were that easy."

"Then let me do some more persuading and give me your answer when you're ready."

"Yes," she sighed just before his lips captured hers again in a toe-curling kiss. She enjoyed the persuading. The deciding, not so much.

"Too tight!" Noah wriggled free of Cassidy's hug and glanced over his shoulder at the approaching school bus the following morning. "And boys don't hug."

"Unless it's your little teddy," Emma guffawed, then flung her arms around Cassidy and squeezed. "Love you, Aunt Cassidy," she whispered before tearing down the road to the bus stop.

"Beuford loves you, too." Noah toed a circle in the dirt.

Cassidy raised a brow. "Just Beuford?"

"Me, too!" he blurted, then flung himself into her arms again, the judgmental classmates in the approaching bus forgotten. A lump rose in her throat as he clung to her. "Will you be here to pick us up?"

"I always am."

His thin face relaxed. "Don't forget the Flamin' Cheetos!" he shouted, then followed his sister up into the bus.

The door swished closed and the vehicle rumbled off. She watched until the yellow bus disappeared, then climbed up into Daryl's pickup and drove slowly back to the cabin. Her eyes stung. Her shoulders hunched. She'd barely slept last night as she'd mulled over her options, uncomfortable with another request from Daryl, one which would stifle aspects of her life's work.

It was different this time, though, and there was more at stake. But was it enough to make her stay?

Starting up the country store helped her connect to this land and this large, loving extended family. The heart-melting pictures the children drew her, their growing happiness as they embarked on family excursions, their cooking catastrophes that ended in giggles and sticky messes added up to such joy. She loved them deeply.

As for Daryl, no one made her feel more cared for and accepted. His arms felt like home, his kisses the world. The love she felt for him was no longer the youthful spark of their college years, but something sturdier. Meant to last.

After drifting around the globe, she'd finally found where she belonged, the place she'd like to settle...yet if she stayed, would she eventually feel stifled? She didn't want to put Daryl and the kids through more heartbreak. Whatever she decided, she'd need to commit to it.

Back in the cabin, she lifted the Crock-Pot lid and sniffed. She added more bay leaves to the simmering beef stew she'd begun before waking the kids for school. Before making breakfast alongside Daryl. Before a delicious goodbye kiss when the kids disappeared to dress.

Her daily routine.

One she could keep the rest of her life.

Leanne's dream.

Guilt shaded her happiness as she delivered folded laundry to the master bedroom. Leanne should be here, and Cassidy should be in Delhi, Chad, Guatemala… Her sister's flip phone caught her eye. Wanting some connection, she grabbed it and opened her sister's email app again.

Clicking through folders, she stopped on "Drafts" and realized they'd never thought to check it. She glanced inside. The top saved note was addressed to her, dated several months before the accident.

Heart pounding, Cassidy opened the draft.

Dear Cassidy,

I've written this letter dozens of times and I can never get it right. There's a lot I have to say, and it begins with I'm sorry, ends with I love you and has a lot of stuff in between that's confusing and hard to express.

Growing up, I always felt inferior to my talented sister. Everything came easy to you, grades, friends, Pa's love. I struggled in school and never could win Pa's favor. The gifts he gave you, like the old camera, made me jealous. It wasn't much, but we didn't have much. What little he scraped together always went to you, even if it was just a smile after one of his sixteen-hour shifts.

You were special, and I was nobody. Since you introduced us, I'd had a secret crush on Daryl and I sought him out after you went overseas. When things went too far, I admit it, I felt glad. I was sure you'd never be happy tied down to a rancher, a life I wanted when all you'd ever talked about was getting away from the Rocky Mountains. Daryl's family had more money and stability than ours. He was the secure future I needed and when you walked away from it, I thought I'd be doing you a favor by taking a man completely wrong for you.

I didn't intend on getting pregnant, but it helped me marry Daryl. My wedding was the happiest moment of my life except that I couldn't share it with you, my best friend, my moon sister. Remember all those nights we used to climb onto the roof and make a wish on our favorite moon? I thought I'd made mine come true, but I was wrong. Daryl doesn't truly love me, no matter what he says. I hoped he'd come to love me, but his heart has always been yours, and I was dead wrong to get in between you.

I saw the hurt in your eyes when you returned from Bosnia. I knew I was wrong thinking you'd have been unhappy in Carbondale and Daryl would be better off with me... Yet the damage was done, and I was pregnant and married. I was too young and maybe too weak to stand up and undo the wrong I'd committed then. But not now.

In the end, I hurt everyone, myself included. Now I'm stuck in a loveless marriage, drinking a little too much, going out too often to escape my troubles, with not much going for me except my children and a business venture that will probably fail like my relationship. I want to prove I can provide a secure future for myself and my kids without depending on a man who was trapped into marrying me, but I'm not sure how.

I don't know if you can forgive me, and I'm pretty sure I don't deserve it, even if you do, but I want to tell you I'm sorry, in person. Could I join you overseas while I sort out next steps? The country store that I'm planning isn't the distraction I'd hoped and Daryl's hovering more than ever, sensing something is off. For the sake of the kids, he'll fight to convince me to stay, and I'm not sure I'm strong enough to resist him when I need to for both our sakes.

Anyway, I probably won't send this version either, but it eases the ache in my heart imagining I'd have the courage to email it. I don't blame you if you ignore this, just like I've understood why you avoided talking to me all these years. I'm sorry, Cassidy. If I could do things differently, I would. But maybe it's not too late for us?

I love you, moon sister.

Leanne

Cassidy stared at the blurred screen, her chest tight, her heart shattered. It was almost phenomenal in its strength, this pain that gripped her. Leanne must have decided to call her instead of sending the note. Cassidy swiped at her streaming tears and hung her head, shoulders shaking as she sobbed. She'd never known she'd made Leanne feel inferior and resentful. Her sister's betrayal finally made sense.

She grabbed her coat, snatched up the car keys and raced outside, devastated and needing distance to think. With a white-knuckle grip, she drove silently, twisting around the mountain roads, up and over, down and around.

"Why, why, why?" she moaned aloud, her breath coming in jagged gasps. Her whole body jerked and shook as she cried. "Why did we lose each other?"

Heaviness built in her chest to an unbearable degree. A fog fuzzed her brain and spots appeared on the edge of her vision.

A horn blared, and she yanked the car back in her lane, heart beating out of her chest, narrowly missing an oncoming tractor-trailer. She slammed on the brakes. The momentum, however, sent her veering onto the shoulder and down into a shallow ditch. At last, the vehicle rocked to a stop. The engine hissed in the sudden quiet.

Voices rose, echoing in her ear.

Hers and her sister's.

In an instant, Cassidy was back in the white Jeep, Leanne beside her, as she drove at breakneck speed down Avalanche Road to make her sister's flight. She had a ticket to Tennessee, where she planned on staying with an old childhood friend.

"Don't leave him, Leanne," she heard herself say, tearing her eyes from the slick road wet with a heavy bout of rain. The wipers swished against the torrent of water streaming down her windshield. "It's not too late."

"It's always been too late," Leanne argued back. Red blotches covered her face. "Daryl and I were never meant to be. Leaving him, getting you here, is my chance to make it right."

"You don't need to do that. I told you, I forgive you."

Leanne reached over and squeezed Cassidy's hand on the wheel. "I don't deserve it. Not yet. With me gone, you two can finally be together... It's what you've always wanted, isn't it?"

"No," Cassidy had denied despite the gnawing suspicion her sister was right. "I want you to stay together. Think of the children."

She put on her blinker, intending to take the next turnoff. She'd agreed to bring Leanne to the airport only as a stall tactic.

"I am thinking of them!" Leanne cried. "They're unhappy seeing Daryl and me so miserable. Why do you think I leave half the time? I don't want them to see us arguing. I'm going to give them a new life once I figure out my own. Please understand... Let me go..."

"No! You're being selfish—like always."

Leanne's sharp intake of air snapped Cassidy's attention back to the road. Entrenched in their argument, she failed to notice a sharp turn and cranked the wheel too late. Tires squealed. The SUV swerved. A bone-jarring crash, then black...

It cast Cassidy back to the present. She scrambled from her car, stumbled toward a tree and grabbed the trunk, embracing it, holding herself up and holding on at the same time. The cries that came out of her were loud and wrenching.

Her last words to Leanne were denying her the life she wanted…calling her selfish for wanting something else.

Worst, she'd driven recklessly. She'd caused the accident.

She'd killed her sister. In more ways than the final one.

"Cassidy?" A firm, gentle hand gripped her shoulder. "Are you okay?" Travis's kind eyes peered from beneath his wide-brimmed sheriff's hat.

"No." She was nearly doubled over by the sudden crushing pain of memory, of loss.

"Are you injured?"

"I'm not the one who's hurt," she cried, thinking of Leanne.

"Is someone else in the vehicle with you?"

"No. Not anymore." She felt as though she was going to collapse to the ground. Just lie there in the dirt long enough to perish, to be with her sister. No. To take her place.

Travis's thick eyebrows drew together as

he glanced from the empty vehicle to her. "I'll get a towing company out here and call Daryl to get you."

"Yes" filled her mouth, but she swallowed it back, tasting only the bitterness of her regret. How could she become a mother to the children she'd orphaned? A partner to the man she'd widowed?

Did she deserve the happiness she'd denied her sister, a sister who never got to feel special with Cassidy garnering all the attention? She'd blamed Leanne for her misery, never realizing her sister had been desperately unhappy, too.

Cassidy needed space. Time to think. One last assignment to help her deal with the guilt and give her time to forgive herself before she faced Leanne's family. Could she live with her culpability in her sister's death if she and Daryl reunited?

How would she tell the kids? Daryl? Would he even want her if he knew the truth? She couldn't answer these questions with the weight on her shoulders. She had to leave Carbondale. Now.

"Cassidy?" prompted Travis.

"I killed Leanne," she blurted in a watery hiccup. "We were arguing, and I wasn't paying attention to the road. I didn't see the turn until it was too late." Another sob shuddered through her body. "Now it's too late, and it's my fault."

"It was an accident." Travis yanked off his jacket and draped it around her shaking shoulders.

"No. We were arguing. I was yelling at her…" Travis might call it an accident, but she didn't see it that way.

"Hang in there, Cassidy." Travis squeezed her shoulder. "It'll all be okay. Let me call Daryl."

"I need to talk to Joy." She didn't dare speak to Daryl or risk blurting out the horrible facts she struggled to process. The first time she left, she'd hurt Daryl; this time was worse. She'd taken her sister from her family. How could they want her now? They'd hate her when they learned everything.

Once she left Daryl a note, arranged for Joy to pick up the kids from the bus stop, she'd board the next flight to Mexico.

Her heart, however, would stay right here in Carbondale.

She had no need of it without Daryl or the children.

CHAPTER FIFTEEN

DARYL RACED UP the steps to his cabin and flung open the door. Anticipation chased away the workday's exhaustion. Had Cassidy made up her mind about them yet? She'd been affectionate this morning. Her stunning smile easy. Relaxed. And she'd hummed their favorite song, the one he'd once hoped they'd dance to at their wedding. He'd smiled for no reason all day and his cheeks ached along with his heart in happiness.

Beuford woofed as Daryl crossed the threshold. Otherwise the cabin lay quiet. Empty.

"Cassidy?" he called, striding through the living room and down the hall to the bedrooms, pulse picking up. "Emma? Noah?"

Silence answered him.

A note filled with familiar script rested on the counter. Cassidy's handwriting. His blood turned to ice. The children.

Dear Daryl,
Emma and Noah are fine and with Boyd
and Joy.

He released a breath and dropped onto a stool. The page trembled slightly in his grasp. Of course Cassidy knew his first worry would be his kids. No one knew him better. Was this a love note? The heaviness in his heart suggested otherwise.

I discovered an email we'd missed in Leanne's drafts folder this morning. It's open on her cell phone's email app. Please read it before reading the rest of this note.

He blasted across the living room to the bedroom, note in hand. The dark cell phone screen lit when he tapped the space bar. An email, addressed to Cassidy, appeared. His gut clenched as he read Leanne's apology, her regrets, her feelings of inadequacy growing up and her decision to move on from a marriage that reinforced her sense of not being good enough.

Queasiness roiled inside. She'd thought she'd gain the status she'd wanted by marrying him. Instead his love for another left her feeling second best. Daryl swore under his breath. Fury over his mistreatment of Leanne, his neglect, his ignorance of her needs, overtook him. He'd gone through the motions, had devoted himself to their family and made romantic gestures, but she'd seen the emptiness behind them and beyond, to a life without him, one he would have fought to prevent thinking the upheaval might harm the children.

He dropped his head in his hands and the note crinkled against his damp forehead. He'd wounded both Fulton sisters. Rather than wait for Cassidy's decision, he'd doubted and betrayed her. Instead of addressing Leanne's discontent, he'd simply tried appeasing it.

He hadn't deserved the love both women gave him.

Did he deserve it now from Cassidy?

She had to be as wrecked as he after reading the email. The urge to find her, hold her, comfort her, gripped him.

Where was she?

He returned to the note.

I'm sorry for what you're feeling after reading the email.

His throat clamped tight. Typical Cassidy to think of him first.

But know you did the best you could in your marriage. You were a devoted husband and an incredible father. Leanne's unhappiness began long ago with a different father, one with good intentions, but bad choices. I wish he'd never singled me out, had never taught me to only be satisfied with being the best, had made Leanne believe she was special in her own way. She deserved better, but her role in your marriage shouldn't be dismissed either. Please don't beat yourself up, my love. She chose you, a wrong decision, but a conscious one. Your heart picked me, and I'm not sure you could divide it, no matter how hard you tried. I certainly couldn't.

His heartbeat ratcheted up. Cassidy called him her love. Was she about to declare it and a wish for their future?

However, I've decided to take the assignment and am flying to Mexico as you read this note. What happened be-

tween you and Leanne showed me that a relationship must be entered into without reservation, without looking back or wishing for something, or someone else. I want to be certain we're on firm ground and won't have regrets. Right now, I don't think I could ever take Leanne's place. You deserve a marriage based on the same unconditional love you give everyone lucky enough to receive it. I'm sorry, more than I can say...
Yours,
Cassidy

Daryl clenched his hand and the note crumpled into a ball. So, he thought, what he'd hoped would be the best day of his life had turned to crap. Cassidy was gone, putting her life at risk in a dangerous assignment. *She might say she's yours, but she's not. Not yet.*

Hadn't he always known this was the risk he was taking as long as he let himself fall in love with her again? That she might never be able to settle down with him? Ever?

You pushed her too hard, he told himself. *Pushed her away. Now she might never want a relationship with you, but at least you have Emma and Noah.*

With a groan, he lurched to his feet, trod heavily to the door and grabbed his keys. He needed his kids.

And Cassidy. More than he'd ever thought possible.

Minutes later, he strode inside the main house and found his children playing Monopoly with Sierra, Maverick, Joy and Pa.

"Pa!" Noah toppled his chair as he bolted from it to reach Daryl. "Aunt Cassidy's gone!"

Daryl swooped his son up, then threw an arm around Emma, clasping her tight to his side.

"I wanted her to stay forever," Emma cried. "Why does she have a stupid job?"

"It's her dream," Daryl answered, voice thick. "What she loves to do."

He looked up and caught his father's grave eyes on him, Maverick's frown and Sierra's and Joy's matching concerned expressions.

"Doesn't she love us?" Noah wriggled loose, and Daryl set him on his feet.

"She can love both," he assured them, tasting the truth as he spoke it.

Cassidy was wrong. He didn't love her unconditionally. If he had, he would have accepted all aspects of her work and tried to be a part of it. Instead, he'd tried to mold her to his insecurities, the anxiety that had him holding tight to those he loved rather than letting them be free to come or to go. Staying was always sweeter when it came without precondition, without expectation, without pressure...with only love.

"Will she come back?" Emma sniffled.

"Yes," he vowed. Cassidy might not return for him, but she'd never abandon the children she loved as her own.

"Son?" Boyd shoved back his chair. "A word?"

Daryl hugged his kids, then followed his father onto the porch. They stood at the railing and stared at the dark sky. The night sounds echoed around them; the last of the crickets, an occasional owl, wind whirring through tall pines. It spun the wind chimes, and their hollow clang tolled inside him.

"Cassidy stopped by on her way out and told us about you two."

Daryl gaped at his father. "Sir?" He'd dreaded telling his family about him and Cassidy, worried they'd judge him for not mourning long enough and moving on too fast. Those weren't the actions of the "good" man he'd strived to be for his adopted family.

"You're a fool if you let her go a second

time. Some might say it's too soon, but you've loved that gal for years. Make it forever. Don't throw away your chance with her."

Daryl stared at his father's stern profile before he recovered enough to reply, "She left me."

"Go after her."

"You'll be shorthanded."

Pa shrugged. "We'll manage. Maverick's shoulder's good enough for ranch work at least. He'll fill in until he's cleared to return to bull riding."

"What if they clear him while I'm away?"

"We'll figure it out. No more sacrificing yourself to do the right thing."

"What?"

"You're a Loveland. You don't have to go above and beyond to prove it."

"I don't—" He cut off at his father's head shake.

"Should have talked to you about this long ago. Lovelands don't pry, but I saw how much harder you pushed yourself than your siblings, how much you blamed yourself for mistakes, how you returned home from college instead of pursuing your dreams. We needed the help then, but I shouldn't have accepted it."

"No, Pa. I owe you. What you did for me…"

Boyd waved a hand, cutting Daryl off. "*I* can't repay *you* for the joy you give our family. We were going through a rough time with Ma and the last thing I needed was another one to look after, but you were special. Saw it right off. Responsible. Determined. Resolute. I knew you were meant to be my son. The day my cousin brought you here was the luckiest day of my life."

Daryl's chest tightened. "Was the luckiest day of mine, too."

"I wanted you to be part of the family, not part of the ranch hand crew. No more doing what's 'right' all the time. If that means leaving home to court your deceased wife's sister, then so be it." Boyd cleared his throat. "I love you, son. You're the best Loveland of all of us."

The "Clemmons" in Daryl evaporated, leaving him weightless. Buoyant. A Loveland through and through. "I love you, too, Pa." He hugged his father, then reared back, surprised his tough-as-boot-leather parent shook. "Pa? What's troubling you?"

His father turned away, shoulders hunched.

Boots stomping up the stairs diverted Daryl's attention.

"Hey, Pa. Daryl," called Travis. "Is Cassidy around? I stopped up at the cabin, but no one was home."

"She left the country."

Travis's eyebrows rose. "Was that a planned trip? She didn't look in shape to go anywhere."

"What do you mean?"

"She had a minor car accident earlier. Refused medical care, but she was shaken up. She regained some of her memory and confessed to causing the accident with her sister. Believes she killed Leanne."

Shock locked up Daryl's joints. "Why would she think that?"

"Said they were arguing and she wasn't watching the road. Missed a turn and went off the road. I talked to our forensics team again and the skid marks prove it was an accident. She won't be charged."

"She's already punishing herself," Daryl bit out, imagining Cassidy's anguish, the blame she must have heaped on herself after remembering her and Leanne's last moments. The words in her note returned to him. *I'm sorry, more than I can say.* Guilt drove her abrupt exit to Mexico; not him.

Travis stomped back down the stairs. "Got to get back to work. We've got a lead on the cattle rustlers. Daryl. Your car is at Tim's

Auto Body. Keep me posted about Cassidy. She's a good one. Don't let her get away."

Daryl stared after Travis as he disappeared into the dark. A choking sound snapped his attention back to his pa. "What's got you upset, Pa?"

"Me," spoke a soft voice behind them.

Daryl whirled, along with Boyd, to spy Joy's approach. She slipped an arm around her husband, who buried his head in her hair and held her tight against his side.

"My cancer's back and it's spread."

Her news struck Daryl in the chest. Blunt force. "I'm sorry."

"Don't be," Joy whispered, fierce. "I've got a lot to live for. I'm not going to leave this one after I finally found him again." She caressed the side of Boyd's face.

"Wouldn't let you, even if you tried, darlin'," Boyd said, hoarsely. "Wherever you go, I'll follow. When we go, we'll go together and not before."

Daryl strove to speak over the lump in his throat. Here was the kind of courage, the love, the devotion he should have given Cassidy. And now she was headed into danger, alone, thinking the worst of herself. He ached to hold her and reassure her, to take away the blame she must feel and replace it with love.

"We can't control how much time we have with each other, but we have a say in what we do with it. You got me, son?" Boyd wiped his eyes with his sleeves and peered at Daryl.

Daryl nodded. Boyd would stand by Joy's side to fight cancer just as Daryl should have accompanied Cassidy on her dangerous assignment. He'd been a coward to refuse her offer, letting his hang-ups, his insecurities, get in the way of love.

"And we'll watch the kids while you're away—however long you need," Joy offered. "I don't start chemo until after Thanksgiving, and my new iron pills are boosting my energy."

"Thank you," Daryl choked out, overwhelmed.

"So why are you still standing here?" Boyd demanded. "Go be with your woman, however she'll let you, and be darn grateful for that."

"Yes, sir!"

Maverick blocked Daryl's dash inside the house. "Going somewhere?"

Daryl counted backward from ten, eyeing his interfering older brother. "Out of my way, bro. I've got to say goodbye to the kids and find a flight to Mexico."

"Way ahead of you. I was here when Cassidy stopped by." Maverick thrust a printout at Daryl.

His eyes widened when he read the flight number for a plane departing to Mexico in just two hours.

"Glad to see I didn't waste my money." Maverick's lips curved in his typical "I got this" smile and he stepped aside.

"Anyone ever told you you're annoying?" Daryl said through a grin.

Maverick shrugged. "Lost count."

"How about 'Thank you'?"

"Not nearly enough."

Daryl grabbed his brother in a one-armed hug. "Thank you."

"Better hurry," Maverick called as Daryl headed inside. "Don't want to miss your flight."

Daryl eyed the clock, his jaw set. "Not a chance."

CASSIDY CREPT TOWARD a dark building for her 3:00 a.m. meeting with a Nuevo León cartel member. Through contacts she'd cultivated in off-grid ventures this past week, he'd agreed to speak only on condition of anonymity, and alone. The hairs on the back of her neck rose. What if someone tipped off the vicious gang?

In such moments, her thoughts centered on safeguarding the story, ensuring information she'd collected made it out, even if she didn't. Now she pictured Emma's face, and Noah's... how devastated they'd be if anything happened to her. As for Daryl, she hadn't dared let herself think of him since leaving Carbondale or risk losing her focus for missing him.

A shadow stirred and detached itself from the building. The outline of a large man materialized. "Senorita! Over here!"

She forced herself to still the nerves tightening inside her and hurried across the cracked asphalt. Beneath her long-sleeved shirt, the wire she wore stuck to her clammy skin. "Approaching target," she whispered to the crew listening in a van on the next street. Technically, she'd hadn't broken the agreement. She'd arrived alone. Like she'd told Daryl, though, this wasn't her first rodeo. She'd be a fool not to arrange for backup if things went south.

Sickly sweet fumes poured off her contact as he waved her through an open door. Tequila. And not the good kind. The man was around six feet with a ropy build exposed by a ragged muscle shirt and cutoff shorts. His feet were bare. A Jaguar Warriors insignia tattoo, his cartel's symbol, adorned the side of his neck.

"Alejandro?"

"Sí." He shoved a thick lock of dark hair from his forehead. "You have the money?"

She nodded. *And a gun...* "Thank you for meeting me."

Normally, she didn't engage in "checkbook journalism," but the chance to meet with a cartel member was too good to pass up.

Alejandro waved her to a rickety chair before dropping onto a scarred stool. An ominous metal hook dangled from the ceiling, a bare light bulb beside it. A length of stained rope was strewn across the earthen floor. Otherwise, the rest of the small, one-story adobe building was empty.

"Tell me how you became part of the cartel."

"Aren't you going to record me or something?" Alejandro's bloodshot eyes narrowed.

"Right!" Hurriedly, she yanked out her cell phone. A frustrated exhale bulged her cheeks. She'd caught herself making similar mistakes on this trip, part of her not as present as needed when every spare thought swerved Daryl's way.

She glanced at the screen, noted the lack of signal for the sixth day straight and accessed her recording app. Hopefully her team could hear her through her wire.

"How old were you when you joined the cartel?" she asked, switching to Spanish.

Alejandro's eyes flicked to the doorway behind her, then swerved back. "Ten."

"That's young."

He shrugged, and his gaze slid from hers.

"Why join? Did you have a choice?" She eyed a spider, as thick as her pinkie toe, skitter up the wall beside her.

"My father was in it." Alejandro crossed himself and his lips moved silently.

"It's tradition? If your father is a part of the cartel, you're expected to be, as well?"

"Not expected. No." Alejandro checked out the doorway again and a silent alarm shrilled inside her. Faint, but insistent.

"If your family is in it, then you should be, too?" she tried again.

"The Warriors are your family. You aren't expected to be a part of it. You just are." He fished a pack of cigarettes from his pocket and offered her one.

She refused with a head shake. "Jaguar Warriors is a business organization and a family."

Alejandro clicked on his lighter and held it to the cigarette clamped between his teeth. "Both. Yes," he mumbled.

"It must be hard to turn on your family." She struggled not to follow his darting gaze over her shoulder.

A stream of smoke curled from Alejandro's nose. "No one betrays the family."

"But you're here. Tell me why."

"I'm no traitor," he growled.

At a sudden noise at the door, she shot from her chair, gun in hand.

"Drop it, senorita," hissed a compact man wearing a ball cap and a suit. He ambled inside. Behind him a couple of muscle-bound sidekicks hulked. One had a gun trained on her. The other slammed the door shut and turned the lock.

"No need to get violent," she said calmly. *Don't panic. Easy breaths.* "I'm only here for information. Let me go and I promise not to speak of our meeting."

The man in the cap guffawed, a menacing laugh picked up by his followers. "Nothing will be said, that I believe. Now. How did you get Alejandro's name? Who ratted us out?"

"I protect my sources." She fought to keep her arm locked and steady, her .38 trained on the leader's chest. Sweat rolled down the side of her face and dripped to her collarbone.

"It's so much more enjoyable when they fight first, *si*?" The leader had a barbed wire smile. Metal-capped teeth and sharp canines. He gestured to the rope. "Secure her to the hook."

"Anyone who moves gets shot." She swung her pistol from the leader to his armed side-kick, then back again. "Drop your weapon, face the wall and stay still while I exit. Got it?"

More laughter.

"Move!" she ordered the men, but a click next to her temple destroyed her hopes of making it out without a fight. The cool metal of a gun pressed into her flesh. Alejandro was armed. She'd been ambushed. Her heart beat so hard she felt it in her toes. Had her team been caught, too? If not, would they arrive in time to save her? She sent a silent prayer for them.

"No. You move!" Alejandro growled in her

ear, pointing to the hook with his free hand. "And drop the gun."

Crap.

She thought she might vomit on the spot. She willed herself to be brave, to be strong, to let this ordeal end.

But they were going to kill her. She knew who they were, what they'd done, and suddenly she knew—they were going to kill her. As soon as the cartel identified the traitor in their midst who'd set up this meeting, that gun would blast off her head.

Was this how her life ended? If so, she'd go out guns blazing. She made as if to drop the gun and fired a round into Alejandro's shoulder instead, spinning him so he tumbled.

She didn't think—she was on automatic. Her jaw ground, her temples pulsed and her blood roared in her ears. She fell along with Alejandro, using him as a shield. Gunfire exploded around her. She kicked the table down and crouched behind it.

"Don't shoot!" Alejandro hollered, his hand pressed tightly over a shoulder wound.

"Let him go," growled the group's leader. "You'll never get out of here alive."

"I wasn't either way." She prodded Alejandro to his feet with the butt of her gun. "Drop your weapons and line up against the wall. Any attempt to stop me and Alejandro dies."

Grim laughter boomed as the men exploded in mirth.

"No, senorita. You die!" With blunt force, Alejandro swatted the gun from her hand and it flew several feet away. He forced her arms behind her back, trapping her.

Before he could make good on his threat, someone kicked the door. It crashed open and bounced off the opposite wall and there stood Daryl, legs braced apart, arms raised, pistol pointed at the men with guns still trained on her. "Drop your weapons. Carefully. The police are on their way."

The two goons cast wary eyes at the dark windows.

"You lie," the leader sneered.

"Wanna bet? Stick around and spend the rest of your filthy life rotting in jail."

Caught in Alejandro's viselike grip, Cassidy looked at Daryl and saw a man she'd never seen before. The expression on his face should have been enough to terrify the man who held her. In combat boots and camo pants, his shoulders and arms frighteningly huge, biceps rounding out of a tank top, he looked like a wild man.

He glared over the barrel of the gun, his eyes narrow, and a set to his jaw told her he was going to act. There was no question. He didn't look at her, but at Alejandro, and her fear evaporated. She believed in him. She knew, in that instant, that he would risk his life for her, but he'd never put her at risk. Never. If he was going to make a move, she wouldn't be in danger.

"You have one second," Daryl barked.

She caught his eye, silently communicating that she loved him. Believed in him. Then she dropped her head to the right to give Daryl a clear shot at Alejandro.

"Back off, man—"

Daryl took his shot. She broke free as Alejandro collapsed behind her, nearly making it to Daryl when footsteps pounded outside and armed men piled in the doorway. Gunfire erupted. Pain exploded in her side, the force toppling her forward. The ground rose up to meet her, hard. The world grew quiet, dark, cold and still…or was that her?

Then—

Nothing.

"MORE ICE, PLEASE," Cassidy heard someone say in English. Someone male. Someone in a tunnel, the voice faint. Indistinct. Her eyelids resisted her attempt to open them. Had one of her team members rescued her?

Her brain ached as she struggled to make sense of her situation and one name blazed in her mind's eye.

"Daryl," she whispered, memory rushing back. "Daryl." He'd somehow found her in Nuevo León and rescued her. Miraculously, she lay in a hospital bed, injured but alive.

"I'm right here, darlin'." A familiar, calloused hand wrapped around hers.

Her lids fluttered open and she gasped as Daryl's handsome face swam into view. "What...?"

"Am I doing here?" Dark circles pouched beneath his eyes and his hair stood on end as if he'd raked his fingers through it for hours. He looked as if he hadn't slept in days, yet she'd never seen his eyes glow as bright with relief. "I came to find you. Took me almost a week. Would have preferred reuniting at a swanky hotel rather than an abandoned building full of criminals."

"The high life." She attempted a smile. "I'll have to speak to my travel agent."

Daryl chuckled and smoothed a strand of hair out of her eyes. "You did warn me."

"How did you find me?" The words came easier now, her thoughts sharpening along with her senses. Besides the pain, she noticed the large bandage covering her torso, the beep of her heart on a bedside monitor, the babble of Spanish-speaking voices and the antiseptic scent common to all hospitals.

"Brenda told me who you were planning to meet but they'd lost track of you a week ago. I've been chasing you down ever since."

"You shouldn't have come." Her voice was barely a croak and even that scraped her throat raw. "Emma. Noah."

"Are just fine with Joy and Boyd," he assured her.

"But you." She fought back the tears that threatened. If not for Daryl, she might not have survived the ambush. "You could have been killed."

"So could you." His lips flattened in a straight line before he added, "Wasn't about to let that happen."

She marveled at him. Daryl had been there for her from the moment of her accident, despite his own grief. He hung in there, putting everyone else's needs ahead of his own. He wasn't just trying to be the better man to prove himself worthy of his adoptive family...

he *was* the better man. She'd never question herself when it came to a life with Daryl again. "My team?"

"Injured," Daryl said simply, gripping her hand. "One dead. The cartel got them before you. Hugo, the driver, played dead but he only had a flesh wound. He'd already called the police when I found him."

"Are the cartel members dead?"

"One of 'em. Arturo something or other. Other ones are in custody."

"You took down Arturo Servando 'La Tuta' Fuentes?" she breathed. Her eyes bulged.

"Tutu?" Daryl shrugged, unimpressed. "Doesn't sound so tough."

"'Tuta,'" she corrected. "He's one of Mexico's most vicious cartel leaders and on the FBI's most wanted list. He's plenty tough."

Daryl's shoulder lifted and fell again. Despite her pain, one side of her mouth kicked up. Tough cowboy. To look at his hardened features and set jaw, you'd never know he played Clumsy the Clown for his kids as easily as he took down drug lords.

"How's the pain?" he asked, pressing his lips to her brow.

She tilted her head to look up at him. "It's there. Did I get shot?"

Daryl frowned. "Yes. You had surgery this morning. None of the organs were hit, but the bullet was close to your spinal cord." He reached for the call button.

She stopped him. She didn't want to be hazy and medicated with the man she loved beside her...not until she understood why he'd acted out of character and come for her. "Not yet."

With aching tenderness, Daryl brushed the damp gathering on her eyelashes. "You need something. You're crying."

"Because of you," she said, tears coming faster in spite of the fact she was so, so happy. "I'm glad you're here."

"Me, too. I should have come with you in the first place."

"But you have the ranch to worry about, the kids. I get it."

"I worry about you, too."

"Thanks for your concern...?"

"And love. I love you, Cassidy. I love everything about you, who you are, what you do, how you affect me... Holding you is the most comforted I've ever been, and I've never felt as safe crying as when I've cried right next to you."

"Daryl," she sighed, reaching for her vulnerable tough guy. "I love you, too. I've never stopped loving you."

He sucked in a fast breath, slid an arm around her and eased onto the bed beside her. When she turned her face, his brown eyes were enormous. "I love you more than I thought I could love a woman. My life started when you walked into the bookstore and re-started when you opened your eyes in the hospital room," he said hoarsely, his voice a mere whisper.

"I loved you from the moment the safety pins holding your old backpack together broke," she said, snuggling close. "Instead of being embarrassed, you asked the librarian for a stapler, closed the gap and didn't miss a beat in telling me why you preferred Dorothea Lange's photography to Ansel Adams's." She smiled at the memory. "Your dignity, strength and unconcern for others' opinions made me want to be admired by you, to be loved by you, although you're still wrong about Ansel Adams."

"You have lousy taste, then, except in men, of course." He nuzzled her neck and spoke directly in her ear. "I shouldn't have let you walk away a second time. Shouldn't have let my insecurities override my love. I love you.

I'll never regret my years with Leanne because of our beautiful children. But this can be a fresh start."

Joy detonated in her heart, filling it with bright sparklers. They fizzled, though, as she contemplated the confession she needed to make. "Are you sure?"

"I've never been surer about anything. I want this. If you take dangerous jobs, I'll go anywhere you want to go."

"But, Daryl, you love Loveland Ranch. The life you've built there."

"Don't you realize I love you more? I need you in my life. You and my kids. Lord, Cassidy—I don't care where that happens as long as it happens. Once you know how much you love someone, no one else will do."

"Daryl," she said in a whisper. "What if you change your mind? What happens if something goes wrong? You have to remember, I never thought anything terrible would happen to—"

He put his finger to her lips. "Shh," he said. "I want you to trust me. You know you're safe with me."

"You are handy in a corner," she half joked, then squeezed her eyes closed and gathered her courage. "There's something you need to know, first."

"You didn't kill Leanne."

Her lids flew open.

"Travis told me what you'd said."

"She wanted me to watch the kids while she stayed with a childhood friend, and we argued." Cassidy drew in a long breath, trying to calm her rapid-fire heart, and looked away from Daryl. "I called her selfish. Those were my last words to her."

"You know what mine were?" At the deep vein of pain running through Daryl's voice, her gaze snapped back to him. "'If you're not coming home tonight, don't bother coming home again.'"

"Oh, Daryl!"

A muscle twitched in his clamped jaw as he battled the powerful emotion gripping him. "I was a terrible husband."

"I was a terrible sister."

"You came home the moment she asked for help," Daryl countered.

"Actually, I was trying to stop her."

Daryl stroked the side of Cassidy's cheek. "I would have done the same."

"I killed your children's mother." She turned away. "You must hate me."

Daryl lightly pressed his index finger beneath her chin and guided her face back his way. "I could never hate you. And I don't blame you. Neither will the children."

"If it wasn't for me, Leanne would be alive."

"Maybe, but she still would have left us. At least you tried to stop her. It's time to let go of our guilt."

"I don't know if I can."

"In your note, you said you could never take Leanne's place. I agree."

She winced. The harsh truth at last.

"You have your own space in our family, one we'll create together. We'll build a new cabin. A new life. Please, Cassidy. I don't care how far you travel as long as this—" he tapped her heart "—stays with me."

"It always has." She cupped his bearded face and brought her lips to his, kissing him softly at first, then more passionately until they both gasped for air. "I love you so much I almost ache with it."

"Or that's your bullet wound talking."

She chuckled softly. "True…"

Daryl rested his forehead against hers. "All of my old feelings returned when I saw you again and I fought them. It felt like I was cheating on Leanne. I figured I'd let you go once, I could do it again. I never thought my feelings would become even more powerful. Seeing you with my children, my family, the community…I only fell harder."

She sniffed a little, and another tear rolled down her cheek. "I feel like I'm betraying Leanne, too. But I think, in the end, she wanted us to be together. She wanted to right the wrong she'd done."

"As do I. Come back home. I make a mean mac-n-cheese…"

"That's debatable, but you have other, laudable attributes."

"Like…"

"Your Clumsy the Clown character."

"Sounds sexy."

Cassidy drew in a breath, trying to steady her tremulous voice. "Oh, he is. And goofy, and endearing and lovable. I also kinda liked you as Rambo, too."

His eyes glinted. "Did I turn you on?"

"You saved my butt."

"Guess that's more important."

"And you turned me on…but you—just you—Daryl Loveland, is who I love most. Yes. I'll come home with you."

"Marry me."

"Now you're pushing it."

His lips lifted in an amused smile. "Marry me, *please*…?"

When she nodded, he kissed her again, tenderly, and she kissed him back, ecstatic. She wouldn't need to step into her sister's shoes to be part of this beautiful man's life. He loved her and wouldn't try to make her conform to his life or anyone else's. She was free to choose her own path, and she wanted the one that led back to Carbondale, to the love and joy that'd long awaited her there.

* * * * *

Get 4 FREE REWARDS!

We'll send you 2 FREE Books plus 2 FREE Mystery Gifts.

Love Inspired® books feature contemporary inspirational romances with Christian characters facing the challenges of life and love.

FREE Value Over $20

YES! Please send me 2 FREE Love Inspired® Romance novels and my 2 FREE mystery gifts (gifts are worth about $10 retail). After receiving them, if I don't wish to receive any more books, I can return the shipping statement marked "cancel." If I don't cancel, I will receive 6 brand-new novels every month and be billed just $5.24 for the regular-print edition or $5.74 each for the larger-print edition in the U.S., or $5.74 each for the regular-print edition or $6.24 each for the larger-print edition in Canada. That's a savings of at least 13% off the cover price. It's quite a bargain! Shipping and handling is just 50¢ per book in the U.S. and 75¢ per book in Canada.* I understand that accepting the 2 free books and gifts places me under no obligation to buy anything. I can always return a shipment and cancel at any time. The free books and gifts are mine to keep no matter what I decide.

Choose one: ☐ **Love Inspired® Romance Regular-Print**
(105/305 IDN GMY4)

☐ **Love Inspired® Romance Larger-Print**
(122/322 IDN GMY4)

Name (please print)

Address _____ Apt. #

City _____ State/Province _____ Zip/Postal Code

Mail to the **Reader Service:**
IN U.S.A.: P.O. Box 1341, Buffalo, NY 14240-8531
IN CANADA: P.O. Box 603, Fort Erie, Ontario L2A 5X3

Want to try 2 free books from another series? Call 1-800-873-8635 or visit www.ReaderService.com.

LI19R

Get 4 FREE REWARDS!

We'll send you 2 FREE Books plus 2 FREE Mystery Gifts.

Love Inspired® Suspense books feature Christian characters facing challenges to their faith... and lives.

FREE Value Over $20

YES! Please send me 2 FREE Love Inspired® Suspense novels and my 2 FREE mystery gifts (gifts are worth about $10 retail). After receiving them, if I don't wish to receive any more books, I can return the shipping statement marked "cancel." If I don't cancel, I will receive 4 brand-new novels every month and be billed just $5.24 each for the regular-print edition or $5.74 each for the larger-print edition in the U.S., or $5.74 each for the regular-print edition or $6.24 each for the larger-print edition in Canada. That's a savings of at least 13% off the cover price. It's quite a bargain! Shipping and handling is just 50¢ per book in the U.S. and 75¢ per book in Canada.* I understand that accepting the 2 free books and gifts places me under no obligation to buy anything. I can always return a shipment and cancel at any time. The free books and gifts are mine to keep no matter what I decide.

Choose one: ☐ **Love Inspired® Suspense**
Regular-Print
(153/353 IDN GMY5)

☐ **Love Inspired® Suspense**
Larger-Print
(107/307 IDN GMY5)

Name (please print)

Address _____ Apt. #

City _____ State/Province _____ Zip/Postal Code

Mail to the **Reader Service:**
IN U.S.A.: P.O. Box 1341, Buffalo, NY 14240-8531
IN CANADA: P.O. Box 603, Fort Erie, Ontario L2A 5X3

Want to try 2 free books from another series! Call 1-800-873-8635 or visit www.ReaderService.com.

*Terms and prices subject to change without notice. Prices do not include sales taxes, which will be charged (if applicable) based on your state or country of residence. Canadian residents will be charged applicable taxes. Offer not valid in Quebec. This offer is limited to one order per household. Books received may not be as shown. Not valid for current subscribers to Love Inspired Suspense books. All orders subject to approval. Credit or debit balances in a customer's account(s) may be offset by any other outstanding balance owed by or to the customer. Please allow 4 to 6 weeks for delivery. Offer available while quantities last.

Your Privacy—The Reader Service is committed to protecting your privacy. Our Privacy Policy is available online at www.ReaderService.com or upon request from the Reader Service. We make a portion of our mailing list available to reputable third parties that offer products we believe may interest you. If you prefer that we not exchange your name with third parties, or if you wish to clarify or modify your communication preferences, please visit us at www.ReaderService.com/consumerschoice or write to us at Reader Service Preference Service, P.O. Box 9062, Buffalo, NY 14240-9062. Include your complete name and address.

LIS19R

THE FORTUNES OF TEXAS COLLECTION!

18 FREE BOOKS in all!

Treat yourself to the rich legacy of the Fortune and Mendoza clans in this remarkable 50-book collection. This collection is packed with cowboys, tycoons and Texas-sized romances!

Get 4 FREE REWARDS!

We'll send you 2 FREE Books plus 2 FREE Mystery Gifts.

FREE Value Over **$20**

Both the **Romance** and **Suspense** collections feature compelling novels written by many of today's best-selling authors.

Get 4 FREE REWARDS!

We'll send you 2 FREE Books plus 2 FREE Mystery Gifts.

Harlequin® Romance Larger-Print books feature uplifting escapes that will warm your heart with the ultimate feel-good tales.

FREE
Value Over
$20

YES! Please send me 2 FREE Harlequin® Romance Larger-Print novels and my 2 FREE gifts (gifts are worth about $10 retail). After receiving them, if I don't wish to receive any more books, I can return the shipping statement marked "cancel." If I don't cancel, I will receive 4 brand-new novels every month and be billed just $5.34 per book in the U.S. or $5.74 per book in Canada. That's a savings of at least 15% off the cover price! It's quite a bargain! Shipping and handling is just 50¢ per book in the U.S. and 75¢ per book in Canada.* I understand that accepting the 2 free books and gifts places me under no obligation to buy anything. I can always return a shipment and cancel at any time. The free books and gifts are mine to keep no matter what I decide.

119/319 HDN GMYY

Name (please print)

Address   Apt. #

City   State/Province   Zip/Postal Code

Mail to the **Reader Service:**
IN U.S.A.: P.O. Box 1341, Buffalo, NY 14240-8531
IN CANADA: P.O. Box 603, Fort Erie, Ontario L2A 5X3

Want to try 2 free books from another series! Call 1-800-873-8635 or visit www.ReaderService.com.

---

*Terms and prices subject to change without notice. Prices do not include applicable taxes. Sales tax applicable in N.Y. Canadian residents will be charged applicable taxes. Offer not valid in Quebec. This offer is limited to one order per household. Books received may not be as shown. Not valid for current subscribers to Harlequin Romance Larger-Print books. All orders subject to approval. Credit or debit balances in a customer's account(s) may be offset by any other outstanding balance owed by or to the customer. Please allow 4 to 6 weeks for delivery. Offer available while quantities last.

Your Privacy—The Reader Service is committed to protecting your privacy. Our Privacy Policy is available online at www.ReaderService.com or upon request from the Reader Service. We make a portion of our mailing list available to reputable third parties that offer products we believe may interest you. If you prefer that we not exchange your name with third parties, or if you wish to clarify or modify your communication preferences, please visit us at www.ReaderService.com/consumerschoice or write to us at Reader Service Preference Service, P.O. Box 9062, Buffalo, NY 14240-9062. Include your complete name and address.

HRLP19